THEY NEEDED PRISONERS

Carl Lyons started to squeeze the trigger, then eased off. The man was firing rhythmically and had no idea what he was doing. His eyes held the same mindless, glazed look as the others.

Lyons confronted him. "What are you doing?"

"Serving the Great Hikari," the man replied, a vacant fixed smile plastered across his face. "Are you one of us?"

"I don't think so."

"Then what are you doing here?" the man asked, looking disturbed. "Are you serving Hikari?"

Lyons shook his head. "No, I'm serving justice." Without further comment he hooked a left jab into the gunner's jaw.

As he gazed down at the prisoners, Lyons felt a sense of satisfaction. Blancanales would have two minds to probe. The only thing that bothered him was he didn't know how much of those brains were left after the Great Hikari's indoctrination.

DON PENDLETON'S

MACK BOLAN®

STONY MAN™

STRANGLEHOLD

A GOLD EAGLE BOOK FROM

WORLDWIDE®

TORONTO • NEW YORK • LONDON
AMSTERDAM • PARIS • SYDNEY • HAMBURG
STOCKHOLM • ATHENS • TOKYO • MILAN
MADRID • WARSAW • BUDAPEST • AUCKLAND

First edition September 1998

ISBN 0-373-61920-0

STRANGLEHOLD

Special thanks and acknowledgment to
Jerry VanCook for his contribution to this work.

STRANGLEHOLD

PROLOGUE

The closest William "Bobcat" Buchanan had been able to come to describing the contradictory atmosphere in the editorial offices of the *Retained Warrior* magazine was straight out of Dickens. "'It was the best of times,'" he finally said out loud, "'and it was the worst of times.'" In the dim glow of the reading light on the desk, he watched Colonel Samuel K. White nod silently.

For a moment, neither man spoke. Buchanan turned away to the wall, pondering the joy and sorrow that seemed to fill his heart simultaneously. The joy, he knew, came from the fact that he was about to embark on a mission. The sorrow was the result of what had happened to the last man who had undertaken that mission, a man who had been a friend to both Buchanan and White.

Buchanan crossed his legs and looked back at the gray-haired man behind the desk. Colonel White opened a drawer, produced a large Jamaican cigar, struck a kitchen match and rolled the flame over the tip. Buchanan studied his face in the light from the match. Colonel Samuel L. White, ex-Marine, looked exactly like what he was—an aging, battle-scarred warrior. A much decorated officer, the colonel had seen combat during World War II, Korea and the early years of Vietnam. When the Corps had forced his retirement in the late 1960s, the battle-hardened old warhorse had hit the mercenary trail in Africa and South America, then returned to the States to become publisher of his own magazine. He'd been sitting behind this same desk, in this same office where he published the *Retained Warrior,* ever since.

Thick blue clouds of smoke came from the long cigar as White dropped the match into an ashtray. He smiled, then leaned back in his chair. "Spence was a good man, Bobcat. All of us will miss—" The sudden purr of an automobile engine on the quiet street outside the window caused him to halt in mid-sentence.

Both men's eyes shot to the windows. The magazine's offices were in an isolated industrial section of Boulder, Colorado. With the exception of the nighttime goings and comings that the magazine itself generated, traffic in the neighborhood this late at night was an unusual occurrence.

Buchanan watched a set of headlights flash onto the office windows, remembering the old adage "One man's paranoia is another man's caution." A glance at White showed even more lines than usual on the wrinkled face. Both Buchanan and White had made enemies over the years, and it never paid for men with enemies to ignore unusual occurrences regardless of how insignificant they might seem at the time.

Buchanan turned back to the window in time to see a light-colored panel van pass by and keep on going.

White looked back to his companion as soon as it was obvious the vehicle wasn't stopping. "Spencer Kiethley was a good man," he said. "We'll all miss him. I understand you're stepping in where he left off?"

Buchanan nodded.

The colonel took time for another puff on the cigar, then narrowed the ice blue orbs below his crinkled forehead. "See if you can find out more about what happened to him while you're there, Bobcat. The whole thing stinks to high heaven, if you ask me."

"Agreed, sir," Buchanan said. "On both counts."

White clamped the cigar between his teeth and spoke around it. "As far as the magazine goes, you ought to get several good stories out of this gig. You'll be in charge of what, a dozen Gurkha training officers?"

"Thereabouts, sir."

The colonel chewed on the end of his cigar. "Any new angle on the Gurkhas is always good for three thousand words or so. And we could use a story on the weapons the Sierra Leones are using. Russian, aren't they?"

Buchanan nodded again. "Mostly. Old AKs, Makarovs, the like."

"Well, do me a story on that. And write up any missions you go on yourself, of course."

"Anything else?" Buchanan asked.

White puffed the cigar again and shrugged. "Your call," he said, letting the blue gray smoke drift out of his mouth and upward toward the ceiling. "You're an experienced writer and a good soldier. Whatever you think will sell magazines."

Buchanan glanced at his watch, and White caught the movement. "What time is your flight?" the publisher asked.

"It's at 2305. I'd better get going." He stood, walked to the ancient wooden coatrack in the corner and pulled on his trench coat. With a quick salute, he reached out and grasped the doorknob.

"Bobcat," White said.

Buchanan turned back toward the desk.

"Be careful down there. Spencer Kiethley was more than just a good man. He was one smart, well-trained, tough son of a bitch." He paused for effect. "Whatever got him could get you." Buchanan nodded, opened the door, stepped into the hall and headed for the street. He paused at the door to the sidewalk to button his coat and buckle the belt around his waist. Instinctively he conducted a mental inventory of the weaponry on his person. In the right-hand pocket of the trench coat he carried a 2-shot .32-caliber Davis derringer loaded with Winchester Silver-Tip hollowpoint bullets. In the left-hand pocket was one of Cold Steel's massive new five-inch Voyager folding knives. Buchanan reached into his pocket and ran his thumb over the opening stud on the thick clip-point blade. He was researching the new knife for a future article.

Light snow began to fall outside as Buchanan pushed the bar on the glass door and stepped out onto the sidewalk. He paused, making sure the door swung shut again and the lock clicked, then performed another personal ritual. Reaching into his open collar, he grasped the woman's wedding ring suspended around his neck. He thought briefly of the woman who had worn it when alive, and the memory brought both love and sadness.

"I am with you, Ellen," Buchanan said. "And you are with me." His voice was a whisper so low that even if someone had been next to him on the sidewalk, he wouldn't have been overheard.

Forcing his mind away from his wife, whom breast cancer had claimed two years earlier, Buchanan headed toward the parking lot on the corner. He breathed deeply as he walked along in the cold Colorado night. Then the sound of footsteps behind him—almost inaudible—registered suddenly in his brain. He resisted the urge to immediately whirl; he could tell by the sound that the feet were still too far away for their owner to be a threat.

And they might be a diversion for something ahead.

Squinting under the streetlights, Buchanan scanned the night as he walked on. He saw nothing out of the ordinary. Finally he glanced over his shoulder. As he turned, he saw a flash of movement in the doorway to his side.

He turned back toward the dark figure with the grace and speed that had earned him his nickname. The Davis derringer leaped into his hand. His thumb found the hammer, but before he could cock the single-action weapon a fist slammed into his sternum.

Air shot up from Buchanan's lungs and out his mouth. He pushed out hard with his belly, trying to correct the vacuum that had been created in his chest, as the derringer was ripped from his fingers. His left fist jabbed out, striking what felt like a jaw. He heard a crunch and then a grunt, but his punch slowed his attacker for only a moment. The shadowy form drove another fist into Buchanan's abdomen, and he bent double.

Gasping for air, Buchanan fished into the trench coat for the knife as a second shadowy figure joined the first. Buchanan lashed out at the dark form with a front snap kick that caught the second man in the shin. He heard another grunt, but the shadow kept coming.

An arm wrapped around Buchanan's neck. He flipped his wrist to open the knife but something—a hand, arm, shoulder—got in the way and stopped the blade halfway out of the handle. The knife snapped back closed.

Another fist struck Buchanan's ribs. A moment later, the blade was pried from his fingers like the derringer had been.

Buchanan heard the footsteps again. Running now,

they were close. As he continued to gasp for air, a shoulder struck him squarely in the back and then he, the two men in front of him and whoever had blindsided him from the rear went pummeling to the sidewalk.

"Better give him the gas," a voice said. "He's not being very cooperative."

"Would *you* be under the circumstances?" another voice answered.

Buchanan rolled hard to his side, trying to get out from under a tall shadow that was reaching into the pocket of a plaid sport coat. He kicked blindly up into the air and felt his foot meet flesh. Another grunt echoed down the street, then one of the other men chuckled as he pinned Buchanan's shoulders to the concrete. "He doesn't give up easy," the chuckler said. "I'll say that much for him."

"If he gave up easy, we wouldn't want him," the tall man in plaid answered. Buchanan caught a brief glimpse upward and saw that he now held some kind of canister. "Hold your breath," the tall man ordered the other two as he stuck the can under Buchanan's nose.

Buchanan held his breath, too, as a sharp spray exited the canister. But the tall shadow had positioned the nozzle directly under his nostrils, and the stinging fumes shot up his sinuses anyway.

His muscles went instantly limp. Soft, fluffy clouds glided over his brain as he entered another world. The man on top of him stood, then stepped back. Buchanan tried to look up—to see their faces—

to see which of the enemies he had made over the years had finally caught up to him. But his eyes refused to focus.

Closing his eyes, he relaxed and let the gas take effect. As if from somewhere far away, he heard a voice ask, "Want us to load him in the van, Ironman?"

Ironman? Buchanan thought.

William "Bobcat" Buchanan's last conscious thought was that he couldn't recall ever making an enemy of anyone called Ironman.

CHAPTER ONE

Stony Man Farm, Virginia

It was a no-nonsense room, a room that had everything it needed and nothing it didn't. It was a room in which decisions were made, the repercussions of which rippled across the globe as sure and unstoppable as ocean waves. Indeed, it was a room in which history was written, a place where the fate of the world often hung in the balance.

It was Stony Man Farm's War Room.

Hal Brognola, director of the Sensitive Operations Group, heard the door swing shut behind him as he walked to his chair at the head of the conference table. Seated to his right was Phoenix Force leader David McCarter. Next to the Briton were the other members of Phoenix Force: Rafael Encizo, a square-faced Cuban exile; Gary Manning, a Canadian explosives expert; Calvin James, the team's medic and edged-weapon aficionado; and Gulf War veteran Thomas Jackson Hawkins, the youngest, and newest, member of the counterterrorist squad.

The men of Phoenix Force had just returned from

a mission in South America and still wore the dirty, sweat-stained camouflage fatigues in which they had arrived. They were *workers* to a man, and along with the trio of warriors who made up Able Team—Stony Man's domestic counterterrorist unit, Brognola had eight of the nine best operatives in the world. Hand-picked from units such as the U.S. Army Special Forces, Delta Force and the Navy SEAL, they were, quite simply, the best of the best.

The big Fed took his seat and glanced to the far end of the table. A tall man, lean yet muscular, with dark hair and even darker features, sat staring his way. The man wore gray slacks and a short-sleeved black polo shirt that stretched tight over his chest and biceps. Here and there along the forearms that rested on the table in front of him, Brognola could see dark round spots—bullet scars—the marks of battles past.

The man's name was Mack Bolan, and he was also known as the Executioner. A lone wolf by nature but a leader of men by demand, Bolan was the ninth in the nine best warriors in the world. And the best.

Faintly, from the other side of the door, Brognola heard the sound of someone tapping the access code into the digital lock. A moment later a buzzer sounded, and the door swung open.

Able Team leader Carl Lyons, known to the Farm's personnel as "Ironman," led the way into the room. Following him was Rosario "Politician" Blancanales, Able Team's psychological-warfare specialist. Hermann "Gadgets" Schwarz, the team's electronics wizard, brought up the rear. In front of

Schwarz was a blindfolded man whose hands were tied behind his back.

The door behind Schwarz had swung halfway shut when an arm was jammed between it and the frame. A moment later a burly man in a wheelchair threw it open and wheeled into the room. Aaron "the Bear" Kurtzman, Stony Man's computer genius and head of the Farm's cybernetics team, wheeled toward the empty space to Brognola's left. A computer keyboard sat on the table in the space that had no chair. Kurtzman rolled up, set the brake on his wheels and immediately began to type.

Lyons and Blancanales took seats at the end of the table next to Bolan while Schwarz helped the blindfolded man into a chair.

Brognola broke the silence. "Let's get started," he said.

He nodded to Kurtzman, then turned toward Schwarz. "Take the blindfold off."

As Kurtzman continued to tap the keyboard, Schwarz untied the knot in the black cloth at the back of the bound man's neck. His wrists still cuffed behind his back, William "Bobcat" Buchanan opened his eyes, then closed them again against the bright lights of the War Room.

Brognola studied the man. By the looks of his clothing, he had to have put up quite a fight. Most of the buttons on his shirt had been torn away, and the man from Justice could see a woman's white-gold-and-diamond wedding ring suspended from a chain around his neck. He wondered what it meant.

Schwarz glanced at Buchanan's handcuffs, then up to Brognola.

The big Fed shook his head. "Not yet. Let's wait and see what kind of temperament he's in when he comes out of it."

The director didn't know what the men of Able Team had drugged Buchanan with, but it hadn't all worn off yet. Bobcat was still groggy, but that wasn't necessarily bad. He had gotten his nickname as much for his fast temper as for the speed that had made him famous within the shadowy world of mercenaries, and letting him gradually warm up to what was happening might not be a bad idea.

Kurtzman suddenly quit typing. He sat back in his wheelchair, then reached forward and tapped one more button. The large wall screen behind Able Team lit up. Lyons and Blancanales swiveled in their chairs to face the screen. Schwarz spun Buchanan that way, then joined them.

"Where...the hell am I?" Buchanan slurred quietly. He closed his eyes, then opened them again.

"Item one," Brognola said as the screen focused on a subway station filled with Oriental men and women hurrying toward the trains. "The Tokyo subway." Suddenly an explosion sounded on screen, and a cloud of fumes began to fill the subway station. The cameraman taping the events switched angles to focus on an abandoned suitcase against a wall. The top of the suitcase had blown off, and clouds of gas streamed from a metal canister that had been concealed inside.

The sound of the explosion had stopped the crowd in its tracks, but that lasted only a moment. The men and women of the Tokyo subway system were all too familiar with what was happening. Panic took over. The fast-paced walks became death sprints for the exits. Screams and curses rose from terrified mouths. Those who stumbled, fell, and those who fell were trampled.

Then the screen went black.

Brognola turned to the men at the table. "The Followers of the Truth cult, thought to be inspired by the Aum Shinrikyo, whose leader was arrested back in 1995 after his devotees released nerve gas in the subway. This tape was mailed to all the Tokyo television stations and newspapers. The Followers of the Truth set a new record this time—261 killed and an additional two thousand with lung injuries." He nodded to Kurtzman again.

The computer genius typed more. The screen changed to show well-known TV anchorman Augustus Garvey seated behind a news desk and wearing a dark brown suit. "The *Washington Chieftain* reported today," Garvey said, frowning into the camera, "that a number of classified U.S. documents has been discovered abandoned by the United Nations in Somalia." The scene switched from Garvey to show UN peacekeepers carrying boxes toward waiting transport trucks.

Garvey's voice rolled on. "The source of the discovery, as well as the number and sensitivity of the documents, has not been disclosed.'' The tape froze for a moment, then Garvey disappeared.

A series of numbers appeared on the whitened screen, then Garvey returned. He sat behind the same news desk but now wore a blue pin-striped suit. "Veteran journalist and adventurer Spencer Kiethley was reported missing and assumed dead in Sierra Leone today,'' Garvey said into the camera. "He was on assignment to help train government troops in the ongoing operations against Revolutionary United Front rebels, and a convoy in which Kiethley was riding was reportedly attacked on the road between Freetown and Marampa.'' Garvey went on to the next story, and Kurtzman tapped a button blacking the screen once more.

For a moment it was silent in the War Room. Then Brognola said, "Three apparently unrelated incidents. At least we thought so until two hours ago.''

He turned to Kurtzman. "Want to take it from here, Bear?''

Kurtzman nodded and cleared his throat. "Routine cross-reference of recent events was what tied them all together,'' the computer ace said. He wheeled back from the table a few inches and grabbed the lapels of his wrinkled white lab coat with both fists. "Spencer Kiethley is the key. He was in Somalia doing a story for the *Retained Warrior* magazine, found the abandoned documents and blew the whistle to the *Chieftain*.''

Buchanan had been gradually coming back to his senses, and at the sound of the magazine's name his eyes finally cleared. "Where the hell am I?" he demanded. "And who the hell are *you*? And what the hell do you know about Spence's death?"

Brognola tapped Kurtzman on the shoulder as the computer man started to speak again. Kurtzman waited.

"I'll answer your questions as best I can," the big Fed said, looking at Buchanan. "First I can't tell you where you are. That's why you were blindfolded. And I can't tell you who we are. Just that we're on the same side that you're on." He paused, then said, "Were you awake enough to catch the news items on-screen?"

Buchanan nodded. "Yeah."

"Okay, then. Just keep listening and you'll learn all we know about your buddy Spencer Kiethley."

Buchanan fell silent. He looked angry, but even more than that, he looked confused.

Kurtzman continued. "Some way, we don't know how, Kiethley discovered the documents the UN had abandoned. He evidently turned them back over to UN authorities, then flew to Tokyo. Sources there tell us he arranged a meeting with the police investigators who were working the subway gassing."

Gadgets Schwarz frowned. "Okay, Kiethley ties the three things together," the electronics wizard said. "But what does it all mean?"

Kurtzman shrugged. "We don't know yet. Anyway, Kiethley flew straight from Japan to Sierra Leone, where he was scheduled to take charge of twelve Gurkha training officers, which he did." Kurtzman paused, frowning over his eyeglasses. "Then, phone records show a half-dozen calls to the *Washington Chieftain* during the three days he was in Sierra Leone. All but the first call were collect."

Carl Lyons shook his head. "It doesn't make sense. The *Chieftain* is a radical, crybaby, left-wing rag. Not the sort of paper a guy like Kiethley would want to talk to unless he didn't have any other choice. Besides, you said he turned the documents back over to the UN in Somalia, Bear?"

Kurtzman nodded. "I tapped into their computers and found the report. It's confirmed."

David McCarter leaned forward and crossed his arms on the table. "The fact that he contacted the *Chieftain* means he wasn't satisfied with the reaction he got from the UN," the former SAS commando said. "And where does the Tokyo gassing fit into all this? Why did Kiethley go to Japan?"

Brognola shrugged. "Those are the things we need to determine," he said. "And it's a cinch that Kiethley won't be telling us."

The big man at the other end of the table hadn't yet spoken, which was his way unless he had something important to say. Because of this, and because of his aura of strength, people listened when Bolan spoke.

All heads turned his way as Bolan cleared his throat. "Why?" he asked quietly.

Brognola pulled the well-chewed cigar stub from the breast pocket of his jacket and shoved it between his teeth. "Why what, big guy?" he asked.

"Why do you say it's a cinch Kiethley won't clear all this up himself?" Bolan said.

For a moment silence fell over the War Room. Then Brognola turned to Kurtzman. "That's right," he said. "We've been assuming that Kiethley is dead simply because the news report assumed so. But his body hasn't turned up. He could still be alive."

Calvin James shook his head. "He might be," the black Phoenix Force warrior said, "but it's not very likely. Those Revolutionary United Front boys are nothing more than bandits disguised as revolutionaries. They wear blue bandannas and word on the streets is that they got the idea from the Crips."

"That true?" T. J. Hawkins asked.

James shrugged. "Who knows? They're every bit as dangerous as the Crips. Their primary objective is to line their own pockets. And they aren't known to keep prisoners alive."

Carl Lyons nodded his agreement, then turned to face Bolan. "I've got to concur, Striker," he said, using the Executioner's Stony Man Farm code name. "They've got a history of torture and murder. If Kiethley's lucky, his death came quick. If not..." Lyons's voice trailed off, but the implication was clear.

Brognola narrowed his eyes. "Striker, do you think he's alive?" he asked simply.

Bolan shrugged. "Maybe, maybe not. I'm just saying there's no concrete evidence that he isn't."

"Is there more to this than you're telling us?" Brognola asked.

"No. Just a gut feeling I've got. Probably nothing."

Buchanan was wide-awake now and looking at Bolan. His hands still behind his back, he leaned forward. "I don't know who you are, big man," he said, then glanced around the table. "Fact is, I don't know who *any* of you are."

"Like the man said," Bolan said, nodding toward Brognola, "we're on the same side as you."

"Is that *all* you're going to tell me?" Buchanan asked.

"That's all we *can* tell you," Brognola said.

"Oh, okay," Buchanan said sarcastically. "So what I'm to believe is that this is some big-time top secret government installation that handles the tough assignments. One of those James Bond deals—even the CIA doesn't know you exist, right?"

Brognola didn't smile. "You've pretty much hit the nail on the head, Buchanan."

Buchanan's eyes widened. He looked around the table again, at every face. "You putting me on?"

"No."

His gaze finally settled on Bolan. "I must be going nuts," he said. "Why am I inclined to believe you?"

Bolan shrugged. "Because you can sense the truth, maybe."

Buchanan nodded slowly. "But what do you want from me? Why did you bring me here?"

"Does this mean you're willing to help us?" Brognola asked.

Buchanan looked Brognola in the eye. "I ought to

be royally pissed," he said. "I've been kidnapped, drugged to the point where I feel like I just got off a three-day drunk and for all I know I could be in Hong Kong, Hog Waller, Arkansas, or Antarctica right now. But for some reason, I'm not mad. Like I said, maybe I'm deranged. Maybe whatever you doped me with killed my reason. Whatever it is...I trust you."

He turned to Bolan. "Particularly you."

James grinned. "The man has that effect on people."

"Yeah, whatever, " Buchanan said. "The main thing is, if there's a chance Spence is alive...I want to help."

"We'll give you that chance," Brognola told him.

"Okay," Buchanan acknowledged. "I said I trust you. Now, how about showing me it's a two-way street by taking these things off?" He leaned forward over the table, holding his handcuffed wrists up behind him.

Schwarz looked at Brognola, who nodded.

The Able Team commando pulled a handcuff key from his pocket and unlocked the cuffs.

Brognola turned to Kurtzman. "What do we know about the Followers of the Truth?" he asked.

"In a nutshell," Kurtzman said, "the cult is a conveniently contrived cross between Eastern and Western religions, with the usual cult aspect of worshiping a megalomaniac leader."

"The Great Hikari," Brognola said.

Kurtzman nodded.

"Do we know his real name?" the big Fed asked.

Kurtzman shook his head. "But I'll get on it."

"Do that," Brognola said. "There may be a link to the other two events from that end, as well."

He turned to McCarter. "David, take your men to Somalia and find out the truth about the abandoned classified documents. I want to know exactly how something earmarked classified could be overlooked like that. If anything is still 'loose,' get hold of it."

He turned to Lyons. "Carl, you, Gadgets and Pol are heading for Washington. Turns out that the *Chieftain* reporter who did the story is an old friend of yours." He couldn't help smiling as he bit into the cigar stump. "Ira Rook. You remember him?"

The smile that spread across Lyons's face was anything but nice. "Oh, yeah," the big ex-cop said. "And I've wanted a chance to talk to him unofficially for years."

Brognola turned back to Buchanan. "What do your friends call you?" he asked.

Buchanan was rubbing his wrists. He frowned. "Depends on who they are," he said. "The guys I work with, soldiers, it's usually Bobcat."

The director shifted his gaze to Bolan. "I think if you look up the word 'soldier' in the dictionary," he said, "you'll find Striker's picture in the margin.

"Calling him Bobcat okay with you?"

"As long as he knows who's in charge," Bolan replied.

Brognola nodded. "And you can call him Pollock," he said. "Rance Pollock." He paused, then went on. "Bobcat, you were on your way to take Kiethley's place as chief training officer in Sierra Leone, right?"

"Right."

"And you said you trust this guy? The one we've been calling Striker?"

Buchanan turned to face the big man at the end of the table. "Yeah," he said. "I like to think I have a few talents left as I hit the end of middle age. And one of them is I know a real man—an honest man— from a bullshit artist." He stared hard at Bolan. "Unless I'm wrong, in which case it's time for me to check into the old-soldiers' home. Anyway, all of you guys are for real."

"I'm glad you feel that way," Brognola said, "because the big guy at the end of the table that you trust is going to Sierra Leone with you as your new assistant in charge of the Gurkhas." He chomped down on the cigar until it almost broke in two. "But, Bobcat...?"

Buchanan turned back to face the director.

"Like the man said...just don't ever forget who's *really* giving the orders."

CHAPTER TWO

Sierra Leone

Heavy foliage lined both sides of the roadway as the rust-ridden Jeep CJ-5 made its way along the narrow route. In the back seat of the vehicle, Mack Bolan kept the fingers of his right hand wrapped around the pistol grip of the AK-47.

The Jeep had arrived on the runway of Lungi Airport, Freetown, Sierra Leone, just as Jack Grimaldi, Stony Man Farm's number-one pilot, set the wheels of the SR-71 on the tarmac. Grimaldi and the plane—commandeered from the USAF by Brognola through the orders of the President himself—would wait at Lungi in case the Executioner needed them on short notice.

Two Gurkhas had hopped through the open doorways of the Jeep. Each man carried a pair of AK-47s, and before they even offered a greeting they handed Bolan and Buchanan each one of the rifles. Which didn't surprise the Executioner. They were in Sierra Leone now. Violence could flare up at any time, in any place.

As the CJ-5 continued down the road, Bolan's left hand unconsciously patted the lump under his arm. Since Buchanan had contracted with the Sierra Leone government to help the Gurkhas train the country's elite troops, they had encountered no problem bringing weapons into the war-torn West African country. The Executioner's Beretta 93-R rode in a well-worn customized nylon shoulder rig, ready to spit 9 mm death through its attached sound suppressor. At the other end of the decibel spectrum, and resting in a hip holster on his other side, the Executioner's trademark .44 Magnum Desert Eagle stood just as ready for action.

But the weapons Bolan had chosen for this jungle expedition didn't stop there. Hanging from his belt on the left, and tied across his thigh with a sturdy length of parachute cord, was a black Kydex sheath. Protruding from the top of the hard space-age plastic was the black micarta grip of the huge fighting knife known as the COMTECH Crossada. With a twelve-inch blade and a seventeen-and-one-half-inch overall length, the Crossada was a cross between a bowie knife and an Arkansas toothpick. A hole in the integral cross guard provided for the optional quillions the Executioner carried in his jacket pocket. When screwed into the weapon, these quillions formed a cross, giving the Crossada its name. Bolan had chosen the spear-point weapon as much for its ability to chop through thick jungle underbrush as for the fact that one thrust-and-pump motion would end the attack of the strongest enemy.

The Executioner tried to stare through the thick leaves and branches as the Jeep bumped over the rough ground. They were headed for the Sierra Leone Commando Unit training base some forty miles from the country's capital. To get there, they had to pass through areas of thick jungle that held almost as many Revolutionary United Front gunmen as it did leaves on the trees. And as Calvin James had said before they left Stony Man Farm, calling themselves the RUF was a thin attempt at making the men politically respectable.

In actuality the RUF was composed of cutthroat opportunists who'd kill their own mothers for a dime.

Beside the Executioner, Bobcat Buchanan sat watching the other side of the road. Bolan had been impressed that the man had immediately known to watch his side while the Executioner scanned the other. Buchanan hadn't had to be told, which meant he was well trained.

The Gurkhas sat in the front seat, the one who had introduced himself as Jessie behind the wheel. "That doesn't sound Nepalese," Buchanan had said, referring to the Gurkha's nationality.

"It isn't," Jessie had said. "But you couldn't pronounce my real name."

The other Nepalese soldier had slid into the passenger's seat and said, "Call me Dax. It isn't my real name, either, but one I saw in a movie long ago."

Bobcat had chuckled. "*Molomondo.*"

"The very one!" Dax had cried.

Now, as they jolted over the rough terrain, it felt

as if they were riding a stagecoach through the Old West. Bolan studied the Gurkhas in front of him. They wore OD green jungle hats with colored bands, Portuguese camouflage BDUs cut French style and rubber-soled boots with canvas uppers. The tip of the leather-covered wooden sheaths of the Gurkhas' traditional fighting knife, the *kukri,* could barely be seen. Both men wore their fierce-edged weapon in a cross-draw fashion and had pistols strapped to their green web belts.

As they continued on in the hot African afternoon sun, Bolan listened to the chirps of unseen jungle birds and the laughter of invisible monkeys hidden in the trees. Every so often a colorful butterfly flew from one side of the road to the other.

Jessie slowed the Jeep as they neared a sharp curve, and suddenly the birds and monkeys fell silent.

The Executioner's sixth sense—an instinct that had been honed over the years by too many attempted ambushes to remember—suddenly went on full alert.

"Incoming!" Bolan shouted as the first rounds of automatic fire burst from the trees to the left of the road. Several rounds struck the front tires of the Jeep, and the rubber exploded, sounding like more gunfire. The vehicle swerved, and the Executioner was thrown against Buchanan. In the front seat Jessie fought the wheel, valiantly trying to keep the Jeep upright as more autofire opened up on the other side of the road. The vehicle was on two wheels as it whirled around the curve, with Jessie continuing to wrestle for control.

Ahead Bolan saw that a huge boulder had been rolled into the middle of the road. "Jump!" he shouted, knowing instinctively that the Gurkha driver would never successfully maneuver the damaged Jeep around the obstacle. Rising to his feet, he dived over the side.

Bolan hit the ground on his shoulder, the AK-47 flying from his fist. His momentum carried him down into a narrow ditch at the side of the road, then up the other side into the trees.

Mud caked the jungle floor, making sick sucking sounds as the Executioner rolled through it. He felt something hard strike his ribs and stop his roll, looked up and saw that he'd come to a halt beneath the hot barrel of a Russian-made SGMB 7.62 mm wheel-mounted machine gun. Above the barrel the RUF gunner, identified as such by the blue bandanna he wore, looked down in surprise.

Bolan rolled to his side, drew his Desert Eagle from the hip holster under his bush jacket and angled the weapon toward the RUF man.

The bandit let up on the machine gun's trigger and clawed for the pistol at his side, but he was too late. Bolan squeezed the Desert Eagle's trigger. A 240-grain hollowpoint round struck the man between the upper lip and nose and blew the back of his head into the trees.

The Executioner twisted onto his belly as a flash of white appeared in his peripheral vision. His eyes focused quickly on a white T-shirt above a ragged pair of camouflage trousers. This man, too, wore the RUF's trademark blue bandanna, tied over his head pirate style, and held a Soviet SKS. He saw the big American and dived face forward into the mud.

Bolan pulled the trigger again. Another big .44 round struck one of the wheels beneath the SGMB, then whined off into the trees. Correcting his aim, he angled the weapon toward the RUF hardman, who had come to a halt less than a yard from his boots. As the man tried to raise his head out of the wet earth, the Executioner tapped the trigger again and took him out with another .44 Magnum hollowpoint round.

Bolan kept the Desert Eagle at the ready as he reached down with his other hand and retrieved the fallen SKS. His AK-47 had been lost when he hit the ground upon leaving the jeep, and he could put a rifle to good use. But just as he feared, the barrel had been jammed with mud when the man at his feet had dived under the machine gun. He didn't have time to clean it out, and to try to fire it as it was would mean a burst barrel. He stood as much chance of killing himself as any of the enemy.

The Executioner dropped the useless weapon. On the other side of the road, as well as from farther down the road on the same side, the gunfire continued. He glanced at the wheel-mounted SGMB. The machine gun was fine for an ambush such as the one the RUF bandits had planned, but now that the battle had taken a more traditional jungle-fighting turn, it would prove far too clumsy and indiscriminate. If he fired blindly through the trees, he could just as easily kill Buchanan or the Gurkhas.

For a brief moment, the Executioner wondered if his three allies were even still alive, then pushed such unproductive thoughts from his mind. Wondering would do no good. What he needed to do was to go find out.

Bolan holstered the Desert Eagle and drew the Beretta with his right hand. With his left he unsheathed the Crossada knife. If he couldn't have the advantage of superior firepower, he would have to rely on stealth. The near silent Beretta, and the totally silent Crossada, would fill that bill quite well.

The Executioner scanned the area. He couldn't see far, but sensed he was at the forward line of the ambush. If not, anyone the Jeep had passed would have come up on his rear by now. Cutting deeper into the jungle, away from the road, he walked silently for what he estimated to be twenty to twenty-five yards, cut ten yards farther down the road, then began to make his way quietly back. With any luck he should come up on the enemy's rear, now.

The gunfire on both sides of the road had died down to sporadic shots by the time he saw the next bandit. The man in the blue bandanna faced away from him, kneeling. The stock of another Soviet SKS rifle was pressed to his shoulder and aimed through the trees.

Bolan stopped, squinting through the leaves. He brought up the Beretta and sighted down the barrel.

His finger was already moving back on the trigger when another flash of blue caught his eye, then two others.

At least three more RUF hardmen were hidden in the thick leaves and branches, both within six feet of the target in his sights.

Slowly, cautiously, he lowered the Beretta, then holstered it. The sound suppressor was just that—a suppressor, not a silencer as it was often mistakenly called. It would go a long way toward quieting the 9 mm blast, but at such close range the noise might still be heard by the other bandits. There might only be the three more RUF men he had seen. Then again, there might be thirty more stretched shoulder to shoulder nearby. No matter how many there were, Bolan couldn't afford to alert them.

Bolan transferred the Crossada to his right hand. He no longer needed quiet: he needed silence.

Letting the bulky leaves and branches keep him hidden, the Executioner moved slowly in behind the nearest RUF bandit. In one swift motion he reached around the man's face with his left hand and covered his target's mouth. Bolan jerked the head in his hand backward, exposing the throat. At the same time the Crossada came around on the other side.

The spear-point blade had a primary sharpened edge of ten inches. The "false" edge measured eight. For all practical purposes the weapon was a double-edged fighting knife.

Bolan drew the false edge across the hardman's throat, severing both arteries and veins in one smooth

slice. The larynx separated with the other components of the neck and turned what the man had intended to be a scream into a soft, wet gurgle.

The Executioner lowered the corpse to the ground.
With a swift and silent lateral movement, he was on
the next man in line. Wrapping a hand around the
mouth again, he thrust the point of the Crossada deep
into the bandit's left kidney. Pumping twice, the Executioner withdrew the blade and inserted it into the
other side of the man's lower back.

The second bandit collapsed to the muddy grass,
as dead as the first.

Bolan paused as shots rang out down the tree line.
More gunfire came from the other side of the road,
then the jungle fell silent once more.

The third RUF hardman Bolan had spotted raised
his rifle to his shoulder, sighting down the barrel at
some target the Executioner couldn't see through the
leaves. The big man lunged forward, thrusting the
Crossada up and out. The tip of the massive blade
entered the bandit's floating ribs, cracking bone and
carving cartilage as it shot on through to the heart.
The SKS fell from his fingers.

Bolan saw a new flash of blue as he withdrew the
knife and let the corpse fall of its own accord. Two
heads turned simultaneously, and for a moment the
Executioner wished he'd kept the Beretta in his opposite hand.

He moved in, quickly closing the gap between him
and the nearer RUF hardman. He brought the Crossada high over his head as the man tried to spin and

bring a Russian-made PPSh submachine gun into play. But the bandit had only partially made the turn when the twelve-inch blade came chopping down onto his scalp.

The heavy steel didn't stop until it had reached the bandit's shoulders. Bolan jerked it out and turned on the man to his side.

The RUF hardman saw what had happened to his companion and froze, his AK-47 aimed at the Executioner's chest but held in hands paralyzed with fear. Bolan took advantage of the momentary pause to plunge the Crossada into the bandit's sternum. The point punctured the soft tissue and kept going. Bolan felt the blade pause momentarily as it encountered the spine, then it slipped off to the side and emerged through the bandit's back. Bolan rode the body down to the ground as it slumped to its back.

The Executioner's eyes searched the jungle for more of the telltale blue bandannas as he tried to jerk the Crossada free. But the blade was lodged firmly in the man's chest and wouldn't budge. Bolan's hand shot to the Beretta in the shoulder holster. He paused long enough to make sure no more of the enemy were in the immediate vicinity, then left the 93-R holstered and grabbed the Crossada's grips with both hands and pulled. Finally the blade began to move. Slowly at first, it finally exited from the body. Wiping the blade across the man's shirt, the Executioner stuck it back in the Kydex sheath and grabbed the AK-47 as the gunfire across the road picked up again.

CHAPTER THREE

Ethiopia

David McCarter glanced out the window as Charlie Mott, Stony Man Farm's number-two pilot, guided the converted C-17 Globemaster III across Ethiopia's Ogaden Desert. The large McDonnell Douglas transport plane had been chosen to deliver the men of Phoenix Force to Somalia for two reasons. First McCarter and his fellow commandos were bringing along enough equipment to be totally self-sufficient in the war-torn nation, and they needed the storage area the modified C-17 provided. And second the Globemaster was serving as partial cover. Mott also had a load of Peace Corps provisions that he would deliver to make it appear that was the real reason the transport plane had arrived.

McCarter continued to stare out of the window. The Globemaster was low enough now that he could see the checkpoint at Dolo. A moment later they had passed over the border village and entered Somalian airspace on their way to Mogadishu.

The Phoenix Force leader felt a twinge of sadness

for the people of Somalia. For the past five hundred years Somalia had been its own worst enemy. Until the early sixteenth century, Mogadishu had been a thriving stopover in the Arabs' Indian Ocean trading network. Then the Portuguese had come to destroy both ports, and in turn to seal the fate of the country. Somalia had declined rapidly after that, lapsing into anonymity on the world scene.

And there it had stayed ever since.

The Phoenix Force leader sighed as the big engines quieted further. The roll of the dice, the draw of a card. The student of history soon began to suspect that history itself was that—a game of chance. A crapshoot, so to speak. Random occurrences seemed to set into motion the events that divided flourishing nations from those that became impoverished. The wrong attack by the wrong enemy at the wrong time could bring destruction to a country for centuries. Drought, famine, pestilence—they could end a flourishing culture just as fast. Sometimes the enemy was man, sometimes nature. Somalia had seen its share of both, and together the two adversaries had conspired to keep the country destitute.

McCarter closed his eyes for a moment. A card game. A crapshoot that busted many nations while bankrolling others. With the right chain of events, with Lady Luck smiling on certain soil, a formally unorganized or defeated people could become a world power. The absence of war for a period of time that enabled the buildup of military strength rather than its depletion, favorable weather to ensure that crops sprouted plentifully and with regularity and a few decades free of serious disease could build a Roman Empire, a Great Britain or a United States of America.

Charlie Mott spoke up, breaking into McCarter's brief reverie. "Two minutes to drop."

Behind him McCarter heard boots moving across the cargo area. At first the Phoenix Force leader had considered just jumping his team into Somalia with their weapons and other equipment. But their primary mission was to find out about the abandoned UN documents, and that meant they'd be working at least some of the time in public. A good cover would be necessary, and an illegal entry into the country would mean they'd be on the run after landing.

They couldn't afford that complication. Not on this type of mission.

Therefore, the Phoenix Force leader had decided that only their equipment would descend via parachute. They would continue on to the airport at Mogadishu and deplane using false passports provided by Stony Man Farm. The passports listed them as a team of journalists and photographers who had hitched a ride on the C-17. The story should also give them good reason to be touring the country.

McCarter glanced at Mott. The pilot wore his usual mirrored sunglasses and green-and-yellow baseball cap. The faded leather bomber jacket that was equally part of his rarely changing wardrobe was draped over the back of his seat.

"Thirty seconds," Mott said. "Get it in gear, guys."

The plane kept a steady speed and altitude as McCarter turned to see T. J. Hawkins and Calvin James slide open the cargo door. Gary Manning and Rafael Encizo hurried up. Both men wheeled a dolly ahead of them that bore several crates. Cargo chutes had been affixed to each box.

"Fifteen seconds."

Quickly and efficiently Encizo and Manning began to hand the static lines to James and Hawkins. The two commandos at the door quickly snapped the lines to the door frame, then stepped back.

"Ten...nine...eight..."

As soon as Mott reached zero, the men of Phoenix Force began to shove the crates through the doorway. McCarter shifted his gaze back to the window, watching the chutes open as each box in turn hit the end of its static line. The top of each crate was marked with a bold red number designating its contents. As box number 4 hit the end, it snapped the line. The chute remained closed, and the crate began an end-over-end tumble toward the ground.

McCarter frowned. "What was in number four?" he called back into the cargo area.

Manning pulled a list from the pocket of his khaki safari vest. "MREs," he said. "Looks like we'll be sampling the native cuisine on this one."

"Looks like," McCarter agreed. He turned back to the window, continuing to watch as the chutes floated the rest of the cargo earthward. Along with the other equipment they had brought, the crates contained pistols and rifles for each man. Until they retrieved them, Phoenix Force was armed only with small folding knives. The knives looked more like working blades but could kill if pressed into service by an experienced hand.

Fifteen minutes later Mott set the wheels down on the tarmac in Mogadishu. McCarter grabbed his camera bag, opened the cabin door and dropped down. He heard the cargo door open, then the boots of the other four commandos fell to the runway behind him.

The heat of the war-torn African country was sweltering, and McCarter felt it rise from the tarmac through the rubber soles of his hiking boots. He glanced over his shoulder. Hawkins and Encizo carried briefcases that contained laptop computers. Camera bags hung from Manning's and James's shoulders, and the big Canadian was further burdened with a tripod. All of the men of Phoenix Force wore blue jeans or khakis and either photojournalist vests or safari jackets.

The Briton grinned. The warriors from Stony Man Farm looked more like newsmen than newsmen, like something straight out of a Banana Republic or Eddie Bauer advertisement. McCarter started toward the terminal and a sign that read Customs—Private Craft in several languages, including English.

Reaching the glass door under the sign, McCarter swung it open and stepped back, letting the others pass through. He followed.

If the heat had been bad outside, it was worse in

the small customs office. A lone ceiling fan twirled overhead, too slow to circulate the hot air. McCarter pulled the canvas hat from his head and used it to mop his brow.

Behind the counter at the end of the room stood a thin black man in a Somalian customs uniform with lieutenant's bars on the shoulders. Manning was the first to reach the window, and he plopped down his passport and shoved it through the opening.

The lieutenant used deft and well-practiced fingers to riffle through the pages of the passport. He glanced up quickly, comparing the picture to the man who had posed for it, then brought his stamp down hard and said, "Next."

Encizo stepped up, and the procedure was repeated. One by one the men of Phoenix Force cleared Somalian customs and stepped to the side of the room to wait.

McCarter came last, opening his passport to the picture and handing it through the window. The document claimed he was a British freelance photographer. The customs officer brought the stamp down with a thud and handed it back.

The Briton walked over to join the rest of the team. Their entry had gone smoothly—not that he'd expected it to be otherwise. Stony Man Farm utilized the best team of forgers in the world for such documents. But in addition to the slick credentials, Brognola had been able, through his position in the U.S. Department of Justice, to call in a favor from a friend in the CIA. The friend had contacted a friend in Somalian customs and the path had been prepared in advance. They should have no trouble.

He glanced back at the lieutenant behind the window. The man grinned, and McCarter nodded back. It seemed unusual that a man with any rank would be working the window, and McCarter now suspected that he wasn't a regular. In fact he was probably the CIA contact Brognola had utilized to ensure a smooth entry.

Yes, David McCarter thought as he lifted his luggage, things were going smoothly. Too smoothly?

As if to answer McCarter's doubts, the door to the terminal proper suddenly opened, and a brawny, bearded black man wearing the uniform of a customs captain blocked the doorway. He glanced from one man to the next, eyeing their luggage and equipment at the same time. "You are newsmen?" he asked in heavily accented English.

McCarter and the others nodded.

"I learned English in London," the man said with a smile, "and I have visited America. There I learned certain slang or colloquial terms." He paused. "Would you like to hear my favorite?"

McCarter stiffened. Something wasn't quite right. He nodded. "Certainly. Give us your favorite."

"Bullshit," the captain said, his smile fading. He then drew a Tokarev pistol from the holster on his Sam Browne belt.

The door through which the men of Phoenix Force had entered the terminal opened, and McCarter turned to see four more customs men, all carrying submachine guns.

"Bullshit you are newsmen," the captain said again. "He nodded toward the door. "My name is Captain Berber. And now, you will all come with me."

Washington, D.C.

THE FLIGHT from Stony Man Farm in the Blue Ridge Mountains of Virginia to Washington, D.C., never took long. Particularly when you had at your disposal an AV-8B Harrier II Plus, the world's only in production V/STOL—vertical or short takeoff and landing—aircraft. Flown by a Stony Man blacksuit pilot trainee, the craft had barely risen into the air when it set the men of Able Team down again in the U.S. capital.

Carl Lyons had rented a Chevy Conversion van at the airport, and they had actually spent more time in the ground vehicle on their way to the *Washington Chieftain* building in downtown D.C. than they had in the air.

Lyons propped the empty cardboard refrigerator box against the white trash bin in the alley behind the *Chieftain* building. He leaned the dolly against the brick of the building's rear wall. The Able Team leader's eyes rose to a window several floors up. It was a bad angle, but just over the sill, he thought he could see the bald spot on the back of a brownish-gray-fringed head.

Ira Rook had begun going both bald and gray during the years since Lyons had last seen him.

Lyons closed the garbage bin's lid, brushed the dust off the sleeves of his plaid sport coat, then turned and walked to the end of the alley. Gadgets Schwarz and Rosario Blancanales were waiting back on the sidewalk.

"You still want to try this straight, Ironman?" Blancanales asked. "We could just snatch him off the street like we did Buchanan."

"No, let's give him every opportunity to cooperate first," he said.

The three men turned the corner and entered the main entrance of the building, stopping briefly to flash their U.S. Justice Department credentials at the security desk. Brognola provided all Stony Man Farm operatives with such ID for those times when missions required the illusion of police authority and covert action.

The security man at the desk wore a powder blue uniform shirt two sizes too small for his bloated torso. His darker blue slacks were even tighter and threatened to burst at the seams. He looked up at the Justice Department IDs thrust down into his face with awe. "Can I give you directions?" he asked around a mouthful of doughnut.

Lyons shook his head. "We know where we're going," he said. Before the man could reply, he led the way into the busy newsroom.

The clicking of computer keyboard keys filled the air as Lyons led the way through a maze of desks separated from each other by clear plastic dividers. Men and women occupied the tiny office cubicles, typing with both hands and trapping telephone receivers between their shoulders and ears. Most were too busy to even look up as the three strangers passed.

The Able Team leader reached the elevators on the far side of the newsroom and pushed the Up button, staring at the door. The sight brought back memories. Ira Rook. Elevators. As Lyons waited for the car to appear, he let his mind travel back over the years.

Suddenly he was a young rookie LAPD cop again. He was in a black-and-white cruiser and had just let Wally Dobbs, his middle-aged training officer, out in front of the four-story apartment building where Dobbs's girlfriend lived. The older man would be no more than thirty minutes, he had promised Lyons.

A moment later Lyons had heard the first scream. Looking out the window, he saw an elderly woman point up in the air with one hand and cover her mouth with the other.

Lyons stepped out of the cruiser and followed the woman's gaze. Teetering near the edge of the roof of the apartment building was a scantily clad young woman. She looked down at the sidewalk as a crowd began to gather, men, women and children taking advantage of the free entertainment.

The old woman who had screamed suddenly grabbed Lyons by the arm. "Do something!" she demanded. "It's your job!"

Lyons looked back up at the young woman on the

roof. As a rookie fresh out of the academy, he was forbidden to take any serious action without his training partner present. Turning toward the front steps of the apartment building, he took them three at a time and stopped just inside the first-floor door.

It was at that point that Lyons realized he didn't know either the apartment number of Dobbs's girlfriend or her name.

Through the glass door Lyons saw that more people had gathered. Someone shouted, "Jump! Jump!" and the rookie cop fought the urge to race back outside and beat the ghoul with his fists. Instead, he hurried to the elevator and took it to the top floor, then sprinted up the final set of steps to the roof.

The door at the top of the stairs had been left ajar, and Lyons eased it open quietly. Not wanting to startle the young woman, he emerged onto the chat-covered roof slowly and saw her standing just beyond an air duct, facing the street. The diaphanous pink nightgown she wore fluttered in the breeze with a gentle peacefulness that defied the urgency of the situation.

Lyons moved slowly toward her, stopping twenty feet away. "Hello," he said as softly as he could.

The girl never even turned to look at him.

She jumped.

The elevator door at the *Washington Chieftain* building suddenly opened, bringing Lyons back to the present. He stepped inside, waited for Schwarz and Blancanales to follow, then pushed the third-floor button. As the car rose, his mind drifted back to the past again.

As the girl had fallen and the crowd screamed below, the young Lyons had rushed instinctively to the edge of the roof. Looking back on it now, he knew he had been only partially aware of a snapping sound and lights flashing behind him. He had reached the edge of the roof in time to see the girl hit the ground. Another flash of light to his rear finally caused him to turn, and he'd done that in time to catch yet another flash bulb in the face. As his pupils readjusted after the flash, Carl Lyons got his first glimpse of Ira Rook behind the camera.

Rook had been a stringer for the *Los Angeles Times* in those days. He had also, Lyons would later learn, lived in the same apartment building as Wally Dobbs's girlfriend and from which the girl had just leaped to her death. When the call had come into the *Times* that there was a jumper on the roof, the editor who answered the phone recognized the address and immediately called Rook.

The *Chieftain*'s elevator stopped on the third floor, and Lyons, Schwarz and Blancanales stepped off. The Able Team leader led the way down a tiled hall, but his mind was still on that night so many years ago.

Wally Dobbs had arrived on the roof ten minutes after the girl had jumped. His face as white as a ghost's, he had pleaded that Lyons save his marriage by telling their captain that the training officer been down the street buying cigarettes instead of in his girlfriend's apartment.

As for Ira Rook, he'd been doing his best to make a name for himself and land a big-time news job. Over the next few days the *Times* had run his pictures of Lyons, and the girl diving over the edge of the roof. Each day a new Rook story accompanied the photos, and each story questioned the way Lyons had handled the incident. Rook called the young cop "insensitive, callous and uncaring" and made an art out of turning fact into fiction. He took tiny details of the incident and twisted them into whatever he wanted them to imply. When he couldn't find anything to be twisted, he simply invented things. The fact that Lyons was a rookie who had violated department policy by acting without his training officer present was stressed in each article.

For a while Lyons was the most hated cop in L.A. The end result was that he received sixty days without pay and narrowly escaped being fired altogether.

A frosted-glass window in the top of the door read Washington Chieftain, Ira M. Rook, Senior Editor. Lyons stopped, curled his hand around the knob, and took a deep breath.

A year after the girl's death Ira Rook had his own column at the *Times,* and the public had long ago forgotten Carl Lyons. Lyons went on to make a new name for himself as one of the best detectives the City of Angels had ever produced. The city forgot the girl who had jumped.

Carl Lyons didn't.

The former Los Angeles PD detective opened the door and stepped inside, followed by his teammates. The chubby, balding man behind the desk looked up, his face a mask of surprise and anger. Lyons closed the door and turned back to Rook. He didn't speak; he just looked.

"I don't know who the hell you think you are," Rook said, "but people knock before they come into my office."

Lyons walked slowly to the desk, still staring at his old nemesis. Besides going gray and losing much of his hair, Rook had put on weight. But he was as short as ever. He wore striped suspenders over his white shirt, and the knot in his tie had been loosened. "You happen to remember me, Rook?" Lyons asked.

The man leaned forward over his desk, cradled his flabby chin in his hands and snorted. "Well, no," he said sarcastically. "But then you don't look important enough to remember. Who the hell are you?"

"We're special agents with the U.S. Department of Justice, Mr. Rook," Schwarz said politely.

"Wooo!" Rook said, pursing his lips obscenely.

Lyons looked at the floor, chuckled and shook his head. "Guys," he said over his shoulder, "you remember that I said we should try this the easy way first?"

"I remember," Blancanales said.

"That's what you said," Schwarz agreed.

"I changed my mind." Lyons drew back his fist and drove it into Rook's jaw.

The man flew back against his chair, closed his eyes and lapsed into unconsciousness.

Able Team went to work like different components of one highly efficient, well-maintained machine. Blancanales walked to the window behind Rook's desk and slid it open as Schwarz unbuttoned the blazer he wore to expose a long length of rope coiled around his waist and chest. He began to unwrap it as Lyons lay the unconscious Rook on the floor and bound his hands and feet with plastic handcuffs.

Blancanales moved to the hall door, grasped the knob, then turned back. "He really *didn't* remember you, did he?" he asked Lyons.

Schwarz echoed Rook's words, chuckling. "Ironman's not important enough to remember."

Blancanales disappeared into the hall, closing the door behind him. Lyons finished binding Rook and helped Schwarz fashion a harness around the editor's shoulders with the rope. When they had finished, they dragged the man to the window.

Lyons looked down in time to see Blancanales fishing the refrigerator box out of the trash. He stood the cardboard container on its end under the window and opened the flaps at the top.

Schwarz looked at Lyons. "I better go down with him. We don't want him banging his head."

"Might do him some good," Lyons said.

Schwarz laughed. "Rook's obnoxious, repugnant and belligerent. He lies in his stories, and he's representative of the worst journalism has to offer."

Able Team's electronics expert paused for breath. "But he's not a criminal, Ironman. He's not a terrorist, and he's not plotting to overthrow the government of the United States of America."

"Don't be so sure," Lyons said.

Schwarz went deadpan again. "So...I suppose we better kill him, then?"

Lyons snorted. Schwarz knew he had no intentions of harming Ira Rook—at least not seriously. The shot to the jaw had been deserved, and a long time coming. But Schwarz was making a point—a point that Lyons might already understand but that could never be emphasized too much: none of the warriors of Stony Man Farm ever let personal feelings interfere with their work. They never had, and they never would. It simply wasn't the way a professional behaved.

The Able Team leader wrapped the rope around the desk several times for support, then helped Schwarz lift Rook over the windowsill. The electronics whiz stuck one leg though the opening after him and then the other. With Rook held securely between him and the wall, Schwarz wrapped his arms around the man and let Lyons lower them to the box.

Schwarz swung out and dropped to the ground as his feet drew even with the top of the box. He and Blancanales guided the unconscious editor inside, closed the flaps, then lifted the box onto the dolly.

Upstairs, Lyons unwound the rope and dropped it to the ground. He closed the window, left the office and walked back down the hall to the elevator. Two minutes later he had joined his teammates in the alley.

"He's liable to wake up, Ironman," Schwarz cautioned as they wheeled the box down the alley to the street. "And we forgot to gag him."

"I didn't forget," Lyons stated.

"But if he comes out of it, he's going to make noise," Blancanales said, glancing up and down the busy sidewalk as they emerged from the alley.

"No, he won't."

Schwarz and Blancanales glanced at each other.

As if to straighten out the confusion himself, Rook suddenly started to move inside the box.

Lyons reached up, opened the flap, then drove a fist out of sight inside the cardboard.

The movement stopped.

"We can't kill him," the Able Team leader said, "but I couldn't resist one last shot."

Able Team rolled the boxed newspaper editor down the sidewalk to the corner, crossed the street and wheeled him up to the van. Schwarz slid the door open and Lyons and Blancanales tossed the box— not too gently—inside.

A moment later the van was speeding away from the *Washington Chieftain* building.

CHAPTER FOUR

Sierra Leone

The Executioner paused, listening, trying to decide exactly where the gunfire on his side of the road was coming from. It wasn't easy in the cacophony of explosions that echoed through the trees.

Then, as suddenly as the rifle fire had started again, it stopped.

Slowly, carefully, Bolan made his way to the tree line, dropping to one knee as he peered through the entangled branches, vines and leaves. On the road, stalled and with the right front tire hanging in shreds from the rim, was the Jeep CJ-5. Blood covered the front seat and behind the vehicle he could see the deep channels the tires of the fishtailing vehicle had carved into the muddy road.

Bolan squinted into the sun, trying to focus his eye on a dark lump on the far side of the vehicle. He knew it was a body, but he didn't know whose. As his eyes cleared, he made out the lines of a small, bent and misshapen man wearing a large *kukri* knife.

Jessie. Blood still poured from the wounds in his chest and neck, but his eyes had closed in death.

The Executioner scanned the roadway and tried to look deeper into the trees on the other side. He saw no sign of Bobcat Buchanan or Dax.

Neither man had taken cover on his side of the road. If they had, he would have encountered them by now as he moved along the line of RUF men. And they hadn't been hit with Jesse or they'd be on the road, dead. Which meant they had to have taken refuge in the trees on the other side. The fact that there appeared to have been return fire earlier told Bolan they had weapons—either the AKs they'd had in the Jeep or other rifles they'd taken from the RUF bandits.

At least they had been alive and in possession of weapons a few moments ago, before the firing suddenly stopped again. Did they still have the guns? Were they still alive? Or was that the reason the road had quieted?

The Executioner stayed just inside the tree line, trying to maneuver toward a spot across from a break in the trees on the other side of the road. Maybe he could see more from there. He had taken less than ten steps when a patch of blue rose directly in front of him.

Bolan had no time to bring the sights of the AK-47 in line with the body that held the Russian Makarov 9 mm pistol. In one swift and smooth motion, he brought the stock around and up against the RUF gunner's jaw.

A loud crack echoed through the jungle as the man slumped to the ground unconscious. The Executioner uprighted his rifle, aiming at the man. His index finger was moving back on the trigger when a flash of movement caught his eye on the other side of the road. He paused.

Peering through the dense foliage, Bolan saw Buchanan step from the trees across the road, followed a moment later by Dax.

Bolan frowned. Neither man was armed.

A second later the reason became obvious. The barrels of two AK-47s appeared through the branches, then two men in blue bandannas. Another armed man stepped from the trees on the other side of the road.

The man directly behind Buchanan was over six feet tall and 240 pounds. He stuck two fingers into his mouth and cut loose with a long shrill whistle.

Farther down the tree line, on Bolan's side of the road and in the direction he'd been heading, another RUF hardman stepped out of hiding onto the road.

The bandits directly behind Buchanan and Dax jammed their rifle barrels into their prisoners' kidneys and prodded them along. The other two men met in the middle of the road, standing back to back as their eyes scanned the trees on both sides.

Bolan knew why. They were looking for him.

The two men in charge of Buchanan and Dax grabbed them by the shoulders and turned them. Buchanan's captor instigated a staring contest as sweat dripped from the bandanna around his forehead.

More moisture stained the armpits of his tight khaki military tunic. Finally tiring of the contest, he screamed in English, "Where is he? Where is your friend?"

Buchanan shrugged, held his hands out palms up, then snorted. "That is an incredibly stupid question to ask under the circumstances. How the hell should I know?" Hooking a thumb across the road, he shrugged. "In the trees, maybe?"

His insolence earned him a rifle butt in the gut.

Buchanan twisted toward Bolan as he fell to his knees. He leaned forward, emptying his stomach. But as he did, the American mercenary-journalist winked at the tree line.

Beneath his feet, the Executioner heard the man he had butt-stroked begin to stir. He looked down to see the man's eyes open and trying to focus.

In a moment the bandit would remember where he was and what had happened. His natural instinct would be to shout a warning, which would give away the Executioner's location. But if Bolan shot him, the round would lead the RUF hardmen to him just as surely.

Bolan drove the stock down into the man's head, rendering him unconscious. He looked across at Buchanan and Dax as the heavy man in front of Buchanan turned to the two men still standing back to back.

He barked orders in Krio, the local language. Then, turning back to Buchanan and Dax, he spoke in English again. "Change the tire on the Jeep! Do it now!"

Bolan watched the two men break position and start toward his side of the road. The big man kept his rifle on Buchanan and Dax as they moved to the spare tire mounted on the rear of the vehicle. The other man turned to face the trees across from Bolan, his rifle pressed against his shoulder and ready.

The Executioner knew they were ninety-nine percent sure he was on the opposite side of the road from which they'd been. But that one percent of doubt was enough to keep one man preoccupied.

Good. It was all the advantage the Executioner would need.

Bolan drew the Beretta 93-R with his left hand and flipped the selector switch to semiauto. He watched the two men in blue bandannas enter the tree line ten yards down. They would split up if they knew what they were doing. One would head toward him, the other away. When they'd satisfied themselves he wasn't in the first "sphere" of the search, they'd move deeper into the jungle, then head back to meet each other in the middle of the search area again. A good search plan. The only problem with it was that the Executioner *was* in that first sphere.

And the RUF hardmen about to enter it would never leave it alive.

The big American dropped to a crouch, moving five feet farther from the road and into a thick growth of brush. He paused for a moment, setting the Beretta on a clump of grass and drawing the Crossada knife.

Pulling the quillions from his pocket, he swiftly threaded them through the hole at the base of the blade to form the cross guard, then jabbed the huge piece of steel into the soft mud. With both hands he scooped the wet earth onto his face, then arms. More mud went over his bush jacket and trousers until they were the same color as the jungle floor. Grabbing fistfuls of the vegetation around him, he pressed them into the sticky mess that now covered his face and clothes. Most of it fell off, but enough stayed to effectively break up his outline and further camouflage him.

He had barely finished his camouflage when he heard the quiet footsteps enter hearing range. The RUF hardman headed his way was moving along the exact line Bolan had predicted and, unless the thick foliage was distorting the sounds, was less than twenty feet away.

The Executioner waited.

The man's blue bandanna, easy to spot in a jungle of browns, greens and yellows, appeared first. Ten feet to his right and five feet in front, Bolan remained still, letting him come. If the bandit didn't spot him before he got into knife range, he'd use the Crossada. If the RUF man did see him, he'd be forced to use the Beretta and hope they were far enough from the other bandits that the quiet 9 mm cough would go unheard.

The RUF man moved on with painful slowness. As he neared, the Executioner could make out the whites of his eyes beneath the blue. The brown orbs in the center of the white darted nervously back and forth as the hunter searched for his prey, never knowing that the prey was stalking him, as well.

Bolan dropped even lower, to all fours, resting his weight on his wrists as his hands held both knife and gun up and pointed toward the target. Like a cat, patient yet anxious to spring, he continued to wait.

When the gunner drew directly across from him, he struck.

The Executioner flew through the air, the Crossada extended in front of him. As the spear point made contact with the RUF man's ribs, he threw his opposite arm back and around in a classic saber-fencing counterbalance move.

The knife buried itself to the quillions in flesh as the man turned shocked eyes toward his attacker. He opened his mouth to scream but a fire-hydrant spray of crimson poured forth instead.

The Executioner reached out, wrapping his arms around the man and lowering him silently to the ground.

Through the trees he could hear the sounds of Dax and Buchanan changing the Jeep's tire. Deeper in the jungle and many yards ahead, he could barely make out the sounds of feet moving quietly through the grass.

Bolan dropped deeper into the thick growth again, moving silently along toward the footsteps. Twenty yards catercorner from where he'd left the last man, he saw the other RUF bandit, who faced the opposite direction.

Three feet behind the man, Bolan rose to full neight. He brought the Crossada up behind his right ear and around in a horizontal arch.

For a moment it looked as if the twelve-inch blade nad missed the RUF man completely. The bandit froze in place, then a thin red ring appeared, encircling his neck. A moment later the man toppled to the muddy jungle floor.

Bolan unscrewed the quillions and dropped them back into his pocket. Sheathing the Crossada, he turned back to the road.

The Executioner transferred the Beretta to his right hand as he made his way back through the trees, walking as fast as possible without making enough noise to be heard from the road. When he reached the tree line he saw Buchanan and Dax stand up. Buchanan still held the tire iron he'd used to replace the lug nuts.

The heavyset RUF bandit still covered the two men with his rifle. He barked something in Krio to the man guarding the other side of the road, and the bandit turned and jogged to his side. "We can wait no longer," he told the two captives in English. "Your comrade has deserted you." He stuck his fingers in his mouth and whistled again.

Bolan flipped the Beretta to 3-round-burst mode as the heavy bandit raised the AK-47 to eye level and sighted down the barrel at Buchanan and Dax. He stepped to the very edge of the tree line as the bandit growled, "And now you die."

"Wait a second!" Buchanan said.

The bandit lowered the rifle momentarily.

As quick as a flash, Buchanan brought the tire iron back and threw it.

The makeshift missile struck the RUF hardman square between the eyes, and the man hit the ground like a felled oak.

But the final gunner was too far away, and as he turned toward Dax, Bolan could see an expression of resignation on Buchanan's face. The man was a soldier who was prepared for death, and now would face it honorably and without showing fear.

The RUF man swung his rifle toward Buchanan and the Gurkha and flipped off the safety.

Bolan stepped out of the trees, aimed the Beretta at the bandit's head and drilled him with a 3-round burst.

Both Buchanan and Dax turned toward the Executioner. Dax opened his mouth in a wide grin that showed two even rows of white teeth.

Buchanan shook his head. "I'm liking you better and better all the time, Pollock," he said. His eyes traveled up and down the Executioner, taking in the mud, leaves and twigs that had served to camouflage him. "Although I've been meaning to talk to you about your personal hygiene."

CHAPTER FIVE

Somalia

David McCarter trailed Captain Berber out of the customs room into the main terminal of the airport. The other members of Phoenix Force followed. The armed guards accompanying the burly black captain brought up the rear.

McCarter studied the man as he walked. Berber's arms were held wide like those of bodybuilders, whose latissimus dorsi muscles have been highly developed. His back was wide, the trapezius muscles shooting at a forty-five-degree angle from the corners of his shoulders to his head, almost completely eliminating his neck. The man lifted weights. Lots of weights. That was clear.

They turned a corner in the terminal and started down what appeared to be a little-used hallway. The captain reached in his pocket as they walked, fished out a large key ring, then stopped in front of a steel door. Inserting the key, he swung the door open, stepped back and motioned McCarter to enter.

The other customs officers stayed in the hall. Letting their subguns fall to the ends of the slings around their shoulders, they took up positions against the wall.

McCarter stepped into the room, followed by James, Hawkins, Encizo and Manning. He glanced around, and saw a combination office-gymnasium. At one end of the room was a battered metal desk. Papers were scattered across the top, and a clear plastic photo cube showcased pictures of Berber, a woman McCarter assumed to be his wife and at least a half-dozen children of varying ages.

The Briton's suspicions about the captain's weight training were confirmed by the contents of the rest of the room. Thousands of pounds of weights were scattered across the floor, on plate trees, benches and other equipment. One bench lay inside a steel power rack, a seven-foot Olympic bar resting over it. McCarter quickly counted up the plates in his head as he waited for the captain to enter. The bar held a full basic Olympic set—310 pounds.

The captain entered the room, nodded the other men toward a bench along one wall, then waved them toward it.

McCarter led the way again, taking a seat at one end of the bench. Manning dropped down next to him with Hawkins on the Canadian's other side. Encizo and James took seats on the other end of the bench.

The captain marched to a position directly in front of them and stopped, flexing his pectorals. The material of his shirt threatened to rip across his chest before he relaxed. He looked at each of the Phoenix Force commandos in turn, for some reason giving Manning a longer once-over than the others, then addressed the team as a whole. "You will give your passports to this man," he said, nodding to McCarter, "who will then give them to me."

McCarter took the passports as they came to the end of the bench and handed them to Berber. By now he had figured out what all this was about, and it had nothing to do with improper passports or their not being journalists. It was a simple case of the captain "shaking them down." McCarter was now certain that the lieutenant they had dealt with earlier was the CIA man. It was clear that Berber was not, but the captain outranked the lieutenant.

The Phoenix Force leader wasn't surprised then, when the captain glanced quickly at the first two passports and said, "These documents are not in order."

"The hell they aren't," Hawkins growled. "Listen, you self-important—"

Berber's eyes flamed as they jerked toward Hawkins.

McCarter cleared his throat, silencing Phoenix Force's youngest member. "Captain Berber," he said evenly, "we apologize. We thought we had the correct documentation of our arrival and departure."

Berber turned his attention to the end of the bench and smiled. "Ah, a more reasonable man."

"I try to be," McCarter replied. "Tell us…exactly what needs to be done to rectify our mistake? How do we get our documents into a presentable fashion?''

Berber lowered his eyes to the ground and sighed dramatically. ''I am afraid it is impossible,'' he said sadly. ''That would require a complete background check on each of you—a costly procedure and we are *such* a poor nation.'' He shook his head again. ''Then we would have to contact your governments and request they reissue you each new documents. More cost to us. And the procedure is painfully slow. You might have to remain in custody for several weeks.''

Hawkins mumbled something under his breath.

Berber's eyes shot to Hawkins again and narrowed.

McCarter turned to Manning. ''Tell T.J. to quiet down,'' he whispered out of the side of his mouth. He turned back to the front, but in his peripheral vision he saw the big Canadian elbow Hawkins lightly in the ribs.

''Captain Berber,'' McCarter said, ''surely there must be some way to handle this situation. We can't afford several weeks. We are journalists who have come to show the world the suffering Somalia is experiencing.'' He paused, then went on. ''That's our only objective. We aren't criminals, Captain. We are honest men who simply made a mistake in our paperwork.''

Berber turned to the side, clasping his hands together behind his back. His back was so broad they almost didn't reach. He paced back and forth in front of the bench several times, his face a mask of concern. Finally he stopped and turned to face them again. He laced his fingers together, turned his hands downward and cracked his knuckles.

Huge horseshoe-shaped triceps muscles popped out on the backs of his arms as the joints popped.

"Perhaps there is a way," Berber said. A thin smile played at the lips nearly hidden behind his thick beard. He shifted his eyes from McCarter to Manning again, studying the Canadian closely.

For a moment McCarter wondered if the captain might be a homosexual who was attracted to the big Canadian. Then the truth dawned on him. Berber was proud of the body he had developed with the weights in this room, and Gary Manning was Phoenix Force's resident weight lifter. Berber had taken note of the Canadian's own barrel chest and heavily muscled thighs.

Quite simply Berber was wondering who was stronger, him or Manning. It was no different than one bull encountering a new one and wondering if he still had first pick of the cows. Or a rooster grown complacent in the barnyard, and wanting to make sure he was still cock of the walk.

Berber wanted to know who was stronger, all right. But that wasn't his *primary* reason for detaining them. Not by a long shot.

"I have an idea," McCarter said.

Berber's head shot back to him.

"I realize the procedure to correct our documents will be expensive. So why not let our newspapers defray the cost? And while the procedure is in progress, we could operate on the passports we have now. With your permission, of course." He cleared his throat. "I mean, Captain, we will need our passports at hotels and other places. No one will spot the discrepancies—it took an expert such as yourself to do that. Even your lieutenant thought our papers were in order." He smiled pleasantly.

Berber frowned as if considering such an arrangement for the first time. "I do not know," he said. "It is highly irregular." He paced back and forth a few more times, then suddenly his face lit up with sudden thought. "I have it."

"Yes?" McCarter said, leaning forward.

"We will leave the decision to Allah."

For a moment the room fell into silence. Then Manning said, "I'm sorry, I'm afraid I don't understand."

Berber smiled happily. "We will let Allah show us a sign as to whether I can trust you," he said. "The price for each of you—to correct your passports, of course—will be 350,000 shillings." The captain's face gleamed with greed.

McCarter had to fight not to shake his head. The price itself was illustrative of just how poverty-stricken Somalia had become. For all of them—the whole team—it would cost less than roughly fifty dollars.

"You will give me the money now," Berber said, holding out five thick fingers.

McCarter reached into his pocket and pulled out a

roll of Somalian bills. He peeled off the appropriate amount and stuck them in the captain's hand. He stood as Berber pocketed the money. "Thank you," he said, and started toward the door.

Berber reached out and grabbed his shoulder. He shook his head violently back and forth. "No!" he said. "We must wait for Allah's sign."

McCarter stopped. "And what exactly will that be, Captain Berber?" he asked.

Berber's eyes returned to Manning. "Allah has spoken to my heart," he said, glancing to the east. "He has said that if this man—" his eyes returned to Manning "—can beat me in a bench-press contest, then you are to be trusted."

McCarter looked at Manning. The Canadian was big, but not as big as the Somalian customs captain. Then again, size wasn't always the determining factor as to strength.

"Let me get this straight," McCarter said. "If our man wins, we can go on with our business in Somalia while our background checks are conducted and new passports issued. But if you win, it means Allah says we can't be trusted and we have to stay in custody until we're cleared?"

"Or not cleared," Berber said, nodding.

"What about the money I just gave you?" McCarter asked.

Berber smiled. "Allah has ordered me to keep it regardless of who wins."

"Surprise, surprise, surprise," Hawkins said in a fairly good Gomer Pyle voice.

Manning looked at McCarter and shrugged. "Well, we might as well find out," he said.

Berber's face looked like he'd just won the lottery. He began to unbutton his shirt.

McCarter turned to the wall, considering his options. He had grown weary of the captain's games, and was tempted to simply knock the man unconscious, do the same to the guards in the hall and lead Phoenix Force out of the terminal and on to the mission. But that would mean that as soon as Berber awakened, Phoenix Force would be hunted by authorities for the rest of the mission in Somalia—a complication he wanted to avoid if at all possible.

Turning back, he saw the captain naked from the waist up. Muscles rippled like tiny tidal waves under his ebony skin.

"We will both take two warm-up sets," Berber said to Manning. "Then there will be three lifts." He grinned. "I will give you the advantage of going last, since you are my guest."

Phoenix Force watched as Berber walked to the bench and slid under the bar. He lifted the 310 pounds, and began pumping out reps as if he were lifting feathers.

McCarter watched the captain hit his twentieth repetition and set the bar back in place, aware that he had to make a decision. He didn't know if Manning could out lift Berber, but two things he *did* know.

First the men of Phoenix Force couldn't afford to remain in custody for any extended length of time—

they had a mission to perform. Second McCarter knew that if they overpowered Berber and simply knocked him out, they'd soon be wanted men. So if he chose escape as the best option, they would have to silence the captain more effectively.

Berber rose to his feet and grinned, stretching his chest muscles as he walked away from the bench. McCarter reached into his pocket, his fingers slipping around the plastic handle of the Spyderco Delica knife as he made his decision.

It wasn't a decision he liked. But it was one that had to be made. Phoenix Force couldn't afford to remain in Berber's custody. But neither could the Phoenix warriors afford to be pursued. So if they had to fight their way out, they would have to make sure Berber, the guards in the hall and even the lieutenant they had dealt with earlier were in no condition to report the incident.

The Phoenix Force leader withdrew his hand from his pocket, leaving the Delica where it was for the time being. He turned to Gary Manning as the big Canadian slid under the bar for his first warm-up set. "Beat him, Gary," McCarter whispered under his breath. "You'll be saving his life."

Washington, D.C.

ROSARIO BLANCANALES SAW the sign on the other side of the intersection as he waited for the traffic light to turn green: U-Lock Self-Storage.

As soon as the light changed, he pulled the van

past the corner, paralleling the ten-foot chain-link fence that circled the storage facility. He turned into the driveway and guided the van through the open gate.

Blancanales scanned the concrete driveway. Halfway down one of the lines of storage sheds he saw a Datsun 300Z parked along the fence. Several other vehicles had been parked in front of the rental garages, but none was close to the Datsun.

He glanced over his shoulder, and the glance brought a smile. It didn't really matter how close the other vehicles were—Lyons's last punch had ensured that Ira Rook would stay asleep a while longer. When the men of Able Team unloaded the cardboard box in a few minutes, it would appear to anyone watching that they were simply dropping off something in their storage space just like any of the other renters.

Blancanales pulled to a halt just behind the Datsun. He waited as a dark-complected man in a lightweight suit stepped out of the smaller vehicle. Leo Turrin, Stony Man Farm's top undercover operative and Washington lobbyist, grinned as he walked toward the van.

Turrin approached the driver's side as Blancanales rolled down the window. Handing over a key, the little Fed said, "Number 307, my psy-op expert friend. We've got the place set up like you wanted." He paused. "Need anything else?"

Blancanales shook his head as he took the key. Without looking, he handed it over his shoulder into the back of the van. An unseen hand took it.

Turrin leaned in the window a little farther, nodded to Lyons and Schwarz, then returned to the Datsun and sped away.

Blancanales threw the transmission into Drive and guided the van past the numbered doors along the rows of storage compartments until he reached 307. Behind him he heard the side door of the van slide open, and a moment later Gadgets Schwarz was inserting a key into the padlock that secured the corrugated overhead entrance.

Blancanales killed the engine and pulled his walking stick from where he'd wedged it between the passenger's seat and console. An expert in the stick-fighting art of *bo-jitsu,* he had also studied the Filipino stick-fighting systems and many of the European stick-and-dagger arts. That was because he had found the cane to be an invaluable tool over the years. Low-key and unobtrusive, it differed from most weapons in that it could be carried openly in polite society without eyebrows rising.

His fingers wrapped around the cane's brass duckhead grip as he got out of the van and closed the door behind him. Schwarz had already returned to the van and was helping Lyons unload the box by the time Blancanales got around to the sliding door. It was a two-man job—a third just got in the way—so he stepped to one side.

Besides, he had other matters to attend to at the moment.

Turning away, Blancanales took a deep breath. Soon Ira Rook would return to the land of the conscious, and it would be time for the act to go on. Which meant Blancanales needed to get into character. He closed his eyes for a moment, then opened them again. He looked out at the street, letting his vision focus on a yellow Ryder rental truck in front of a storage garage several tiers away. Half-consciously he saw a young man and woman struggling to unload a mattress. Breathing deeply again— in through his nose and out through his mouth—he leaned forward on the duck-head grip of the cane and continued staring at the rental truck, seeing it and yet not seeing it, his mind focused inwardly on the part he was about to play.

As the team's expert in psychological operations, it had fallen on Blancanales to oversee this leg of the mission, Ira Rook's interrogation. It was an interrogation that would be tricky to put it mildly.

He continued to get into character and mentally outline the path he wanted the next few hours to take. His objective was to extract information from Rook—information that the obnoxious little editor wouldn't give up willingly. If Rook had been a criminal, that would be no problem; Blancanales had ways to make him talk. But as Schwarz had pointed out to Lyons, Rook *wasn't* a criminal. A perfectly disgusting human being perhaps, but no criminal.

The bottom line was that Rook was a citizen of the United States who wasn't guilty of any crime. He didn't deserve to be harmed. Which meant a physical interrogation was out.

Blancanales shook his head. What he was about to

do might well be construed as mental torture, and
that bothered him. He had always had a concern for
people, and he wished there was some other way to
obtain the information he needed. But if there was,
he didn't know it. The greater good had to be considered, which made some compromise necessary.

The Able Team psy-op expert jerked his mind
away from the moment of self-doubt. Such overin-
trospection was never productive once the decision
to use a certain tactic had been made.

Blancanales took one last deep breath, then turned
toward the open overhead door. Inside he saw Lyons
and Schwarz standing on the sides of the refrigerator
box. The rectangular room had been furnished to
look like an office. Wall-to-wall carpeting covered
the concrete floor. A divan rested against one wall,
a matching stuffed easy chair against the other.
Bookshelves lined two of the walls, and at the far
end of the cubicle stood a desk with papers piled and
scattered across the top. Several filing cabinets stood
behind the desk, and Blancanales could see a paint-
ing or two.

The Able Team psychological-operations man
couldn't help but smile. Leo Turrin had done a ter-
rific job of making the storage compartment look like
an office, and he had pulled out all the stops to create
a convincing atmosphere. "Windows" had even
been attached to the walls in several spots around the
room—the blinds, of course, were pulled down as
the apertures led to bare concrete.

Blancanales stepped into the garage and pulled

down the overhead door behind him. As it descended, he saw that wood panelling had been affixed to it to make it look like a permanent wall. The photograph of a door stood just to the left of center.

He leaned his cane against the wall and looked around. It all looked phony right now, but it would look real enough as soon as he dimmed the lights Turrin had installed.

The sound of something scraping against cardboard sounded from inside the box, followed by a low moan.

Lyons nodded to Blancanales, who looked at Schwarz. The electronics whiz gave him a thumbs-up. Lyons and Schwarz reached into their pockets and produced panty hose. Pulling them down over their faces to obliterate their features, they headed for the divan and took seats.

Blancanales dimmed the lights with one hand as he pulled his own panty hose over his face with the other. The room fell into a dull, eerie glow that simulated nighttime. When Rook came to in a few seconds, he would get the feeling he had been unconscious for several hours rather than minutes.

It was all part of the scenario Blancanales had worked out to disorient the man.

Blancanales walked to the cardboard box, reached up and opened the flaps. Without further ado he pulled down on the flaps while one foot swept the bottom into the air.

For a split second the cardboard box was airborne, then it slammed into the carpet with a dull thud.

Grabbing the bottom of the box, Blancanales jerked hard like a magician sweeping a tablecloth from beneath a table of dishes.

Ira Rook shot out of the box with a timid yelp.

Blancanales wasted no time. Squatting in front of the belligerent newspaper editor, he grabbed the man under the arms and jerked him to a standing position. With one swift motion he swept Rook off his feet again and hurled him into the overstuffed armchair directly across from Lyons and Schwarz.

"What's—" Rook started to whine.

"Silence!" Blancanales shouted at the top of his lungs. His voice held an odd, indiscernible accent. Maybe French, maybe Italian, maybe something else—it was impossible to make out.

"You guys..." Rook said uncertainly. "You aren't Justice Department—"

"I said *silence!*"

Rook followed the order; his lips slammed shut.

Blancanales stepped in front of the chair. Reaching down, he hooked a thumb under Rook's jawbone and pulled up.

Rook looked like a fish on a hook as his eyes opened wide in horror.

"You're correct that we aren't with the Justice Department," he said in a low, threatening voice. "But from now on you'll speak only when spoken to." He paused. "Is that clear?"

Rook nodded as best he could with Blancanales's thumb jammed halfway into his head.

Blancanales leaned down, pressing his nose into

Rook's. His voice dropped even further, becoming a sinister, barely audible whisper. "Good," he said. "If you forget it, you'll die."

Rook began to tremble.

Blancanales straightened and turned toward Lyons and Schwarz on the other side of the room. Using his body to block Rook's line of vision, he gave the other two Able Team men a thumb's-up to let them know Rook was responding as hoped. Then, twirling dramatically, he shoved his nose into that of the man in the chair again. "What is your full name?" he demanded.

"Rook," the newspaper editor whispered. "Ira Rook."

"Your full name!" Blancanales yelled at the top of his lungs.

Startled, Rook screamed back. "Mason!"

"Do not raise your voice to me!" Blancanales thundered. "Mason what?"

"Ira Mason Rook," Rook whispered. "That's my...full name?..." His voice trailed off as if he weren't sure.

Blancanales stepped in and raised his hand as if he were about to strike the fat little man. Rook winced.

Able Team's psychological expert dropped his hand and laughed sardonically. "Where do you live?"

Rook started to answer, but Blancanales interrupted him. "Where do you work?"

"The...*Chieftain*," Rook whined softly. "The *Washington Chieftain*."

"You live at the *Washington Chieftain!*" Blancanales roared. "You *live* at a newspaper? Don't play games with me, Ira Mason Rook! You will regret the day you tried that!"

"I...I'm sorry...I thought you asked—"

"Answer the question! Where do you work?"

"Work? The *Chieftain*. I—"

Blancanales reached down, grasped Rook by the collar and hauled him to his feet. Shoving his face into the other man's again, he shouted, "You have already told me that! I asked you where you live!" He dropped the editor back into the chair.

The questioning went on in that vein for a good five minutes with Blancanales always keeping Rook off balance as he fired one query after another. At first the newsman had been frightened. Then he had become terrified.

By the end of Blancanales's first series of questioning, he had become little more than a whimpering bowl of jelly.

Blancanales suddenly quieted and began to pace back and forth across the room in front of Rook. He kept watch on the man out of the corner of his eye. At first Rook followed him back and forth like a cat watching a table tennis game. But gradually his interest shifted to the men across the room on the sofa.

Blancanales shot a glance that way in time to see Schwarz draw a Cold Steel Peacekeeper II fighting knife from under his jacket. Slowly, deliberately, he began to clean his fingernails.

Rook's gaze was locked on Schwarz. Blancanales studied the man's face and posture trying to get a fix on just how disoriented Rook was.

Was it time to get down to the real questioning? There was no way to be completely certain, and if he played his hand too soon it could blow all chances. But everything about Rook—his voice, body language and the terror in his eyes—told Blancanales the time had come.

"Tell me about Spencer Kiethley," Blancanales demanded.

Ira Mason Rook looked up into Blancanales's panty-hose-covered face and began to talk.

Stony Man Farm, Virginia

AARON KURTZMAN'S primary objective during this mission was to identify and locate the Great Hikari. The self-professed god had been in hiding since his cult's first subway gassing over a year ago, and neither the Japanese police nor military—both of whom were working on the case—had had any luck finding him. Earlier in the day Kurtzman had broken the codes and hacked his way into Japanese police files only to find that the police knew little more than he about the cult leader. He had finally worked his way into the files of Japanese military intelligence and initiated a scan to access any intel on Hikari.

Kurtzman settled into his chair. The search had

come up with something—but he didn't know what. At the top of the monitor he saw a picture of the Great Hikari. The man wore a bright Japanese ceremonial robe. His long hair was pulled back into a braid, and wispy chin whiskers fell from his face. But beneath the photo the file entry was all in the Japanese characters known as *kanji*.

Kurtzman's fingers flew across the keyboard, typing in the words Quick-Cross. A moment later he had accessed a language-translation program of his own recent creation. Faster than any of the previous such programs on the market, Quick-Cross also held the capacity to maintain 188 complete, separate languages, even given the complexity of Chinese, Russian or English. Within seconds it would eventually be able to translate an entire document written in Hebrew or Swahili into Japanese, French or whatever language one preferred.

So far Kurtzman had found time to enter only a few of the world's most common tongues into the computers at Stony Man Farm. But English and Japanese had been among the first.

He stopped typing and sat back against the padded backrest of his wheelchair. As he watched the screen, it divided into two parts. The photo of the Great Hikari and the kanji beneath it shrank and shifted to the left-hand side of the monitor. On the right-hand side an identical picture of Hikari appeared. But below this photo the words were in English.

The computer genius shook his head in mild disgust as he read. It wasn't much. Like the police, Japanese military intelligence had the picture of the man in his ceremonial kimono and a few speculations on who the Great Hikari might actually be. But they had no solid evidence, or even any good leads to go on.

Kurtzman closed his eyes and rubbed his temples. In the blackness he saw the picture of the Great Hikari that both police and military had in their files. If it was the only picture either agency could come up with that meant photos of the cult leader were scarce.

He opened his eyes and looked again at the pictures of the Great Hikari on both sides of the monitor. Somewhere there was a key to learning the man's identity. Somewhere there was a clue that would get him on the right path to discovering who the cult leader really was.

Twirling his wheelchair to the side, Kurtzman looked down the ramp to where the rest of his cybernetics team worked. At the far end of the bank of monitors sat Huntington Wethers, a tall well-proportioned black man with graying temples. Wethers was creating a personality profile of the average police officer killed in the line of duty in the hope that the results would help keep more cops alive. The results he was finding weren't particularly encouraging—it seemed that the friendlier and nicer an officer was the more likely he was to be shot.

Next to Wethers a lively redheaded woman was tapping the keys of her own keyboard. Carmen Delahunt was in the process of using Kurtzman's probability program to narrow down a list of suspects in a rash of serial killings up and down the East Coast.

On Delahunt's other side, and closest to Kurtzman, was the young man the computer genius needed to talk to. Akira Tokaido was busy, too. The young Japanese American was monitoring all incoming and outgoing communiqués of the Japanese police and military using the Quick-Cross program.

Kurtzman smiled, unconsciously nodding his approval of all three members of his team. So far, he hadn't needed their help on this mission. They had stayed busy with other projects. His people always stayed busy but were ready to leave their other projects and help with the mission as soon as Kurtzman said the word.

They were flexible, and flexibility was the key to success.

The computer wizard wheeled his chair to face Tokaido. "Akira," he called out.

Tokaido's hands stopped in midair over the keyboard. He twisted sharply in Kurtzman's direction. "Yes, bossman?"

Kurtzman waved him up the ramp.

Tokaido jerked the earplug from his ear and let it fall on the portable CD player on the console next to his monitor. He bounded up the ramp in three quick strides.

"You glean anything about Followers of the Truth or the Great Hikari in the Japanese news reports?" Kurtzman asked, pointing at the twin pictures of the

Great Hikari on his monitor screen. "Do we have any other photos?"

"Let me see." Tokaido leaned across Kurtzman, cleared the screen and linked Kurtzman's computer to his own. A moment later a menu appeared. Frowning, the young man worked the cursor down the list until his face suddenly lit up. "Only one item. But it is a television news report. Filmed right before the first subway gassing. Right before the Great Hikari went into hiding."

"Let's see it," Kurtzman said.

Tokaido tapped several keys, then straightened as the computer clicked and beeped, linking into Stony Man Farm's vast library of videotapes. A moment later the monitor became a moving television screen.

Kurtzman watched the short segment. It showed the Great Hikari coming down the steps that led to a Buddhist shrine, surrounded by his disciples. He wore the same kimono as in Japanese police and military intelligence files, and Kurtzman decided that picture had to be a still lifted from the news tape. He watched Hikari stop at the street as one of his glassy-eyed followers opened the door to a limousine, then disappear inside the vehicle. A second later the limo drove away, and the news report went on to something else.

"Let's see it again," Kurtzman said.

Tokaido ran the tape back, then played it once more. This time Kurtzman noticed that all of Hikari's followers had the same distant look in their eyes. Something about the look bothered him.

Kurtzman felt his eyebrows lower in thought. What did he expect? he asked himself. These men and women were cult members, after all. They had been brainwashed. A distant look in their eyes was to be expected.

So why did it bother him?

He had Tokaido rewind the tape again, then watched once more. He got the same uneasy feeling as he stared into the obscure eyes of the cult followers. Only this time the feeling was even stronger.

It was during the seventh viewing of the video segment that Kurtzman suddenly saw what it was that bothered him. This time his eyes chanced to fall on a short man in the background who followed Hikari down the steps. As soon as they reached the ground, the man circled the cult leader and got into the limo on the far side of the screen.

Kurtzman ran the tape back again. "Watch the guy in the red kimono," he told Tokaido. Together they walked through the Great Hikari's celebrated descent down the steps one more time. When the car drove away this time, Kurtzman leaned forward, tapped a key and froze the frame. "Notice anything different about that guy in red?" Kurtzman asked.

The young man nodded. "Yes. His eyes. They're clear and sharp. He doesn't look drugged—or brainwashed—like all the others."

Kurtzman nodded. That had been what bothered him before he figured it out. Not that the other members of the cult looked like they'd been brainwashed. But that this one man *didn't*. "That man isn't a follower of the Great Hikari," he said. "He's a confederate."

Tokaido nodded. "I have to agree."

Kurtzman turned back to the screen. "And I've got a gut feeling that he's the key to finding out who your Great Hikari really is."

CHAPTER SIX

Japan

Toshiro Ohara straightened the lapels of his kimono
and studied his reflection in the mirror. His hair was
pulled tight against his skull and fell in a braid behind his back. The round rimless eyeglasses, and the
pudginess of face he had developed since reaching
prosperity, lent a serious demeanor to his features.

Ohara smiled into the mirror. He looked official
yet kind, competent but compassionate, wise and lov-
ing.

The smile became a laugh. It was exactly the look
he wanted. He looked like the perfect man-god.

Ohara turned away from the mirror and walked
across the bedroom to the bed. Life was truly good,
he had decided during the past two years. Before that
he hadn't been so sure. He took a seat on the edge
of the bed to wait for the new converts he was about
to meet. Had it only been two years since he and
Ichiro Murai had founded the Followers of the Truth
cult? A little less, in fact. Before that they had been
nothing more than small-time criminals—petty bur-

glars, drug dealers, and for a short time numbers runners for the Yakuza.

The cult leader's smile broadened. He and Murai had been con men, too, running the usual hustles and making a little money here and there. Then they had stumbled onto the best con of all.

Religion.

Ohara lay back on the bed and closed his eyes. He and Murai had come upon the idea for the cult by accident, really. A stranger in a saki bar had started them down the path. In a drunken stupor the man—a Buddhist by faith—had mumbled that Eastern religions all had one shortcoming: they concentrated too much on the here and now, offering no salvation or clear reward in an afterlife. They offered no immortality.

Ohara opened his eyes, and the smile returned. He had already learned that the most successful con games offered people something they wanted but didn't think they'd ever get. He and Murai were about to create their own religion, when they were lucky enough to receive one ready made, when the Aum Shinrikyo—Supreme Truth—cult was exposed in 1995, all its followers were suddenly in need of a new leader and fresh direction.

Ohara chuckled deep in his chest, remembering the nights he and his partner of so many years had stayed awake plotting strategy, researching the Aum Shinrikyo so that their own cult would seem the logical successor—and Ohara would be presented as the divinely appointed leader.

Sitting up, the cult leader continued to grin at how simple it had all been. Yes, the Followers of the Truth had given people what they wanted. And in doing so he and Murai had gotten what *they* wanted, too—power and money.

Not that it all didn't have its downside. Ever since the first subway gassing, he had been a wanted man, and he and Murai had been forced to hide out in this ancient castle formerly owned by one of his converts. They had decided on a light security force to protect them, knowing that a large army would draw attention and that no matter how many men he employed the Japanese government would have more. So he had relied more on anonymity than force, utilizing only a half dozen of what they referred to as "lower angels" to guard the doors at night.

Ohara smiled. All of which would change soon enough. Soon he would walk freely wherever he wished. The world would kiss his feet if he asked, or his ass if that was his preference.

Or they would die.

Ohara glanced at his watch. That he should become the leader and figurehead of the cult had been a mutual decision due to Murai's criminal record. His friend hadn't protested. During the years he and Murai had worked the streets, Murai had been arrested more than a dozen times, but Ohara, ironically, had always managed to escape detainment.

The leader of the cult would be in the public eye, and the police would be interested. Therefore Ohara had become the figurehead.

Ohara had sensed a small amount of resentment on Murai's part—after all, who wouldn't have wanted to lead a multimillion-dollar empire like theirs? But that resentment hadn't stopped the man from contributing to the plan. It had been Murai's idea to call Ohara the Great Hikari, "the Great Natural Light."

The power of their cult had grown quicker than he and Murai had ever dreamed it would. Thanks to the demise of Aum Shinrikyo, they had hundreds of thousands of converts on three continents, and they hadn't yet even begun to reach their full potential.

But they would soon.

The Great Hikari clasped his hands behind his head. He had done his homework well before he began to recruit followers. As well as his thorough research of Aum Shinrikyo, he had studied the methodology and tactics of several famous and successful American evangelists. Then Ohara had spent six months following the Reverend Sun Yung Moon, learning more. The final chapter in his studies had been an intense examination of Jim Jones and the People's Church in Guyana. He had wanted the answer to one important question: what had it taken to convince so many people that mass suicide was the only answer?

The answer to the question had come back just as Ohara suspected it would. Although on a much grander scale, the basic premise had been little different than those used in the small-time street hustles he and Murai had run. First Jones had convinced his recruits that the established Christian denominations had lost sight of their purpose, stripping away their illusions of salvation and creating the opening the false prophet needed. The people still wanted salvation, but now they didn't think they'd get it. So Jones had stepped in with a new twist and offered it right back to them and they'd jumped on it.

Jim Jones had offered the people something they wanted but didn't think they'd get. Ohara knew he could do the same thing. And he did.

The phone next to the bed rang shrilly, startling Ohara from his thoughts. He rolled to his side and lifted the receiver from the cradle. "Yes?" he said.

"Your Reverence," Ichiro Murai said sarcastically, "I thought you would want to know. We have just received word that we've broken into the Canadian market. An order for five hundred vials of your blood has come in from Vancouver."

Ohara chuckled. Among other schemes, the Followers of the Truth sold bottles of swine blood that they represented as coming from the guru himself. It went for one million yen per vial, and drinking it was said to guarantee salvation and the highest possible rewards in the afterlife. The blood sold so well that had it really been drawn from Ohara's veins he would have bled to death during the first week it was on the market.

"Very good," Ohara said. "And my bathwater?" For those unable to afford the first-class ticket to heaven, the cult offered an economy flight. Ohara's bathwater, also to be consumed, sold for only two hundred dollars per eight-ounce bottle. It might not provide followers as many jewels in their crowns after they went on to their heavenly rewards, but at least it got them through the gate. The water was as phony as the blood; the cult leader never bothered to dip his body in the vats where the solution was manufactured.

"We are processing an order for two thousand bottles at the moment," Murai said.

Ohara nodded. Money from Canada and the United States was coming in steadily, but it was nothing compared to what he'd have soon. Under the leadership of a man named Carver, he already had followers spread across the two North American countries. Not many, but enough.

The Great Hikari smiled again. At least enough for what he was planning. If things went well, he would soon have the technology to gas millions of people at a time rather than thousands. Which would mean he could hold the entire earth hostage and name the amount of ransom he wanted.

But enough business, the cult leader thought. It was time to reap the benefits of being the Great Hikari. "Where are the two new converts you mentioned, Ichiro?"

Ichiro Murai breathed in disgustedly. "You are growing too fond of the perks of this business, Toshiro," he said. "But they are on their way up. I believe you will be pleased. Particularly with the shorter one. She is top-heavy the way you like them."

"Ichiro," Ohara said, "do not worry about me. I have not lost sight of our objectives."

"Of course not, Your Reverence," Murai almost spit. "Perhaps I find you annoying only because I remember when we were both street bums. Before you became a god."

Ohara started to answer, then decided to simply hang up. Murai and he had been friends since childhood. They had grown up together, and worked the streets as a criminal team as they grew older. Now his right-hand man, Murai was the only follower who held Ohara's complete trust, and certainly the only member of the cult who knew that the cult was a complete sham. Even the men like Carver—unbelievers who were retained to conduct the cult's dirty work—believed the Great Hikari was serious about what he preached.

A soft knock sounded on the door, and Ohara rose, slipping his feet into a pair of zori by the bed. He cast a final glance to the mirror, padded across the room in the straw sandals and opened the door.

The two women were extraordinary.

Ohara studied them silently as they dropped their eyes to the floor. The taller of the two—Reiko, Murai had said her name was—was slender and had long ebony hair that fell past her shoulders like a black waterfall. The shorter woman—Yoshiko—was heavier. But pleasingly so, her breasts unusually large for so small a frame. Ohara felt his pulse quicken. Both women wore the simple white kimonos that new converts were given during their initial induction.

And beneath the kimonos, the Great Hikari knew, they would wear nothing.

"My daughters," Ohara said. "Please enter."

He reached out to take each woman by the hand and guide her into the room. He closed the door behind him, then led them to the bed, positioning one on each side of him.

"Your Reverence," Reiko said, "may I speak?"

"Of course, my daughter."

"I wish to extend my gratitude that you have met with us personally."

Yoshiko nodded enthusiastic agreement. "We understand you are so very busy," she said. "That you greet few new followers yourself." She dropped her eyes. "You honor us."

Ohara looked down at the woman's chest and smiled. "I greet those whom time permits," he said. Yoshiko's kimono had parted slightly, and Ohara strained to see more. "The spirit guides me as to whom should be chosen." The woman drew a breath, and the kimono parted farther, revealing a hint of a shadowed nipple.

Big breasts would always get a woman a meeting, too, Ohara thought to himself.

"Your Reverence," Reiko said, "may we ask a question?"

"Of course."

"We have done as you directed, Your Reverence. We have turned all of our worldly possessions over to your staff to be destroyed. We have forsaken friends and family, Your Reverence." She paused, looking down at the floor. "I am single," she went on. "But Yoshiko has a husband..." Her voice trailed off meekly, then came back. "He has no idea where she is and will worry about her. She is shy and will not ask a favor for herself, so I must ask for her. Could her husband be informed that Yoshiko is safe? That she is in the arms of God?"

Ohara twisted his face into his best fatherly smile. "It shall be done," he said. Reaching for the phone, he tapped several buttons. "Ichiro," he said into the instrument, "please inform the husband of Yoshiko that she is safe." Then he hung up.

Turning back to Reiko, he smiled. "Your concern is a sign of the compassion in your heart," he said, then turned his attention to Yoshiko. "And your timidity in asking a favor demonstrates selflessness." Slowly he reached out with both hands, parted Yoshiko's kimono and placed a palm on her chest between her breasts. Beneath his hand he felt her heartbeat quicken. His own chest pounded, as well.

Ohara looked into Yoshiko's eyes but stared at her breasts in his peripheral vision. He left his hand where it was and twisted to face Reiko. He opened her kimono to reveal a set of smaller, yet beautiful breasts. Placing his other hand over her heart he said, "The heart is the center of love. Breathe deeply. Feel the love that passes between us." He watched both women as their chests heaved in and out. Their eyes took on the glazed fanatical look of the zealot.

"Reach out, my daughters," Ohara said, "touch each other. Feel each other. Feel not only the love that passes between you and myself, but the love between the two of you. It is the key to your salvation.'' The cult leader moved his hands to the sides, cupping one of the small breasts and one of the large as the women both reached up to touch each other. He leaned down, kissing Reiko first, then turned to place his lips on Yoshiko.

''Some drink my blood,'' Ohara said as he slowly slid the women's kimonos the rest of the way off, ''and others my bathwater. But there is another path to the afterlife through me, and because of the love you have exhibited, you shall experience it now.''

THREE HOURS LATER Toshiro Ohara awoke and noted that the sun had gone down outside the window. He glanced to his left and saw Yoshiko. To his right lay Reiko. Both women slept the peaceful sleep of the righteously saved.

Ohara smiled. Yes, life was good. It was good to be a god, and soon he would be a god who held the entire world in his hands.

Slowly, careful not to disturb either of the women, Ohara reached across Reiko and lifted the phone again. ''The husband has been taken care of?'' he asked Murai.

''Oh, yes,'' he replied. ''He is quite dead.''

Sierra Leone

BOLAN WATCHED the deep purple sky lighten to a soft, airy gray as the sun poked its nose over the

Loma Mountains. Beyond the plateaus lay the eastern edge of Sierra Leone, and beyond that, Guinea.

The Executioner reached around the Desert Eagle hanging from his web belt and pulled a bandanna from the hip pocket of his cargo shorts. Rolling it quickly into a sweatband, he tied it around his forehead. It was still fairly cool, but even as high up as they were, the Sierra Leone climate was hot and humid. By the time the sun had fully risen, Bolan knew sweat would be breaking out on his face to sting his eyes. Hearing footsteps behind him, he turned to see Bobcat Buchanan approach.

"Company...assemble!" Buchanan shouted behind the Executioner.

Turning, Bolan rested his right hand on the grips of the Desert Eagle, the other on the hilt of the Crossada knife strapped to his left leg as he watched four hundred handpicked Sierra Leone Commando Unit candidates line up on the large parade ground. The men, all eager to earn their place in the newly formed elite division, stood stiffly at attention. Walking through the lines, inspecting uniforms and checking gear, were the Gurkha training assistants the Sierra Leone government had hired to help Buchanan.

Bolan had to smile. He had worked with Gurkhas in the past, and they had always earned his respect. They were tough little soldiers from the peaks of Nepal, and he suspected they took to the Loma Mountains like mountain goats. The Executioner watched them as they moved through the ranks in their baggy shorts, loose BDU blouses and rubber-soled canvas boots. Each man carried an AK-47 such as the Sierra Leone Commando Unit would use, and a pistol of one type or another hung from their web belts on the right side.

But on the left side of each Gurkha hung a weapon that had brought terror into the hearts of their enemies for centuries—the *kukri.*

Bolan studied the reverse-curved fighting knife. It was capable of chopping off hands, heads and feet, and had done so many times in the past. Over the years the blade, and the Gurkhas' proficiency with it, had taken on mythical proportions. In the Falklands, Argentine soldiers had thrown down their firearms and deserted when word had come down that the Gurkhas had arrived and unsheathed their knives.

Buchanan took a place next to Bolan in front of the men and turned to face them. Like Bolan, he wore khaki cargo shorts, a black tank top and lightweight nylon hiking boots. But instead of a Desert Eagle, a Colt Government Model .45 pistol hung from the web belt around his waist on his right hip. A Cold Steel Black Bear Classic subhilt fighting knife hung on the left side.

Bolan glanced for a moment at the wedding ring around Buchanan's neck and wondered whose it had been. A wife? Mother? He didn't know. But it was none of his business, and he wouldn't ask. It was obviously a personal thing, and if Buchanan wanted him to know, he would tell him.

"All right, gentlemen!" Buchanan yelled. "After PT we'll break into two teams. Team A will follow me to the firing range, where I'll do my best to teach you which end of the rifle the bullet comes out. Team B will stay here with Colonel Pollock and work on close-quarters combat. But first, let's see who's in shape and who isn't!'' He turned to Bolan. ''Colonel, if you'd be so kind?''

Bolan led the men through a series of stretches and calisthenics that had them sweating profusely by the time he turned to Buchanan and nodded.

Buchanan reached up and grasped the whistle suspended around his neck on a lanyard. ''All right, ladies, you think that was hard? At the first whistle you will run in place, lifting your knees high enough to blacken both eyes! At the second whistle you will dive forward onto your bellies! The next whistle will bring you back to your feet running, then we'll start all over again! Are there any questions?''

Roughly three dozen hands shot up in an attempt to delay the torture.

''No questions?'' Buchanan said, ignoring the hands. ''Good.'' He hooked a thumb over his shoulder toward the barracks. ''Anyone failing to keep up will return to the racks and pack your bags. Any *other* questions?''

The last query had been rhetorical, and Buchanan didn't wait for a response. He immediately blew the whistle.

The commando candidates began to run in place for all they were worth. Buchanan whistled again, and they fell forward onto their faces. No sooner had they hit the ground than the whistle had them bounding back to their feet.

Bolan studied the men as they continued the conditioning drill. All were in good shape and with the proper training could make the grade. But the Sierra Leone Commando Unit was budgeted to consist of less than a hundred men, which meant three-fourths of the hopefuls he saw before him now would be unhappily returning to their regular units.

As the men ran and dived, the Executioner moved through the ranks, trying to get a feel for each man's endurance and courage. He had no idea what twists and turns the mission upon which he was embarking might take, and he might be called upon at any time to recruit a small army. Silently he picked out several men who looked to be in extraordinary condition and who showed good reflexes and coordination. One of them, however, caught his eye for a different reason.

The man was tall and slender with wiry muscles and a thin pencil mustache, and the name tag on his left breast pocket read Margai. He was fit, all right—as fit as any of the men on the parade ground, and that's why the Executioner noticed him to begin with. But the reason Bolan kept looking his way was because Margai kept glancing toward a spot in the foliage that surrounded the parade ground. The man's face showed concern. But what gave him away was that twice he saw Bolan looking at him and shot his eyes back to the front.

The Executioner's sixth sense went into high gear.

Something was going on with the man, and he would bear watching.

Buchanan kept them at the running and diving for close to an hour. Nearly fifty men had fallen by the wayside by the time he blew the whistle a final time and called a halt to the exercise. The losers were ordered back to await the bus that would take away the failed candidates each evening.

The rest of the troops sagged in exhaustion, sweat dripping from their pained faces. Buchanan didn't seem to notice. "Team A move out!" he ordered. "Double time!" He turned and led the men away at a trot.

Bolan watched the men of Team A disappear over the berm that separated the parade ground from the rifle range, then turned to his own Team B. "Everyone loosened up, or should we get a little more exercise before we start?"

A few nervous groans sounded from inside the ranks. "All right, form a circle around me!" he ordered.

The Executioner studied the men as they hurried into place. Each of the candidates wore the government-issue Portuguese camouflage BDUs, leather-and-canvas combat boots and black web belts and battle harnesses. A 9 mm Makarov pistol hung from each man's left side. Applegate-Fairbairn double-edged fighting blades had been issued to each potential commando, and the men wore them proudly, either opposite the Makarovs or upside down on the suspenders of their harnesses.

Bolan cleared his throat. "Your government has provided you with one of the finest fighting knives ever designed," he said by means of opening. "It's my job to teach you to use it." He leaned forward and pulled the blade from the sheath of the nearest man. "You have a six-and-one-quarter-inch-long blade made of 440-A steel. It's three-sixteenths of an inch thick and weighs 8.6 ounces. The ergonomically designed handle is made of Lexan, and has lead weights strategically positioned inside it to ensure proper balance." He paused and glanced across the men, making sure they were paying attention. All were—except Margai, who was again looking into the trees.

"What you have, gentlemen," Bolan said, "is a near perfect killing tool. The blade on your side has no other function but to kill men. Do not use it to clean your fingernails, or as a tent stake, or to open a can of corned-beef hash. It was designed as a fighter—pure and simple."

Flicking his eyes back to Margai, he saw the man return his attention to the front.

What was he looking for in the foliage?

"When you face a man and you are both armed with a knife," the Executioner went on, "there are eight planes of motion, twelve angles. Your body opens or closes with each movement. Let's try them. Draw your blades."

Bolan handed the knife in his hand to the man from whom he had taken it and drew the Crossada. Close to two hundred Applegate-Fairbairn blades came out of their sheaths. He led the men through the twelve thrusts and slashes several times, then had them pair up and work together. He watched carefully as the men parried or avoided each attack, noting whose movements were cleanest, most natural.

Margai was one of the better knife men—when he wasn't looking off into the forest.

At noon the Executioner heard a whistle blow inside the barracks. The men of Team A came jogging back over the berm behind Buchanan.

"Chow time!" Buchanan called out. "Reassemble on the parade ground as soon as you've eaten!"

Bolan stood watching as the grateful men hurried toward the mess hall, all eyes focused in the direction of the food.

All except Margai's.

As he walked toward the mess hall, the tall slender man with the pencil mustache was again looking into the trees.

Somalia

GARY MANNING WAS was in no mood to play games, but it didn't look like he was going to have any other choice.

He watched Captain Berber strut across the office-gym flexing his muscles. It was obvious that the man was more than just a little proud of both his body and the strength he'd developed with the weights in this room.

Berber was an egotist, being fueled solely by narcissism. And right now his fuel tank needed filling.

The way Manning saw it, he and the other men of Phoenix Force had two choices. One, he could beat the captain in the bench-press contest, and assuming the man kept his word, they'd be free to go. Or, as McCarter had already insinuated, they could kill the cocky SOB and go on about their mission.

Manning watched Berber slide under the bar and begin pumping out warm-up reps. The problem with killing Berber was twofold. On a moral plane, not Manning, McCarter nor any of the men of Phoenix Force wanted to kill anyone they didn't absolutely have to kill. Being a nuisance didn't mean a man deserved to die. Taking life for trivial reasons not only violated everything Phoenix Force and Stony Man Farm stood for, but it also violated the personal code of each of the men.

But there was also a practical reason for putting up with Berber's narcissism and taking time out to play this bench-press game. Leaving the airport without legal sanction would be a problem Phoenix Force didn't need. The men had their work cut out for them on this mission without the added complication of being hunted as fugitives by the Somalian government.

Manning watched Berber rack the bar and stand, then moved to the bench himself. Sliding under the 310 pounds, he lifted it and lowered it to his chest.

Manning knew that weight lifting was as much mental as it was physical. The big Canadian needed to "get his mind right" if he intended to beat Berber. And if possible, he needed to get Berber's mind *wrong*. Manning took a good look at Berber as he pumped out the practice reps. So far, the captain had no down side to this situation. If he won, he kept the men of Phoenix Force captive. If he lost, he let them go. Big deal. Either way, he lost nothing personally.

That needed to change. Berber needed something to worry about. Something that would not only distract his mind from the task at hand, but physically drain him of strength at the same time.

Manning cranked out fifteen warm-up reps and stood. He looked at the shirtless Somalian captain who had watched him closely during the set and smiled. Then he chuckled. "Captain," he said, "you suppose we ought to put a little money on this just to make it more interesting?"

Berber moved toward the bench for his final warm-up set, his face suddenly turning more serious.

Manning felt satisfaction, knowing he'd hit home.

"How much do you wish to wager?" Berber asked as he slid under the bar. His face had turned to stone now, and Manning could see the concern in his brown eyes. Berber's purpose for forcing the contest had been ego, not wagering. But he'd been backed into a corner now; he wouldn't come off looking quite as sure of himself as he wanted to appear if he didn't agree to a bet of some kind.

Manning glanced to the family picture on the desk. On the other hand, Berber couldn't afford to risk much, either. The Phoenix Force warrior didn't know how much a Somalian customs captain got paid, but in an impoverished country such as this, it couldn't be much. That meant any money Berber lost would take food right out of his children's mouths.

"How much?" Berber repeated as he swung under the bar.

Manning stalled a moment, trying to come up with the perfect amount. He needed a number that was high enough to create stress in the captain's mind— stress that would drain Berber's strength, as well as keep his mind off balance. On the other hand the wager couldn't be so high that Berber was forced to refuse.

"Oh, say around one hundred thousand shillings?" Manning said as Berber reached up to grasp the bar.

The captain's forearms tensed, and he hesitated. "Yes," he finally said. "All right." He lifted the bar and began his reps.

Manning watched closely as the bar went up and down. Berber didn't use quite the same smooth motion he had before. That amount was less than what McCarter had already given Berber for their "bad passports," and a mere pittance to Phoenix Force, but enough to ensure Berber's kids went hungry for a couple of days if the captain lost.

Berber racked the weights and stood, the slightly worried look still on his face. Manning slid under the bar, whistling happily. Berber's spirit was down, so it was time for the Phoenix Force commando to keep it there by exhibiting his own confidence and enthusiasm.

Manning cranked out twenty reps, then bounded to his feet, clapped his hands and said, "All right! Let's do it!" Turning to Hawkins, he said, "T.J., want to spot us? Rafe, how about you and Cal working the plates?" Then, turning back to Berber, he added, "That is, if all that's all right with you, Captain?"

Berber nodded as McCarter took up a position behind the bench and James and Encizo moved to the ends of the bar.

"How much do you want, Captain?" Encizo asked.

Berber's confidence was fading fast, falling victim to Manning's fervor. "Add ninety pounds," he said. "I will begin easy—with four hundred." He glanced at Manning, then quickly added, "I always make my first lift easy."

"Me, too," Manning responded. "But not *that* easy."

Berber frowned at the comment, then dropped onto the bench. Reaching up, he grasped the bar, and took two deep breaths. "Okay," he said.

Hawkins gave him a "lift off." Berber lowered the bar to his chest, pushed it up and handed it back to Hawkins. He sat up.

Manning reached down, grasped him by the hand and hauled him to his feet. "Make it 450, guys," he said.

Encizo and James each added a twenty-five-pound

plate as Manning slid under the Olympic bar. He reached up, nodded to Hawkins and took the bar.

The big Canadian kept a smirk on his face as he lowered the bar to his chest, paused a second, then shot it back up. He racked the weight without help, then stood again. Looking to Berber, he saw the doubt had doubled in the customs man's eyes. "Hey, I'm almost warmed up," Manning said.

Berber took a seat and leaned back again. "Put two more twenty-fives on," he said. "Five hundred pounds."

Manning felt a quick stab of unease in his belly. He had hit five hundred only twice in his life, his best lift being a one-time high of 510. And he had been too busy to train properly in the past few months, which meant he might not be able to do so today.

As quickly as the doubt had come, Manning pushed it from his mind. He didn't necessarily have to hit five hundred. He just had to beat Berber. And if his psych-out plan had worked as well as he hoped, Berber might well miss this lift. Manning might already have won without knowing it.

The big Canadian's hopes for an easy victory evaporated as Berber lowered the bar, then pushed it back up.

Manning kept up his front of confidence as he took a seat on the bench. He closed his eyes, thinking, but kept the arrogant grin on his face. Berber had struggled with his second lift. The five-hundred-pound lift had taken its toll, and he didn't have that much left in him.

"Let's still keep it light," Manning said. "Say...oh, 510." He waited while Encizo and James each added five-pound plates, then moved under the bar. With a deep breath he reached up. Breathing in again, he visualized the bar coming down, then going back up.

A moment later, it did.

Manning sat back up and looked at Berber. The doubt that had been growing in the man's brown eyes was now fear. He didn't know what the captain's all-time best push was, but it had to be about the same as his.

It was time for Berber's final lift, which meant it was also time for Manning to play his psychological hole card.

Before Berber could take his seat, Manning walked casually over to the desk. Picking up the plastic photo cube, he looked at the pictures of the smiling children. "Hey, Captain," he said, "these your kids?"

Berber looked across the room and nodded.

"Nice," Manning said. "You've got a nice family. You're a lucky man."

Berber's face fell even further as he took a seat.

Manning almost felt sorry for the captain. Berber was probably a pretty decent man overall. He'd just let a streak of vanity push him into a corner. He realized that now, and knew that failure to win the contest would cost the children in the photo.

"How much?" Calvin James asked.

Berber glanced at the bar, then to Manning.

The big Canadian grinned back. Berber was close to his limit, whatever that was. He was trying to decide what Manning was capable of. If he chose a weight for his final lift that was too low, Manning would top it. But if he attempted too much, he would fail himself.

"Five hundred fifteen," Berber finally said.

Manning felt his own heart drop. He had been hoping the captain would go higher and miss, and a third lift on his part would be unnecessary.

Berber closed his eyes as he lay back on the bench. His lips moved slightly.

Manning couldn't help wondering if the captain was talking to himself, or God.

The bar went down to Berber's chest, then started up. The captain's arms straightened partway out, then reached the point where the lift became hardest. For a moment it appeared the weights had traveled as far as they were going. Then, with a mighty grunt, Berber pushed the bar on to the end of his arms.

The other members of Phoenix Force shot glances at Manning as Hawkins helped the captain rack the bar. The team often worked out together, and knew one another's capabilities. And they knew Manning would have to beat his personal record by ten pounds if they were going to leave the airport without problems.

"Five hundred twenty," Manning directed. He turned away and saw McCarter standing against the wall. The Phoenix Force leader's hand had disappeared into his pocket, and Manning knew he had to have his Spyderco Delica knife gripped in his fingers.

The bottom line was easy to understand. If Manning didn't beat Berber, Berber would die. And the Phoenix Force warriors would be wanted men in Somalia.

Manning took a deep breath and looked away from McCarter. He couldn't think about that right now—he had to concentrate on the lift itself, and the time for tearing down Berber's confidence was over, as well. Now he needed to concentrate fully on building up his own assurance, harnessing his strength.

Slowly Manning breathed in through his nose and let the air out through his mouth. Again he pictured the lift in his mind, visualizing it going down, then up. But instead of iron on the ends of the bar, in his mind's eye, Manning saw feathers.

When he had completed this mental exercise several times, the big Canadian took a seat on the bench. His mind focused intently now on the matter at hand, he barely noticed that McCarter had taken up a position directly behind Berber.

Manning leaned back and said, "Let's do it." He looked up, glancing from the right end of the bar to the left. At first he saw iron plates on each end of the thick Olympic bar. He narrowed his eyes, and the black plates became fluffy white feathers.

Manning took the bar from Hawkins and lowered it to his chest. With all the strength in his pectorals, deltoids and triceps, he heaved upward. The bar traveled up to the sticking point, hesitated, then shot on to the top.

The men of Phoenix Force broke out in applause.

Manning caught a glimpse of McCarter's empty hand coming out of his pocket as he sat back up. The big Canadian looked at Berber. The man looked as if he'd just lost his wife and best friend on the same day. But Manning could see the captain intended to honor the agreement; Berber was already reaching in his pocket.

Manning took the money from the captain, shook his hand, then took the man by the elbow. Leading Berber back to his own desk, he lifted the photo cube and pointed to a picture in which Berber's children stood facing the camera in front of their mother and father.

With the other hand Manning pressed the bills back into Berber's hand. "This is a present," he said, "from me to your children."

Berber looked at him with gratitude for a moment, then the customs captain's face changed to anger.

Without another word, the Phoenix Force men picked up their passports off the desk and filed out of the room.

Manning was the last to leave. He took a final glance at Berber before closing the door behind him with an arm that wanted to drop off from exhaustion. The man looked as if he'd like to grind them all up and feed their bodies to wild animals.

The big Canadian let his weary arm fall to his side as he followed the others down the hall. Remembering McCarter's hand in his pocket—the pocket where the Phoenix Force leader carried his Spyderco Delica—Manning realized that regardless of how strong he was, Berber would never know just how close his little game had brought him to death.

The big Canadian sighed. The time for games was over now. The real mission was about to begin. And he couldn't help wondering if Berber would be a player again somewhere down the line.

CHAPTER SEVEN

New York

The rented forest green Probe had been stashed in a
Manhattan parking garage ever since its use a month
earlier in a Stony Man Farm blacksuits training exercise. It didn't have much power, and it looked like
a nerdmobile in Carl Lyons's opinion, but it would
do for what he had in mind.

Lyons kept his foot on the accelerator as he guided
the Probe through Brooklyn Heights, keeping his
place in the long train of vehicles heading toward
Prospect Park. Trees lined the road paralleling the
East River, and across the water the Able Team
leader could see one of the most spectacular views
of the Manhattan skyline available anywhere. He
stared briefly, then shot his eyes back to the Datsun
in front of him as the driver slammed on the brakes.
Lyons jerked his foot to his own brake, skidding to
a stop an inch behind the Datsun.

Ahead and behind the Probe, tempers flared at the
sudden delay. Horns honked; voices screamed and
cursed.

Lyons made a few rude remarks himself as he threw the car into Park to wait.

"Relax, Ironman," Schwarz said from the passenger's seat. "According to Rook we've got at least two days before they gas the subway."

Lyons nodded. His mind wondered back to the unusual but expert interrogation Blancanales had put Ira Rook through earlier in the day when they'd still been in Washington. When Rook had broken it had been as if a dam had burst. He'd answered questions without hesitation. The unscrupulous newspaperman had confirmed what they already knew—it had been Spencer Kiethley who had broken the story about the abandoned top secret documents. But Kiethley had told Rook more.

The Followers of the Truth cult had another plot under way to plant sarin gas in a subway. But this time the plot had a small twist to it; the subway wasn't in Tokyo.

It was in New York City.

Traffic began to move again, and Lyons shifted the Probe to Drive. A few minutes later they were cruising down Eastern Parkway, then turning onto Flatbush Avenue at the main entrance to Prospect Park. Signs outside the park advertised the many features inside. The Brooklyn Botanical Gardens, for one, included a "touch-taste-smell" garden for the blind, greenhouse displays, a Dutch Colonial farmhouse built in 1777 and a Quaker cemetery that dated back to 1662. The Probe picked up speed as traffic thinned slightly.

Lyons glanced to Blancanales. Able Team's psychological-warfare expert had been strangely quiet since the interrogation, and now his face reflected deep thought. "What's wrong, Pol?" Lyons asked.

Blancanales shrugged. "I don't know," he said. "Something. Nothing, maybe. Just something about Rook that bothers me."

"Me, too," Schwarz said. "The man's a jerk."

Blancanales shook his head. "No, I mean about the things he told us. I don't know. It seems like...." His voice trailed off, and he shrugged again. "There are some holes. Like this American cult member. Rook said Kiethley told him about the guy. Well, how'd Kiethley know about him?"

It was Lyons's turn to shrug. "Who knows? Maybe the Japanese cops had a line on the man and told Kiethley when he was in Tokyo. What's it matter *how* he knew? It's a good lead."

The men of Able Team lapsed into silent thought. Lyons's mind stayed on Casey Balforth, the cult member they'd been discussing and whose house they were headed toward now. It was here the Brooklyn cell of Followers of the Truth was planning the subway gassing, and Lyons wondered how heavily armed they would be. Able Team might be facing strong resistance or meek compliance. There was no way to know in advance. But Carl Lyons intended to take no chances.

"Weapons inventory," the Able Team leader called out. It was a technique he had learned years before as a member of the LAPD SWAT team. Ver-

bally stating what weapons everyone was carrying
served two purposes: it acquainted other team members with what equipment was available should the
man carrying it go down and his gear be needed, and
it helped mentally prepare each man for battle.

Lyons went first. "Colt Python .357 Magnum,"
he said. "Four speedloaders. Colt Government
Model .45. Six magazines."

Gadgets Schwarz chuckled. "Some things never
change," he said. "Beretta 92 with four extra mags.
Then there's the pop gun." He held up a Smith &
Wesson Chiefs Special airweight. "Two speedloaders." He paused. "Oh, yeah, and my blade." A
Benchmade Emerson Spec War CQC7 liner-lock
folding knife came up in Schwarz's other hand. He
flipped it open with the ambidextrous thumb stud,
then closed it again just as quickly.

"I'm carrying the Beretta, too," Blancanales said.
"Same four-mag setup, but I've got my Walther PPK
for backup. Two extra mags there. And as for cut-
lery..." He pulled out a Cold Steel Culloden, the
lightweight Scottish "sock knife," then returned it
to its neat weightless nylon scabbard. "And I've got
my walking stick. We taking the Calicos in?"

In the rearview mirror Lyons saw Blancanales
glance down to the three hard plastic cases that concealed their Calico 960 submachine pistols. The Able
Team leader hesitated before answering. Each case
carried one of the space-age weapons with a 50-
round magazine already mounted on top of the receiver. The gun itself was suspended in a shoulder

sling, and in an extra magazine carrier opposite the weapon hung a 100-round backup mag. All the men of Able Team needed to do to have 150 rounds of 9 mm ammo at their disposal was to open the case and slip into the rig.

"Ironman," Schwarz said, breaking into the Able Team leader's thoughts, "what about the Calicos?"

Finally Lyons answered. "Let's leave them in the car for now," he said. He turned off Flatbush Avenue into a lower-middle-class residential area and pulled a Brooklyn street map from the inside pocket of his coat. "Unless we see something that makes us think the house is crawling with bad guys out for our blood. Even with the shoulder rigs there's too much chance of them being eyeballed on our way in by some good citizen. And we don't need the NYPD surrounding the house while we're inside."

The men rode on in silence. Lyons opened the map and spread it on the seat between him and Schwarz. Watching it with one eye, he kept the other on the street. After making two more turns, he slowed the Probe. "Should be on that side," he said, pointing across the street. "Right about there."

All three men stared out the window at a light green, one-story frame house as the Probe passed.

"See any signs of life?" Lyons asked.

Schwarz and Blancanales both shook their heads.

Lyons pulled the car to the curb. "We'll get out here and walk back," he said. "Stay up in the yards and on the sidewalk. I don't want this Balforth character seeing us until we're on his front porch."

"Good idea," Schwarz stated. "He's going to make you for a cop for sure in that jacket."

Blancanales chuckled.

Lyons shot his teammate a dirty look as all three men got out of the vehicle.

Lyons led the way down the sidewalk, past a curious mixture of single family homes and brownstone tenement houses. A few people sat out on their front steps, watching the three men curiously as they passed. More than once, the words "cop," "man" and "pig" drifted within Lyons's earshot.

"I'm telling you, Ironman," Schwarz said, "it's that coat."

The Able Team leader ignored him, increasing his pace as he reached the house next to Balforth's address. He cut across the grass, taking the steps two at a time, hearing his teammates behind him. Lyons's hand shot inside the plaid jacket to the grips of the Colt Python on his hip as he raised his hand to knock.

He would give the door one knock, then kick it in. He didn't want to give Balforth time to get out the back or decide that they *were* cops and start shooting.

Lyons never got a chance for the one knock he had planned.

As his fist started down, the first rounds from inside the house came exploding through the door.

Sierra Leone

THE COMMANDO UNIT training center mess hall smelled like a combination of rice, vegetables, meat and sweat.

Bolan and Buchanan leaned back against the rickety wooden wall and let the troops go first, watching silently as the exhausted special-forces candidates fell in at the front of the serving line. Roughly half of the original would-be commandos still remained in camp, the others having fallen out sometime during the day and been returned to their units. The men Bolan saw now looked ravenous. But after the long day he and Buchanan had put them through, they also looked like they might be too tired to lift their forks to their mouths.

Bolan watched the men shuffle down the serving line, pushing their brown plastic trays ahead of them. Four chow attendants—enlisted men who wore white shirts and slacks—stood on the other side of the counter. Also between the men and servers were steel pots filled with rice, fresh vegetables and meat stew. The faces of the men in white glistened with sweat from the steam that rose from the food.

The Executioner glanced around the mess hall. It was a strange building, consisting of a main serving and dining area that looked to have been built from the scrap wood of other structures. It was closed in on three sides, but the fourth had been left open and the roof and walls were of canvas tenting. The long mess tables extended past the concrete floor of the main part of the hall and onto the hard-packed dirt of the tent area. So far, the men who had made it through the chow line had all stayed on the concrete.

Turning back to the line, Bolan saw Margai reach the front and lift a tray. The man looked tired, but didn't show the almost total exhaustion that most of the others exhibited. He moved down the line, accepting dishes and bowls of the native Sierra Leone fare, then walked through the tables, past the concrete and under the tenting. He took a seat alone about halfway to the far end, facing out into the quickly dropping sun.

Every minute or two, Bolan noticed him glance up in the general direction of the spot he'd been so intent on watching earlier in the day.

Bolan elbowed Buchanan lightly in the ribs. "The guy by himself out there," he said too quietly for anyone else to hear. "Name's Margai. You know him?"

Buchanan squinted Margai's way for a moment, then shook his head. "Uh-uh. Why?"

"He's strange," Bolan said.

Buchanan shrugged. "He's just basically a loner is all." He paused, then added, "Unless I'm way off base I'd guess you're a loner yourself."

Bolan shook his head. "No, it's more than that. Something about him doesn't add up. He's been watching the bush all day. Like he's waiting for something or somebody."

The line of men waiting to eat had shortened to less than a dozen now, and the Executioner and Buchanan fell in behind them. Bolan took a tray, then accepted a large bowl of rice and vegetables and another of meat stew. At the end of the chow line he set a large plastic glass of iced tea on the tray, then led the way to the officers' table, where several of the Gurkhas already sat downing their food.

Bolan sat where he could watch Margai. Buchanan fell into the seat next to him.

The Executioner ate silently, his gaze fixed on Margai's back. By now the main area of the mess hall was filled, and several other men had joined Margai on the dirt.

But to Bolan he seemed as isolated as ever.

The Executioner was almost finished when Margai stood, carried his tray to the window that led into the kitchen and cast a quick glance at the officers' table. Hurrying—but trying not to look like he was—the commando candidate exited the mess hall by a side door.

Bolan hesitated for a second. The men had been instructed to return to their barracks immediately after chow, and as tired as they were, there had been no argument. But unless he missed his guess, the Executioner didn't think that was where Margai was headed. At least not directly. And Bolan was pretty sure he knew where the man *was* going.

Not why, maybe, but where. And the why he intended to find out.

The Executioner rose from his seat with the easygoing bearing of a man who might take a short walk, then hit the sack. He dropped his tray of empty dishes on the counter next to Margai's, walked to the opposite of the mess hall where the man had exited and headed out the door.

The sun had fallen, becoming a deep purple glow behind the mountains by the time Bolan had circled the building. He paused at the last corner before turning, pressing his back against the rotting wood and peering slowly around the corner. What he saw didn't surprise him.

Margai was walking hurriedly away from the mess hall in the general direction of the parade ground. Every few steps the man cast a nervous glance over his shoulder.

Bolan let him fade a little farther into the twilight, then darted out from behind the building. He sprinted across an open area to the building that housed the camp's generator and took cover again. By now Margai was perhaps forty yards ahead in the quickly darkening camp. The man appeared confident that he hadn't been seen. Bolan watched him break into a jog and quit looking over his shoulder as he neared the rise that overlooked the parade ground.

The Executioner let Margai disappear over the rise, then came out from behind the generator house and sprinted forward. When he reached the top of the rise, he dived forward onto his belly, sliding the last few feet to the edge.

Slowly he peered down onto the parade ground.

Margai was still jogging—directly toward the spot in the bushes he had watched all afternoon.

Bolan stood, glancing at the sky now and relying on its darkness for cover. He knew the general vicinity in which Margai was headed, so it wasn't imperative that he keep visual contact on the man. Staying low to the ground, he moved down the slope, then forward across the dirt and grass.

Fifty yards before he reached the spot to which he suspected Margai was headed, the Executioner cut into the trees himself. Swiftly and silently he made his way on. The sound of Margai's feet, thrashing through the undergrowth, drifted back through the thick foliage. The thrashing sounds grew louder as Bolan closed the gap between them, then suddenly stopped.

So did the Executioner.

A muffled grunt—the sound a man might make when attempting to lift something heavy—came drifting through the trees. The Executioner moved on, keeping low, until he reached the clearing. In the center of the open area he could see the soft glow of a pocket flashlight. Margai's shadowy form sat on the ground holding the light in one hand, its beam cast downward onto the small white piece of paper in his other hand.

Next to the commando trainee a large boulder had been overturned, and in the glow of the light Bolan could see worms, maggots and other suddenly disturbed insects crawling across the stone's damp underside. The Executioner dropped to one knee, watching silently. He saw Margai look up from the paper with a nervous expression on his face, then stare back toward the parade ground. He looked back down, then glanced deeper into the woods.

The man's body language spoke as loudly as words. Margai had known someone was coming to leave a message for him under this rock and had been unable to avoid looking that way all day. Now the paper he had retrieved gave him orders of some type—something that involved his further deserting the camp and going deeper into the wooded area. Margai obviously didn't like the idea and was trying to make up his mind whether he would follow that order.

The Executioner's hand fell absentmindedly to the grip of the Crossada knife as he considered his own options. He could overpower Margai, read the note himself or force the man to translate it if it was written in Krio. But if it *was* in Krio, the Executioner would have no way of knowing if Margai lied about the contents of the order.

No, it would be better to wait. Unless he missed his guess, Margai would decide to follow the note's orders and move deeper into the forest. Bolan would follow and find out what was going on that way.

After another minute's deliberation in which Margai glanced both ways several times again, he stuffed the paper into the pocket of his fatigue blouse, killed the flashlight and stood. Another soft grunt emanated from his lips as he rolled the stone back into place. With a final look back toward camp, he started deeper into the trees.

Bolan started after him, drawing the Desert Eagle with his right hand, the knife with his left. He had left the Beretta back in his footlocker during the day's training schedule, and if silent action was called upon, the huge fighting knife would have to serve him.

The Executioner stayed well back, following Margai more by sound than sight. In the still night mountain air every twig that snapped under the man's boots pointed toward him. Every dry leaf he brushed denoted his position as definitively as the spotlight from a police helicopter.

Margai led the Executioner down the bank of a mountain stream, through the water, then up the other side. For a mile or so they followed the mountain road that had brought Bolan and Buchanan to the training camp. The big American was able to move in closer, using the thick trees that lined the pathway as cover. Margai finally left the road again, taking a narrow game trail, which led to another stream thirty minutes later. Margai forded, then followed the water course for another two miles. He had quit looking over his shoulder now, confident that he wasn't being followed.

Bolan took advantage of the man's new confidence to move closer. He hurried along, knowing they had to be getting close to wherever it was they were headed. They had been gone from camp for nearly three hours now, and assuming Margai was going back—and the Executioner's gut feeling was that he'd been planted in the camp as a spy and would return—he would need time to arrive before reveille in the morning.

Ahead, Bolan heard Margai's footsteps suddenly halt. He slowed, moving forward. Through the dark trees he could see the side of a mountain, and, as he focused through the dark limbs and leaves, the black outline of a cave mouth began to take shape. In the center of the black hole, the Executioner could see a flicker of light.

A campfire. It had to be. It was too strong and sporadic to be Margai's pocket flash again.

The Executioner moved as close to the cave as he dared, dropping again to one knee as he took cover behind a thick tree trunk. The campfire just inside the opening was brighter now. To prevent night blindness he looked to the sides of the flame, using his peripheral vision to watch Margai move toward it. As best Bolan could make out, there was no one else around the flames. Margai stopped next to the fire. He called out softly in Krio.

A moment later a trio of men wearing blue bandannas stepped out of the opening. The RUF hardmen were well armed, each man gripping an AK-47 in his hands and wearing a pistol and blade of some type on the web belt around his hips.

Bolan aimed the Desert Eagle ahead of him and started to rise. He wanted information from these men, and he would be afforded no better opportunity to get the drop on them without having to kill them. If he acted quickly now, he could step out from behind cover, take the men by surprise, bind them and begin his interrogation.

There was no time like the present. Bolan sheathed his knife and rose to his feet.

He had started to step forward when he heard the faint footsteps in the woods behind him.

Somalia

FROM MOGADISHU, Somalia boasted one surfaced road to Kismayu in the south and another that stretched north to Hargeisa. Throughout the rest of the country the roads were gravel, or simply paths cut through the thick foliage and sparsely vegetated desert areas.

It was on one such gravel road that Phoenix Force had been traveling ever since leaving the airport and Captain Berber. And it was onto one such path that T. J. Hawkins now turned their hurriedly rented 4WD Jeep Wagoneer station wagon.

In the passenger's seat McCarter steadied himself as the vehicle began bouncing over the rugged semi-desert land. They were in the no-man's-land around the Somalian capital city. To the south lay greener terrain with corn and banana fields, and to the north were the herds of sheep, goats and camels of the nomads.

McCarter stared out over the central plateau. Here, there was little of anything.

Hawkins gave the Wagoneer's shocks a torture test as he guided the vehicle down a long, dry creek bed, then hopped it back up the opposite bank. They followed the plateau for a mile or so, then McCarter broke the silence. Pointing to an old and knurled tree growing up through the cracks in the layered dirt, he said, "Head there, T.J. Unless I miss my guess, the crates should have landed just beyond that point."

"All except for one," Encizo said from the back seat. "Number two—the long guns. A gust of wind caught it and took it north."

McCarter turned in his seat. In all the confusion with Berber, he hadn't known that. "You see it land?" he asked Encizo.

The man shook his head. "We'd flown on before it hit," the little Cuban said. "But it was close to the ground. We'll find it."

Hawkins gunned the vehicle up a series of steps cut into the dirt and rock surface by centuries of erosion. Next to the aged tree, he tapped the brake, slowing to a stop.

McCarter squinted through his sunglasses as the sun fell in the west. Perhaps a quarter mile away, between a large formation of boulders on each side of the path, he saw the first of the crates. The cargo chute that had lowered it to the ground still flapped in the light breeze over the plateau.

Hawkins drove on without having to be told. McCarter squinted again as a small brown object appeared ahead in the road. As they drew closer, he could see it was an MRE envelope. Beyond it, he saw several more in a cluster. "Pull over," the Phoenix Force leader ordered. Hawkins did as ordered, riding the brake to a dusty halt on the dried earth.

McCarter turned in his seat. "Rafael, Gary. You and Calvin get out and gather up the MREs. Crate number four must have hit somewhere around here.

They're scattered up and down the road. T.J. and I will meet you at the first crate.''

The three men in the back seat got out.

McCarter saw them gathering up the Meals Ready to Eat envelopes in the mirror fastened to the sun visor as Hawkins drove on. A few minutes later they pulled to a halt between the boulders next to the crate.

"Number two," Hawkins said, reading the bright red number off the top. "Ammo."

McCarter got out, grabbed the tire tool from the rear of the Wagoneer and walked forward. Hawkins drew his Randall Model 2 Fighting Stiletto and cut the cargo chute lines away from the crate. He hid the chute in a thick growth of sagebrush while McCarter snapped the iron bands around the crate's pine lid and pried it off.

John "Cowboy" Kissinger, Stony Man Farm's chief armorer, had packed the crates and outfitted Phoenix Force well. Inside this box, dispersed throughout hundreds of foam packing pellets, they found box after box of 9 mm ammunition. Scattered among them were a few boxes in .40 caliber S&W. The two men began to load the cartridges into the Wagoneer.

The job was finished by the time James, Encizo and Manning arrived, their arms loaded down with MREs. "We didn't find them all," Manning said with a grin, "but we won't go hungry for a while."

McCarter nodded. "Then let's get this crate out of sight and—" He stopped talking, turning suddenly when he thought he heard movement in the boulders to his left. In lieu of having a firearm yet, his hand dropped instinctively to the pocket where he'd clipped the Spyderco Delica knife. His eyes scanned the rocks.

He saw nothing.

"Something wrong?" James asked. The black Phoenix Force warrior had picked up on McCarter's movement, and his own hand had entered his knife pocket.

McCarter shook his head slowly. "I thought I heard something. I suppose I was wrong." He paused. "Get the crate off the road and let's go."

Phoenix Force hid the pine box next to the cargo chute and piled back into the Wagoneer. A hundred yards farther on they found crate number five and unloaded their pistols—Matching Beretta 92 semiautos for James, Manning, Encizo and Hawkins, and a pair of Browning Hi-Powers for McCarter. The Phoenix Force leader quickly loaded one of his Brownings with 9 mm ammo, then paused to study the other. Rather than the 9 mm parabellum ammo the Hi-Power had used since its inception in 1935, this weapon was the newer model in .40-caliber S&W.

McCarter smiled. He had carried Brownings since his days with the British SAS and had fostered only one complaint about the weapon: he would have preferred it in .45ACP. But the .40 S&W was close enough that he'd give it a try. The round, which split the difference between 9 mm and .45, was fast becoming the sweetheart of American law enforcement.

Quickly the Phoenix Force leader loaded eleven rounds into the magazine and popped one into the chamber.

The Wagoneer moved on, stopping next to load fatigues, holsters, belts and other gear. A short row of scrub trees lay near where the crate had landed, and again McCarter thought he heard movement from that direction. He'd had no time to slide his weapons into their holsters yet, and had them stuck in his belt. He hefted the .40-caliber pistol.

With the rest of Phoenix Force assisting, McCarter searched the trees and surrounding area. They found nothing.

"Anyone else hear anything?" the Briton asked.

All four men shook their heads.

"It's that age thing, David," Hawkins joked. "All things considered, though, I'd say you're doing pretty well."

"Just a lizard or something like that," Manning suggested.

"Yeah." McCarter wasn't so sure. He *had* heard something, and his instinct told him it was made by a human. He stuck the pistol back into his belt.

The men loaded into the Wagoneer once more and continued on over the flat, dusty plateau in search of the rifles that had been carried away by the gust of wind. McCarter had pulled a pair of binoculars from the last crate and now pressed them into service to aid in the search. But even with the lenses he had still seen no signs of the rifle crate an hour later.

Finally, an inch away from deciding that the rifles were lost and they would have to continue the mission with pistols only, McCarter caught a glimpse of what looked like cured wood in a canyon ahead. "That way," he told Hawkins, gesturing with the binoculars.

Hawkins pulled to the edge of the steep drop-off and killed the engine. The men of Phoenix Force got out. McCarter focused the binoculars on the wood from the new angle, then dropped them to the end of the cord around his neck. "That's it," he said. "But we'll never get the Wagoneer down there. Hawk, you watch the Jeep while we get the rifles."

The Phoenix Force leader led the way on the slip-slide down the bank to where the rifle crate lay. When he, Manning, James and Encizo reached the bottom, McCarter noticed that the impact of hitting the ground had already broken the retaining band. Slipping the tire tool under the lid, he pried up and was surprised at how easy the nails came out.

A moment later he saw why.

The crate had already been opened. Most of the nails were missing, and those that weren't had been shoved back down the now larger holes. McCarter leaned forward, knowing what he'd see even before he saw it.

The crate was empty.

For the third time that day McCarter heard movement. But this time there was no mistaking it, and the others heard it, too.

Turning, the Phoenix Force leader saw at least forty men suddenly rise from hiding throughout the canyon. Although they carried a wide variety of weapons, all were armed to the teeth. They held their weapons at the ready as they moved forward, encircling the team from Stony Man Farm.

McCarter's hand dropped to the Browning Hi-Power stuck in his belt, but he said loud enough for Hawkins to hear, "Hold your fire. There are too many of them."

The men who moved in were a ragged bunch in a mixture of tattered African and Western dress. They closed to within ten feet, then stopped. Scattered among them, McCarter saw the five M-16s that had been in the crate.

A man wearing a red bandanna tied over his head stepped out from the crowd and stopped, facing McCarter. His left eye bore a black patch, and a gold hoop earring hung from his left ear. His ebony face was almost completely hidden by an unkempt black beard, and what wasn't bore the scars of battles past. A long cutlass hung from a scabbard on his left side, and on the right McCarter saw a Ruger Vaquero single-action revolver with stag grips. The weapon was either a .44 Magnum or .45 Colt—from the distance he was at, he couldn't tell.

The man walked forward and smiled widely, showing two rows of pearly white teeth spattered with gold fillings. All in all, he looked every bit the part of the Caribbean pirate McCarter guessed he was trying to emulate. "I am Captain Jack," the man said, "and these are my men."

McCarter nodded. "We're—"

"My prisoners," Captain Jack finished for the Phoenix Force leader. The smile disappeared, and two of his men escorted Hawkins down the steep bank. He snapped his fingers, and several more of his men rushed to his side. "Disarm them," he ordered, "and tie them up."

New York

MORE THAN ONE MAN fired through the front door of Casey Balforth's house in Brooklyn, New York. That fact was clear.

By the number of holes that suddenly appeared in Balforth's front door and the amount of lead chasing after Carl Lyons, Hermann Schwarz and Rosario Blancanales, there had to be several.

The three Able Team commandos dived out of the line of fire, drawing their weapons as they fell off the porch to both sides. They immediately turned back toward the assault.

Lyons hit the grass and rolled up against the house, the Colt Python gripped tightly in both hands. On the other side of the porch he saw Blancanales. He waited for the gunfire to die down, then looked to his side to see Schwarz. "Take the back, Gadgets," he whispered.

Schwarz nodded, rose to his feet and hurried around the corner of the house and out of sight.

Lyons moved back up onto the porch to the side of the door, transferring the Colt to his left hand. Hooking the weapon around the corner, the Able Team leader fired a full cylinder of .357 semijacketed hollowpoint rounds into the house, then dived from the porch again.

Return fire chased him back to the grass.

Lyons had a speedloader full of fresh ammo into the Python's cylinder two seconds after he hit the ground again. He looked up, seeing that he'd come to rest directly under the front window. The sight didn't make him happy. Anyone inside the dwelling who knew he was there had only to stick a gun out the window, point it down and pull the trigger. They'd stand about a ninety-five percent chance of hitting him somewhere.

No, Lyons decided, this wouldn't do at all.

The fire through the front door continued as the wood began to splinter. Large holes appeared in the door. Lyons twisted and rose high enough to glance over the windowsill into what appeared to be the house's front bedroom. Unless someone was hiding on the other side of the bed or in the closet against the far wall, it was empty. Lyons reached up and pushed against the top of the window. He was surprised to find it unlocked.

The Able Team leader glanced across the porch again and caught Blancanales's attention. He pointed at himself, then at the window.

Blancanales nodded. He curved his Beretta 92 around the corner of the door very much like Lyons had done on the other side a moment before. As he fired off a string of fast semiauto rounds to mask the noise, Lyons lifted the window.

The Able Team leader kept the Python in front of him as he crawled through the opening. His eyes darted back and forth, covering the room. The door to the hallway was closed, but on the other side he could hear the sound of gunfire still exploding in the living room. Silently he breathed a sigh of relief for the extra moment's warning the closed door would give him if someone tried to enter the room.

The main threat right now was from the closet or under or around the bed. Leaving the window open behind him, Lyons quickly checked these potential hiding places as the gunfire in the other room continued. Finding no one in the bedroom, he moved to the closed door. With the Python in his right hand, he reached out and slowly twisted the knob.

No sooner had he turned it than the door flew open in his face. The corner of the door struck Lyons squarely between the eyes, knocking him back over the bed behind him. A tall burly man in a white T-shirt and long, greasy black hair stopped halfway in the room, a huge .44 Magnum Colt Anaconda filling his hand. The weapon resembled Lyons's Colt Python .357—only larger.

At first Lyons thought it was mere surprise he saw on the face of the man with the greasy hair. But as the Able Team leader brought the Python up into play, it looked more like a Vacant sign hanging in the man's eyes.

Lyons's Python jumped twice in his hands, sending a double tap of .357s into the white T-shirt. As the Able Team leader rolled off the bed and onto his feet, the T-shirt suddenly turned crimson.

The burly man in the shirt looked down at his chest, his face still a mask of bafflement. He struggled to bring the Anaconda back up with both hands.

Lyons raised the Python until the sights lined up on the man's uncomprehending face. Squeezing gently, he double-actioned the trigger, and another round drilled through the man's nose and into his brain stem.

The man in the stained white T-shirt was dead before he hit the ground.

Lyons pushed the falling body out of the way and moved back to the door. He flipped open the Python's cylinder, clawing the dead rounds out with his fingernail and leaving the live loads inside. Fresh .357 rounds came from a cartridge pouch on his belt under his jacket and filled the holes. As he slid the cylinder back into the frame, he felt something drip into his eyes. His vision blurred, and his eyes began to burn.

Raising a hand to his forehead, Lyons brought it away again to find his fingers covered with blood. He cursed silently. The door had opened a gash just above the eyebrows. It was nothing a few stitches wouldn't take care of, but it would bleed down into his eyes until he got it bandaged. In the meantime he needed to be able to see.

Lyons reached into the back pocket of his slacks and pulled out a white handkerchief. Rolling it quickly into a headband, he tied it tightly around his head and pushed the cloth hard against the wound. The bleeding didn't stop, but it slowed.

Sticking his head around the corner into a short hallway, the Able Team leader could see part of the living room through another door. One man stood in front of a fireplace, an old but perfectly serviceable .45 Ingram MAC-10 gripped in both hands. The machine pistol jumped rapidly in his hands as he fired round after round through the front door. He had the same distant look on his face as the man Lyons had encountered in the bedroom, and he used the weapon as if someone had flipped a switch, setting him on automatic pilot.

As Lyons watched, the gun ran dry. The man pulled another box mag from his vest and rammed it home with the emotion of a zombie.

Lyons moved out into the hall, keeping his back to the wall and sliding toward the door to the living room. As he got closer, a set of feet, then calves, then knees appeared. The ex–LAPD cop stopped, studying what he could see of the kneeling figure. This man, too, was firing a weapon at the front door. Lyons couldn't see it, but he could see the vibration caused by each recoil in the man's lower body.

Finally reaching the door, Lyons took a deep breath. It had sounded like several men shooting when he'd been outside, and so far he'd seen only two. But he had also seen only half of the living room. Ten more could be waiting silently in the other half, not firing, knowing someone had entered the house and using the two men Lyons had seen as bait.

Lyons shifted the Python to his left hand and drew the Government Model .45 with his right. He took a deep breath. It could be a trap, but there was only one way to find out. A hard smile curled his lips. Besides, he thought. As Native Americans used to say, "Today is a good day to die."

He burst into the room with both guns roaring. The Python jumped twice in his hands as he pumped a pair of Magnum rounds into the man firing the Ingram. Almost simultaneously the .45 blew downward at the kneeling man. Lyons looked down, trying to get his first full look at the man on the floor.

He was a split second too late. By the time he had focused on the man's face, two .45-caliber Black Talon hollowpoint rounds had already destroyed the features. Another MAC-10 fell to the carpet.

Lyons turned his attention to the back half of the living room—the half he had been unable to see. He raised both weapons to just below eye level, scanning his environment.

The rest of the room was empty.

The Able Team leader frowned. It didn't make sense. Even with the fast-firing full-auto Ingrams, there had been too many rounds blowing through the door to be fired by just two men. There were more gunmen in the house somewhere.

Where?

Lyons had only a few seconds to wonder before his question was answered for him. As he stood thinking in the living room, the distinctive pop of 9 mm rounds being fired from a Beretta 92 came from the backyard of the house.

Schwarz.

A second later a cacophony of other weapons joined the Beretta as World War III erupted in the backyard.

CHAPTER EIGHT

Sierra Leone

The Executioner froze in the dark African mountain night, suddenly on alert. No longer was the situation completely in his command. No longer could he simply step from behind the tree and take Margai and the other men in front of the cave prisoner. The footsteps behind him had changed all that.

And now, he heard them again.

Bolan turned slowly away from the cave. He could see nothing behind him, and for a moment he wondered if the footsteps had been his imagination. No, he had conquered and learned to harness his imagination many years ago. An animal moving through the night? No, not that, either. Somewhere over the long course of his career he had developed the ability to unconsciously perceive the difference in movements between four-legged animals and the two-legged variety.

He took another second to consider the situation. Who was the human coming up behind him? The most likely explanation was an RUF sentry who had been posted on the perimeter of this cave camp. If so, the man had to have been far enough away from Bolan and Margai's path that Bolan hadn't seen sign of him until now. But the sentry would also have had to be close enough to hear Margai nearing the camp. Margai had grown increasingly careless about the noise he made as the night grew on and he became more confident that he wasn't being followed.

The sentry had heard Margai but not *see* the would-be commando. Which meant that the guard had, naturally, wondered if whoever approached the camp was friend or foe. The sentry would also have wisely noted that he would be unable to intercept whoever it was before the man arrived at the cave. So the RUF guard had circled, coming up from the rear in case the advancer was an enemy.

Bolan heard the soft brush of a limb being moved aside. The sound came from maybe ten yards away.

Quickly but quietly Bolan holstered the Desert Eagle and drew the Crossada knife from its sheath. He took a quick final glance at the men in front of the cave. All four now sat cross-legged around the fire and had either leaned their rifles up against the cave wall or laid them at their feet.

Crouching, the Executioner moved to his right, following the tree line next to the mountain. Silence was now more important than ever. He couldn't expect to take the men at the campfire alive for questioning if they heard him battle the sentry. And if he tried to take his prisoners before he dealt with the man approaching from the rear, the sentry could stand inside the trees and shoot him like a fish in the barrel once he was at the mouth of the cave and in the firelight.

The Executioner moved roughly twenty feet to his side before cutting back deeper into the foliage, away from the cave. He circled the sentry, taking a page from the man's own book. He would come up from the rear, employ a classic silent sentry-removal maneuver, then replace the knife with the pistol and step out into the clearing to take his prisoners as he'd planned.

The movement to his side grew fainter rather than louder as the sentry neared the spot where Bolan had hidden only moments before. Whoever the man was, he was good. He knew that he was close, and he had no intention of blowing his approach now.

Bolan began cutting back as soon as he sensed that the man had passed him. It was imperative that his movements remain hushed but now he had to be faster, as well. As soon as he reached the edge of the trees, the sentry would look through the branches like he had and see the men in front of the fire. For a brief moment he would wonder what had happened to the prey he had stalked. Then, if he was as sharp as he appeared to be, he would figure it out. He would know that the man he had stalked now stalked him.

And he would turn to fight.

Bolan had to be on top of him before that happened. He couldn't afford the split-second warning a loud scuffle in the woods would provide for Margai and his confederates at the cave. He moved back, looking for signs of both his and the sentry's approach to the camp. A crushed leaf was all he could make out in the dim light, but it was enough. He turned back toward the fire.

Faster now, Bolan moved in. Ahead he could sense the presence of the sentry. He couldn't see the man, but he could feel him. He quickened his pace once more, now risking the slight noise that might announce to the sentry that the tables had been turned and he was about to be accosted from the rear.

Then, as he moved around a thick tree trunk, Bolan saw the dancing flames of the fire once more. Margai and the other men now sat talking in hushed voices. Between them and the Executioner, still in the tree line and peering through the branches just as Bolan had done only moments before, was the dark silhouette of a man's back.

Bolan took a deep breath, readying himself for the final moment of the hunt. He held the Crossada in a saber grip, considering the possibilities as he moved forward. Should the sentry sense his presence and start to turn, Bolan would thrust it through his kidney or ribs or whatever other target presented itself during the man's revolution. If that happened, the Executioner would have to assume that noise would be made and he'd leave the knife in the man, draw the Desert Eagle and step out of the trees, hoping he could still take the men by surprise and shooting if he couldn't.

If, however, the Executioner was able to close the

gap between himself and the sentry while the man's back was still to him, he would cup a hand over the mouth, slice the throat with the mammoth blade, then step out of the trees unannounced.

Seconds seemed like minutes now as Bolan narrowed the field of play, the Crossada held back and ready to thrust. But the sentry heard nothing and continued to stare straight ahead at the men in the mouth of the cave.

At the last second Bolan's fingers shifted on the hilt of the knife, taking a firm hammer grip. He reached around the sentry with his left hand and cupped the man's mouth, shutting off any sound. At the same time the Crossada's spear-point blade circled the throat from the man's other side.

The movements were too fast to even afford the man time to struggle. Bolan felt the forearm of his knife hand make contact with the sentry's upper chest. His wrist hit something hard as he prepared to draw the blade back across the throat.

The Crossada was already moving when the Executioner's instincts screamed for him to stop. The thought pattern in his brain occurred in the twinkling of an eye: he had felt something around the man's neck—a chain—but not an ordinary chain. This one had a ring suspended from it.

Bolan kept his hand over the man's mouth as he spun him. As the man came around, he saw Bobcat Buchanan's face. The diamond in the ring around his throat sparkled in the dim light.

Buchanan's hand had fallen to the Government

Model .45 holstered on his hip. Bolan dropped the Crossada and reached out, pinning the man's arm to his chest.

Slowly, giving Buchanan ample time to recognize him in the darkness, the Executioner took his hand away from the man's mouth. Even in the dim light he could see Buchanan's face had gone pale. "I want to take them alive if we can," he whispered.

Buchanan nodded. "I'm glad you took *me* alive."

Bolan picked up the Crossada and shoved it back into his sheath. The blade had made some noise when he dropped it, enough to cause the men at the fire to stop talking for a moment. But it hadn't been enough to cause further alarm. Now they had resumed their conversation, attributing the sound to an animal or some other unexplained but natural cause.

The Executioner drew the Desert Eagle and nodded to Buchanan, who presented the .45.

Together, the two men stepped from the trees to confront the startled RUF hardmen.

"Nobody move!" Bolan commanded.

For a moment the men sitting around the fire followed the order, staring dumbfounded at the two Americans who held them at gunpoint. Then one of the men, a tall, slender black man wearing the blue RUF bandanna around his wrist like a bracelet, lunged for the AK-47 next to his feet.

Bolan had no choice but to fire, which was only the beginning of what followed.

Somalia

HANDS BOUND behind their backs with leather strips, the men of Phoenix Force fought to keep from falling off the sides as the ancient flatbed truck bounced over the rugged plateau.

Behind the truck Phoenix Force's own Jeep Wagoneer followed. McCarter sat near the rear of the guardless vehicle, wondering which bump they hit would finally be the one to throw him from the bed and into the path of the Jeep. He could see the dozen or so 4WD vehicles ahead of the flatbed, and in the lead, Captain Jack's Ford 350 XLT Lariat pickup. The Lariat's CD player had been cranking out Bob Marley reggae music ever since the former British SAS commando and the rest of the team had been loaded onto the truck.

McCarter tried to recall what he knew about Captain Jack as the truck continued to bounce. Bolan had undertaken a Somalian mission that involved the warlords some months back, and Stony Man Farm had collected extensive intel on them all. Jack, or whatever his real name was, was regarded by much of the world as just another in a long line of petty potentates who all robbed their own people and stripped power and territory from one another whenever opportunity presented itself.

But Stony Man's research had offered another view of the man. Captain Jack, it seemed, was certainly not above stealing and killing. But he was particular about it, never stealing from or killing his own people as the other warlords did. He actually seemed to have some humanitarian goals, as well as the pursuit of wealth. He concentrated on robbing other warlords, foreign military personnel he believed should leave his country and the occasional tourist. He redistributed to the common man much of what he took back, and Stony Man speculated that when, and if, things ever settled down in the war-torn nation long enough for an election, Captain Jack planned to be the new president.

A real Robin Hood, McCarter thought as they bounced on to who knew where. He never hurt the good guys. The only problem was Captain Jack thought the men of Phoenix Force were bad guys.

"Any guess as to where we're going?" Hawkins asked no one in particular. He sat with his back against the truck's cab, and each jolt from the road threw him back against the rear windshield.

"No idea," McCarter replied. "But I suppose we'll be finding out shortly. He looked to the spot where the sun had finally fallen over the horizon. Soon the plateau would be too dark and treacherous to travel. Even if they hadn't reached their destination—whatever it was—they'd have to hole up for the night.

The thought had barely left the Phoenix Force leader's mind than Captain Jack's pickup disappeared into a canyon. The vehicles behind it slowed, creeping forward as, one by one, each descended the steep slope. When the flatbed reached the edge of the drop-off, the driver slowed to a stop. The Wagoneer circled around the tailgate and descended the slope. From where they sat, McCarter and the other men from Stony Man Farm could see the vehicles parked in line at the bottom of the canyon. Most of the forty-odd men had exited the vehicles and stood next to them.

McCarter still didn't know what was going on but he understood why the flatbed had stayed at the top of the plateau. The other 4WD vehicles could make it back up the slope again. If the flatbed went down it, the heavy, clumsy truck would remain there for eternity unless someone jerked it out with a Sherman tank.

As they waited, Captain Jack led a contingent of a dozen men back up the slope to the flatbed. He was smiling again, and his gold-hoop earring glowed warmly in the paling light from the sun.

The warlord and his men reached the truck and jerked McCarter and the others unceremoniously from the bed. McCarter landed on his belly, hearing the familiar swooshing sounds as blades were unsheathed. He felt someone grab the hands bound behind his back. A moment later he felt a blade pass between his wrists, and his hands separated.

"Get up," Captain Jack ordered.

McCarter rolled to one side in time to see the man shove his cutlass back into the scabbard and draw the Ruger Vaquero. He stood, waiting as the other men were cut loose.

Captain Jack prodded McCarter on with not so gentle stabs in the back with the Ruger Vaquero, directing the Phoenix Force leader between two of the vehicles to the other side of the line.

Carefully laid out on the ground, McCarter saw long white sections of eight-inch PVC pipe, cans of pipe cement and several shovels. He knew what was expected of them immediately.

"We thanked God when he dropped the provisions from the sky," Captain Jack said, chuckling. "We quickly saw that there was enough not only for our current use but that some should be stored." He paused and stepped out from McCarter's side to where the Phoenix Force leader could see his face. "But we had no idea that he would send us slaves to do the work for us, too." Captain Jack leaned down, lifted a shovel and handed it to McCarter. "Get busy," he ordered, and stepped back again.

McCarter saw James, Manning, Encizo and Hawkins pushed forward toward the shovels with rifle barrels. A series of orders in mixed English and Somali came from the mouths of the warlord's men as the Phoenix Force commandos began to dig.

As McCarter began to work, he saw several of the warlord's men begin unloading the Wagoneer of the supplies Phoenix Force had already picked up. Others began to saw lengths of PVC, while still others began cementing waterproof caps to the storage pipes.

The sun finally disappeared completely, and McCarter heard the sounds of several of the 4WD vehicles starting. Headlights came on as the vehicles backed around to cast their lights over the area where the men worked.

McCarter felt the sweat trickle down his face as

he drove the shovel into the ground, then tossed the load to the side. He looked up and down the row of men, seeing that Hawkins worked ten feet to his right, with Manning perhaps fifteen feet in the opposite direction. Encizo and James were in front of him, less than ten feet away.

As they continued to dig, Manning whispered to him, "You know they're going to bury us, too, don't you?"

McCarter nodded. "Just as soon as the work is done and we're of no more use."

"Any ideas?" Manning asked.

The sound of a pump shotgun's slide racking a round into the chamber echoed through the night. "Do not speak!" someone shouted.

Then Captain Jack himself appeared in front of McCarter and Manning and directly behind James and Encizo. The warlord pressed the barrel of the Ruger into McCarter's sweating face and cocked the hammer. "You heard the man. Keep quiet."

McCarter and the other men of Phoenix Force went on digging. He racked his brain for a plan. Manning was right. Captain Jack intended to bury them along with the cache of weapons, food and other supplies. As soon as the ditches were deep enough, they'd be forced to carry the PVC storage pipes into the holes. Then they'd be shot where they stood and covered up with the provisions. Or maybe Captain Jack and his men wouldn't want to come across their decaying flesh when they dug the pipes up, and they'd be forced to dig separate graves.

It didn't much matter. Unless they came up with a plan, and quick, they'd be dead.

McCarter dug on, the muscles in his arms, shoulders and back beginning to ache. On the isolated plateau, a hundred miles from civilization, in the glimmer of the headlights, the scene seemed to the Briton to be straight out of *Tales from the Crypt* or some old Alfred Hitchcock movie.

Hawkins had to have had a similar feeling. As they worked on, the newest member of the team began absentmindedly humming the theme from *Twilight Zone*.

"Silence!" Captain Jack said curtly, turning toward him with the Ruger.

Hawkins didn't appear to have heard the warlord. He went right on humming.

Captain Jack was unaccustomed to having his orders ignored. With a scream of rage, he cocked the Ruger's hammer and fired a round down into the ditch where Hawkins was working.

Now it was Hawkins's turn to scream. He fell forward, half in, half out, of the hole. "You shot my foot, you dirty SOB!" he yelled as the work stopped throughout the ravine.

Anger flooded McCarter's veins. He leaped from his ditch, the shovel swinging high over his head.

Captain Jack spun on him like an Old West gunfighter, cocking the Ruger's hammer once more.

McCarter froze in place.

"Oh...my foot!" Hawkins moaned.

Captain Jack kept the gun on the Phoenix Force

leader as he moved toward Hawkins. "If this man, or any of the others, move," he called out to his men, "kill them."

McCarter couldn't see the warlord's men behind him, but he almost felt the many guns that moved to cover him.

Captain Jack turned toward Hawkins as he neared the ditch. He leaned over the side, trying to get a look at the foot he had shot. The cold smile McCarter had seen earlier returned.

Hawkins moaned again, then suddenly there was a flash of movement within the ditch. A split second later Hawkins had scrambled out of the hole and driven a shoulder under Captain Jack's Vaquero and into the man's ribs.

Phoenix Force's newest man looked like an NFL linebacker blitzing to sack the quarterback as he drove Captain Jack backward toward McCarter's ditch. The bandit, taken by surprise, had no time to react and no choice but to backpedal, furiously trying to keep his balance. The Ruger's hammer fell, sending a round harmlessly into the dirt pile behind Hawkins as he propelled the warlord on.

A moment later both Hawkins and Captain Jack came crashing down into the hole on top of McCarter.

McCarter gave way beneath their combined weight, thrashing around in the damp earth. His hand dipped into his pocket and he jerked out the Spyderco Delica, flipping out the blade with a twist of his wrist. Rolling to his side, he felt an elbow catch him in the ribs. He looked up and saw the back of a black neck on top of him. The head atop the neck wore a black bandanna "pirate style."

It was the neck he was looking for.

Reaching over the top of Captain Jack's head with his left hand, McCarter hooked his middle and index fingers into the warlord's eye sockets. His adversary screamed as the former SAS commando jerked up, exposing the throat. The Delica came around, the tip jamming through the skin over Captain Jack's sternum and into the xiphoid process. Another scream issued forth from his lips as the blade lodged in place.

Hawkins had grabbed the bandit's Ruger by now and shoved the barrel under the warlord's nose.

Captain Jack suddenly quieted.

McCarter looked up to see that the ditch was surrounded now with Captain Jack's men. The metallic sound of rifle bolts working drifted down from above.

"Don't shoot!" one of the men shouted. "You will hit the captain!"

"That's right, you lily-livered ring-tailed tooters!" Hawkins called back up. "And even if you don't, we'll kill him with our dying breaths!"

The man who had warned the others not to shoot, a muscular man with a bushy black Afro, mustache and goatee, turned away from the hole and barked orders.

A second later several of the riflemen moved back from the edge of the hole. McCarter saw James, Encizo and Manning suddenly thrust forward. Arms wrapped around their necks and gun barrels were pressed against their heads.

The goateed man looked down and spoke again. "Let the captain go," he said, "or we will kill your friends!"

McCarter chuckled. "It appears to me you intended to do that anyway. So it's you who have something to lose, not us." He paused to let the man consider the situation.

Captain Jack spasmed in McCarter's arms, and the Phoenix Force leader let up slightly on the knife. "Now, you think things over for a few minutes and decide if you think we should find some kind of settlement to this situation that suits both of us."

As the voices above began to mumble McCarter turned to Hawkins. "How bad is your foot?" he asked.

Hawkins's eyebrows lowered momentarily as if he didn't understand the question, then shot back up. "My foot? Old Jack missed it by a yard."

Even under the circumstances McCarter couldn't help but laugh.

The man in charge up top finally spoke again. "I must speak with Captain Jack! I must ask him what to do!"

With his fingers still hooked in Jack's eye sockets, and the Delica lodged shallowly in his chest, McCarter leaned up to whisper in the warlord's ear. "I'm going to let up slightly so you can talk," he said. "But I don't suppose I have to tell you what will happen if you try anything funny."

Jack shook his head back and forth slowly, and no farther than he could without popping his own eyeballs out of the sockets.

McCarter let up a little more on his chest and eyes. "Okay," he called up to the man, "talk to your main man."

"Captain Jack," the man called down into the hole, "it is Alfredo! What should we do?"

There was a brief pause while Captain Jack drew in a long shaky breath before answering. "Alfredo, can you see me?"

"Yes, Captain Jack!" the man called back. "I can see you!"

"Then can you see this man's fingers in my eyes, ready to pluck them out and make me blind? Can you see his knife in my chest, ready to plunge through my heart?"

"Yes, Captain Jack! I can see both his fingers and the knife!"

The warlord drew in another breath, but this time the sound registered disgust, as well as fear. "You can see all this, and still you ask me what you should do?" he called up to Alfredo.

"Yes, Captain Jack! What should I do?"

"Whatever they tell you to do, you bloody fool!" Captain Jack screamed in fury. "Whatever they tell you to do!"

New York

ROUND AFTER ROUND exploded at the rear of the house. They were answered by the 9 mm pops from

Schwarz's Beretta.

Lyons started to rush back into the hall, then remembered Blancanales still in front of the house. Sprinting to the splintered front door, he called through a hole in the wood, "Pol! Don't shoot! It's me!"

The Able Team leader gave it a second to sink in, then threw the door open. "Get around back!" he yelled. "I'm going through the house!"

Blancanales nodded and sprinted around the corner as Lyons closed the door.

Lyons heard footsteps behind him and turned just in time to see one of the men coming back to check on the two in the living room. Instead of an Ingram like the other two had carried, this man had a Japanese-made Shin Chuo Kogyo submachine gun.

But he had the same vacant look to his eyes. And although obviously Occidental, he was also dressed in a bright red kimono.

Lyons had no time to question the strange costume on the Westerner. The man raised the subgun and fired a steady stream of 9 mm rounds his way. The Able Team leader ducked under the barrage by dropping to his knees. He pressed the trigger on the .45 twice, and both rounds found a home in the man's chest.

Lyons was back on his feet by the time the body hit the floor. He moved past it to the door, then looked into the hall. Clear. He had just stepped out when two more men appeared from a doorway at the end.

Both were Westerners, but they, too, wore Oriental clothing and looked as if they might be under the control of some unseen force.

The man in the light blue kimono held a Portuguese Model 48 submachine gun. Lyons dropped him with a round between the eyes before he'd had time to get it into play.

The other man, wearing a plain white *hopi* coat over his blue jeans and black T-shirt, sported a Calico 960 like those Lyons was beginning to wish the men of Able Team hadn't left in the van. Another double-tap of .45s sent the high-capacity machine pistol falling to the hall floor. The man in the *hopi* coat fell on top of it.

Lyons shoved the near empty .45 back into his holster, relying on the Python for protection as he hurried on down the hall. He stopped in front of the man in the *hopi* coat, grabbed a handful of hair and rolled the body off the Calico.

A quick glance at the windows in the top of the 50-round magazine showed him that between thirty-seven and fifty 9 mm bullets remained in the drum.

Gunfire continued to erupt from the rear portion of the house, answered now and then by return fire from the backyard. The Able Team leader moved cautiously now, reaching the end of the hall and the doorway through which the two men in the hall had emerged. Dropping to one knee, he peered around the corner into a kitchen.

Pots, pans, broken dishes and shattered appliances scattered the counters and floors. As Lyons watched, rounds flew through the shattered glass of the back doorway to strike a toaster on the counter next to the refrigerator and send it crashing to the floor. More rounds had created circular holes in the refrigerator door, stove and dishwasher. Two men, one in Japanese dress, the other wearing khaki slacks and a white short-sleeved shirt, lay on the floor in one collective pool of blood.

Amid it all stood four men armed with automatic rifles. They fired through the windows and door into the backyard, ignoring the return fire that swarmed around them like a disturbed nest of angry bees. None of them made any attempt to take cover.

Lyons pulled back away from the door. Every man he had encountered so far appeared to be under a spell of some sort. Whether they had been dressed in Western or Oriental fare made no difference. They had one thing in common: they had all stood firing with zombielike dedication and made no particular attempt to protect themselves. They were either on drugs, or they had fallen victim to the cult's brainwashing.

Lyons peered back around the corner to the kitchen. He needed at least one of the men alive for questioning, but he couldn't take the chance of them hurting his teammates. Not that the other two Able Team commandos couldn't take care of themselves—they could. But they hadn't gone through the transitional thinking process with Lyons right now.

They wouldn't know where their leader stood mentally, and they would be expecting him to cover the flank during this firefight, not just partially but completely.

The big ex-cop walked softly as he entered the kitchen. The first man he came to was big—as tall as Lyons himself and maybe fifty pounds heavier. But the weight was all in his hips and thighs, and he went down hard when Lyons rapped the barrel of the Calico against his skull.

Two of the other three men heard the crack of hard plastic against bone and started to turn. Lyons turned his weapon on the first of the two, a squat man wearing a camel-colored sport coat and navy blue slacks. The man held a French-made FA MAS 5.56 mm autorifle in his hands and tried to bring it into play.

In the brief second before he squeezed the trigger, Lyons heard the man in the camel sport coat say, "Oh, fuck" under his breath. The Able Team leader also saw a different look in the man's eyes: fear. A *clear-eyed* fear.

Lyons held back the trigger, letting the Calico spray 9 mm rounds into the man's heart, liver and intestinal tract. The Able Team leader swung the gun to his side as a taller reed-thin man in another of the baffling kimonos aimed a Finnish M-60 his way. The 7.62 mm weapon spit a wild 5-round burst of fire that missed Lyons by inches.

The Able Team leader held the trigger back again. A half-dozen 9 mm rounds splattered up and down the man's body, ending his career as a brainwashed, religious-fanatic, lunatic-zombie robot gunman.

Not so of the last man standing. Lyons ground to a halt as the man, wearing a martial arts *gi,* continued to fire an old, obsolete Czech ZB-26 LMG. He held the heavy weapon cradled in his hands, the bipod hanging impotently below the barrel as the gun jumped in his arms.

The Able team leader started to pull the trigger to shoot him, then checked himself. The man was firing rhythmically and had no idea what he was doing. Even more than the others, he looked as if he might be on drugs. As Lyons watched, a 20-round magazine ran dry and the man dropped it from the weapon and inserted a new box with the same nonthinking, practiced motions as a heroin junkie tying off and firing up.

He pulled the trigger again.

Lyons had seen enough. He walked up behind the man and tapped him on the shoulder.

The man stopped firing, turned and smiled pleasantly.

The gunfire from the backyard through the windows stopped almost immediately.

"What are you doing?" Lyons asked.

The zombie smile didn't waver. "Serving Hikari," the man replied. "Serving the Great Hikari." He looked at Lyons curiously. "Are you one of us?"

"I don't think so," Lyons said.

"Then what are *you* doing here?" the man asked, looking disturbed. "Are you serving Hikari?"

Lyons shook his head. "No, I'm serving justice."

With no more ado the Able Team leader hooked a left into the man's jaw.

The moronic smile was still on the Hikari follower's face as he hit the floor.

Lyons walked to the back door and opened it. Outside, he saw Schwarz and Blancanales in the backyard. "It's me," the Able Team leader called. "Come in."

He turned back to the men on the floor, staring down at the two men he'd knocked out rather than killed. Good. That was good. He'd have two new brains to probe and find out what they knew.

The Able Team leader reached up, wiping the sweat off his forehead with the back of his hand. Only one thing bothered him.

He didn't know how much of those brains was left after the the Great Hikari's indoctrination.

Japan

REIKO FUKOTO HAD KEPT a low profile during her brief stay with the cult, knowing something big was in the works but not what. Bit by bit she was beginning to piece it all together.

And what she was coming to understand made her ill.

Fukoto took almost ten minutes to rise from the bed of the Great Hikari, moving an inch at a time, careful to make sure that both the cult leader and Yoshiko were still asleep. She moved more swiftly once she was on her feet, slipping into her bathrobe before moving on. She had walked the stretch of floor from the bed to the door many times that afternoon and knew exactly which of the ancient boards creaked and which didn't. Now, as Hikari and Yoshiko lay arm in arm behind her, she followed the zigzag path of silence she had memorized.

Once in the hall, she shut the door carefully behind her. She descended the steps quickly, hurrying down the hall on the floor below the Great Hikari's sleeping chambers toward the office. She had seen the open door when Ichiro Murai had brought her and Yoshiko upstairs to meet the Great Hikari the day before. On the desk she had seen the phone, and she had filed that information in the back of her mind. The night before, she had crept from the Great Hikari's room just as she was doing now, only to find that Murai was using the office to do late-night paperwork. She had been unable to make her call, and as she crept on toward an intersecting hallway, she prayed that the use of the office wasn't a nightly ritual of Hikari's right-hand man.

The Japanese woman heard a sound from down a side hall and stopped in her tracks. Voices—one sounded like Ichiro Murai's—drifted through the quiet castle. She couldn't make out what they said. Then the sound of a door closing ended even the muffled sounds.

Fukoto moved on, hooking an eye around the corner to glance in the direction from which the voices had come. She saw nothing and hurried across the intersecting hall. Memories of the past two days of wild and perverted sex she had shared with the Great Hikari and Yoshiko flooded into her mind. She shuddered, then tried to push the thoughts away. Yoshiko hadn't seemed to mind, appeared to revel in what she still believed to be her "salvation." But Fukoto had seen through the cult's scam even before being brought to Hikari's chambers. She had engaged in the debauchery for other reasons.

Again the Japanese woman shuddered. Sometimes she questioned the things she did. Did the end really justify the means? Sometimes she thought so; other times she didn't.

Fukoto reached the office door and was surprised to find it closed. She leaned forward, pressing her ear lightly against the wood. She heard nothing. But that didn't necessarily mean no one was inside. Should she chance cracking it open? If someone *was* there, and they saw her...

The woman took a deep breath. She didn't know exactly what the Great Hikari was planning, but she had a general idea. Time for her to pass that information along hadn't yet run out, but the clock was ticking. If she wasn't successful this night, it would be twenty-four hours before she had another chance to use the phone.

She *had* to try the door. What if Ichiro Murai was using the office again tomorrow night?

Slowly Fukoto reached out, grasped the knob and gently twisted it. Part of the Japanese woman was relieved when she found the door locked. The other part was disappointed. She took a step back and stared at the lock. A simple snap lock with a hole in the center of the knob, it could easily be picked with a hairpin or similar device.

She hurried back down the hall, pausing again to glance down the corridor from which the voices had come. Ascertaining that the way was clear, she walked quietly back to the stairs. She had both hair- and straight pins in her purse. She would return to the room, retrieve one and come back to the locked door.

Slipping back into the bedroom, Fukoto closed the door behind her. She moved silently to the table by the side of the bed and grasped her purse. She was digging through it when the Great Hikari stopped snoring.

She slipped the robe off her shoulders and let it fall to the floor. She had barely laid back down when the Great Hikari rolled over and opened his eyes into slits. "Mmmm," he whispered sleepily. A hand cupped her breast, his eyes opened wider, and he said, "I have slept enough, my daughter. We should continue with your salvation."

As his lips met hers, Reiko Fukoto knew she wouldn't return to the office, or the phone, that night.

CHAPTER NINE

Sierra Leone

The wrist wearing the blue bandanna never made it to the AK-47 on the ground next to the campfire.

As the RUF hardman twisted to the side for the weapon, Bolan dropped the front sights of the Desert Eagle on center mass and squeezed the trigger. The mammoth .44 Magnum semiautomatic pistol leaped in his hand, a 240-grain semijacketed hollowpoint zipping from the barrel to drill through the RUF bandit's sweat-stained fatigue blouse.

Blood blew out the man's back to shower Margai, who had been sitting behind him. The man's chest jerked and spasmed, then his hand froze in midair an inch from the rifle. His eyes looked up at the Executioner with a puzzled look in them, then the eyelids closed and he toppled over to the ground.

The whole process had taken less than one second, but it had been time enough for a RUF bandit sitting on the other side of the fire to grab his own autorifle. The ends of the man's Fu Manchu mustache rose in a wicked snarl as he sent a wild burst of rounds flying high over both Bolan and Buchanan.

The Executioner was still riding the recoil from the big .44 as he watched Buchanan pivot with the agility of the cat for whom he'd been named. The .45 Government Model pistol spit flame and a round-nosed 230-grain full-metal-jacket hardball round caught the rifleman in the trigger hand.

The bandit shrieked in pain, dropping the weapon, as the bullet traveled on into his intestinal tract. Gut shot, he screamed again and toppled to the ground, his hand clawing for the pistol holstered at his side.

The third bandit scrambled to his feet as Bolan lowered the Desert Eagle and put a lone round into the hardman's head. In the corner of his eye the Executioner saw Buchanan swing the Government Model toward the escaping man and hammer two rounds after him. He led the man too much on the first round, the bullet striking the rocky mountain wall in front of the bandit and sending pebble chips raining through the air. Buchanan overcorrected on his second shot, and the round fell behind the fleeing RUF bandit, who disappeared into the dark mouth of the cave.

Margai had sat frozen through the entire gunfight. Bolan aimed the Desert Eagle at him now, but spoke to Buchanan. "Watch our friend here, Bobcat," he ordered. "I'm going into the cave."

Buchanan already had the Colt's sights on the traitorous Sierra Leone commando trainee. "Be careful, Pollock."

"Careful's the name of the game," the Executioner answered as he hurried toward the black hole.

Bolan ducked to one side as soon as he'd entered the mouth of the cave. Half-expecting to take a bullet, he was a little surprised when no gunfire greeted his entry. Going into the cave that way was risky, but there was no other way to do it.

He gave his eyes time to adjust to the darker environment inside the cave. When they had, he saw that the room he was in was no more than ten by fifteen feet. But the RUF hardman was nowhere to be seen.

A dark, narrow passageway on the other side of the small chamber led somewhere deeper into the mountain. The Executioner drew the Crossada knife and holstered the Desert Eagle. The cavern was small, and the confines of the passage even closer. He had no intention of killing himself with a .44 Magnum ricochet when the big blade would work equally well at such close quarters.

Slowly, carefully, the Executioner crossed the room, the Crossada leading the way. Bolan held the knife in front of him in a saber grip, ready to thrust or back cut should his adversary be hiding just inside the passage and suddenly emerge.

But that didn't happen, and Bolan stepped into the opening.

What little light from outside the cave had made it into the first cavern faded quickly in the passageway. Bolan cursed beneath his breath for not having a flashlight, then pushed the thought from his mind.

Like all missions, you made do with the gear you *did* have available and didn't waste time wishing you were better equipped. A soldier rarely entered battle with exactly what he needed. At least some amount of improvisation was always necessary.

Bolan moved slowly, using his left hand to feel his way down the passage and keeping the Crossada pulled back to his chest, ready to thrust. The walls of the rock hallway were far too cramped to allow slashing techniques should he encounter the RUF hardman. The fact was they were so constricted that the Executioner was forced to turn sideways. A quick stab across his own chest would be the only technique he'd be able to employ. And he would have to strike fast should his adversary be waiting ahead, would have to react before the bandit employed his own weapon.

Silently the Executioner inched on. What weapon would the man he pursued be relying upon? He remembered that all of the men he had seen had been armed with AK-47s, pistols and knives. The man ahead had abandoned his rifle at the campsite, but Bolan had seen the blade and handgun still on his hip as he disappeared into the cave. If he thought about it, the man would resort to his knife as Bolan had. But what if the reality of a possible ricochet didn't cross his mind considering the pressure he was under? He might very well open fire, even in these narrow confines.

A cool, stale odor emanated from the stones as the Executioner carefully picked up one foot and set it down. Try as he might, Bolan found it impossible to move without making some noise. Pebbles beneath his feet crunched no matter how softly he stepped down. His clothing brushed against the rocks, making a soft rustling sound. The slightest sound was magnified a hundredfold in the constricted area, and he knew that any noise at all would warn the RUF hard man that he was being followed.

In the same light the Executioner knew the situation could work for him, as well as against him, and he listened for signs of his prey with ears trained by years of tracking men. He heard nothing, which led him to believe that the bandit had already left the passage and entered another cavern. The fact that he himself was making noise, and hadn't been attacked, strengthened that theory.

Finally Bolan reached the end of the passage. Through the opening he saw faint light, and when he looked up he saw a small opening in the ceiling. Moonlight drifted down into a room slightly larger than the one on the other side of the passageway. Stalagmites grew from the floor so thick they appeared to be cultivated, and water dripped from the stalactites overhead, making soft splashing noises as they hit a pool of water in the center of the cavern.

Bolan scanned the rock room. There was no other way out than the way he had come.

But there was no RUF bandit in the cavern either.

Bolan frowned in the semilight. There had to be another exit. Either that, or the bandit was hiding in some nook, cranny or shadowy corner not readily discerned from where the Executioner stood.

The Crossada in front of him again, Bolan circled the cavern, checking behind the larger stalagmites and scanning the room from every possible angle. Still, there was no sign of the RUF hardman.

Turning back to the passageway, the Executioner shook his head. The man couldn't have doubled back. There was barely enough room for Bolan himself to squeeze through the tunnel.

That left only one possibility.

The Executioner walked to the edge of the pool of water. Cautiously he sat and extended both feet into the dark puddle. He scooted forward, lowering his legs to the knees without touching the bottom.

That was the answer. The pool covered another passageway that led out of the cavern.

Bolan twisted to face the edge of the pool, took a deep breath and lowered himself into the black water. He could see nothing in the darkness, and was once again forced to work by feel like a blind man. A quick dive took him to the bottom, which he estimated to be roughly ten feet. He returned to the surface, took another deep breath and lowered himself under the water again.

Dropping to just below the surface, the Executioner began to move in a circular route around the bank. The Crossada held at his side, he used his free hand to trace along the rock, looking for an opening. When he returned to the spot where he had started, he resurfaced for air, then dropped lower, repeating the same excruciatingly slow search for the exit at a deeper depth.

On his fourth circumnavigation of the pool he found it. The opening was roughly three feet across.

Bolan rose to the surface, grasping the side and breathing deeply again. Not knowing where the passage would take him was a secondary worry at this point. Not knowing if he'd get there at all was primary. The Executioner knew he could get through the opening, all right, but he had no way of knowing whether the passageway would narrow once he was inside. That the RUF bandits knew the escape route well, and the fact that the man Bolan now pursued had evidently taken it and made it through, meant little. The Executioner was several inches broader in the shoulders than any of the bandits he'd seen. He might get caught at some point that never even drew the attention of the smaller men.

But he had no choice.

Dropping back to the opening under the water, the Executioner pulled himself through.

Somalia

"IT APPEARS we have a few details to work out, wouldn't you say?" David McCarter said. He still lay on his back at the bottom of the ditch, with Captain Jack on top of him. The Briton kept his fingers in Jack's eye sockets and the Delica knife firmly embedded in the man's xiphoid process as he awaited an answer from the warlord's men above.

There was a trick to taking a hostage when unarmed or armed only with a hand weapon, a fine line that had to be walked and couldn't be crossed on either side. The subject had to be controlled with pain and the fear of serious potential harm, but no serious damage could actually occur. A little blood—like that seeping onto McCarter's fingers from the punctured skin around the Delica's point—was okay. So was severe pain and terror like that Captain Jack was experiencing with McCarter's fingers hooked around his eyeballs. But the former SAS commando had to be careful not to take it too far, and certainly not to kill Captain Jack.

Any hostage who was accidentally killed, or whom the other enemies believed about to be killed regardless of what they did, became useless.

"Let the captain go!" Alfredo called down into the hole. "We will set you free!"

"And we're to take your word for it?" McCarter asked. "Like I said, I think there are a few details to work out first." He glanced at the polished stainless-steel gun barrel Hawkins had shoved under Captain Jack's nose. The hammer of the single-action Vaquero was cocked, meaning the slightest pressure would send a bullet through the warlord's brain. Hawkins had been careful to angle the gun so the round—a .45 Colt, McCarter could now read on the barrel—wouldn't hit the Phoenix Force leader when it exited Jack's head.

Hawkins was a professional, and he was doing his job just like McCarter was.

But the other members of Phoenix Force—the men above the pit who were in Captain Jack's shoes as hostages—were doing their job well, too. From where he lay, McCarter could see Calvin James. One of the warlord's men stood behind the commando with an arm wrapped around James's throat and a pistol shoved against the back of his head. Yet the man's chiseled features showed no fear.

Manning, likewise, stood stoically awaiting whatever fate might have in store for him, the barrel of a rifle in his ear.

Encizo had accepted death as the most likely end to his violent career years ago when he'd been a member of the anti-Castro Cuban resistance organization Alpha 66. The firm set of the man's jaw showed that that acceptance hadn't wavered over the years.

"What would you have us do?" Alfredo called down into the hole.

McCarter leaned up to Captain Jack's ear again. "Any suggestions?" he asked.

"Yes," Jack choked out. "But first...take your fingers from my eyes." He paused. "Please."

McCarter did as the warlord had asked, grabbing a handful of the man's long hair instead. He kept the Delica where it was, and the Ruger in Hawkins's hand stayed in place under Captain Jack's chin.

The warlord's whole attitude had changed.

"Thank you," he said meekly. "Now, if you will just let me up—"

"Let's cut through that nonsense immediately," McCarter said. "We're still outnumbered and for all practical purposes unarmed. *You* are all we've got, and we aren't letting you go until we're safely away. So I suggest you figure out a way to make that happen."

Captain Jack drew in a deep breath. "I will lose face with my men," he whispered. "But I suppose that is better than being blinded by your fingernails. So take me with you. I will order my men to wait here until we are far enough away that you are safe. Then you will let me go."

"Sounds good to me," Hawkins said.

"But we will keep your supplies."

McCarter dug his fingers back into the man's eyes.

"Except the guns and ammunition!"

McCarter removed both his fingers and the Delica and stood, pulling his hostage to his feet. He shoved the man to Hawkins, who looped an arm around the captain's neck and shoved the Ruger's barrel against his temple. The Briton again recalled the intelligence file Stony Man had on Captain Jack. The man might employ some deplorable tactics against his enemies, but he wasn't automatically against the West like other warlords.

McCarter frowned, thinking. Having an ally such as Captain Jack could come in handy down the line.

"We'll take the pistols, rifles and the ammunition," McCarter said. "We'll leave you the MREs and anything it doesn't look like we'll need right away. And we'll figure out a way for you to save face in front of your men. That's a better deal than you deserve, and a good deal for a man who isn't in a bargaining position."

Slowly Captain Jack nodded his head. "The face-saving I will handle," he said. "When we get to the top, allow me a few words."

McCarter nodded. "Fine. But for now tell your men to let mine go, then stand back and let us come up."

Captain Jack barked out the orders. The faces and weapons around the edge of the hole pulled back out of sight.

As soon as the men had disappeared, McCarter pulled himself out of the hole. The warlord's men had formed a ring around the ditch ten yards away. Encizo, Manning and James had been freed and now wore their pistols and gripped rifles.

McCarter reached down, grasping Hawkins's up-raised hand and helping him and Captain Jack out of the shallow hole.

Captain Jack stood tall, chest out like a statesman addressing his constituents. "Gentlemen," he called out, "we were mistaken about these men. They are our friends!" He paused while a few confused murmurs drifted through the ranks. "At this time I am not at liberty to divulge what we are about to do. But I will explain it all when I return. In the meantime I must go with our new friends on a mission of great urgency." His chest puffed out with pride. "It is a mission that will affect all of Somalia!"

The men ringing them nodded their understanding.

Hawkins had lowered the Vaquero to his side, but McCarter noted it was still cocked. He kept close to Captain Jack, and they moved to the Wagoneer. Captain Jack was placed between Manning and McCarter in the back seat, with Encizo driving and James and Hawkins squeezing into the front with him.

"Jack, you ever think about running for office?" Hawkins asked, turning and resting an arm over the seat as McCarter started the engine.

The warlord was examining the wound to his chest and for a moment he didn't answer. Then, evidently deciding the injury was minor, and realizing that the men who had him in custody had no intention of killing him if he did as ordered, he looked up and grinned. "I do not intend to be a simple warlord forever, my friend. When this civil strife is over, when things have settled down, and when you Americans and other do-gooders have gone home—" he took a deep breath and let his grin widen "—after all that, my friends, I intend to become the president of Somalia."

New York

THE RESPONDING POLICE had to have waited until they were less than a block away from Casey Balforth's house to turn on their sirens. By the time Carl Lyons got to the front window, two black-and-white squad cars were pulling to the curb, followed by a white unmarked vehicle, a magnetic red light spinning on the roof. As Lyons watched, a fourth car—a blue Voyager—pulled up across the street. It bore no lights or sirens.

"What have we got, Ironman?" Gadgets Schwarz asked. Already the Able Team electronics man was helping Blancanales lift the heavy man on the floor.

"Two marked units, one dick car and what looks like an undercover vehicle that must have been in the area," Lyons answered. He knelt and began shouldering the man who wore the martial-arts *gi*. "We'll have to take them out the back," he added. "The front's already covered."

The Able Team leader threw the man over his shoulder in a fireman's carry, walked to the rear door of the kitchen and kicked it open. He heard the loud knock on the front door as he hurried down three concrete steps to the backyard, then cut over to a short chain-link fence. Dropping the man in his arms over the side, he leaped after him.

Lyons saw Schwarz and Blancanales lugging the fat man as his feet hit the ground. Behind them, in the house, a sharp crack sounded as the police kicked the front door in. The Able Team leader helped them lift their burden over the fence, then hoisted his man once more and hurried under a clothesline. His teammates followed, all three Able Team commandos ducking around the corner of the redbrick tenement next to Casey Balforth's house.

Not a moment too soon. Lyons peered back around

the corner to see a pair of officers in blue cut around the back. An uneasy thought crossed his mind. "You close the door behind you?" he whispered to Schwarz. If it had been left open the officers would immediately know someone had left through the back and pursue.

Schwarz nodded. "Yeah, but the lock's broken. They won't notice it for a minute maybe." He drew in a deep breath. "But we'd better get going."

Lyons nodded. He let the two cops behind Balforth's house disappear into the kitchen, then cut into the backyard once more. For a moment he remembered the young men who had been on the porch of the tenement tossing insults their way when they'd crossed to enter Balforth's. They would be busy watching what went on in the front with the cop cars—that's where the excitement was.

Climbing over another fence and ducking another clothesline, Lyons led the way to the back door of a crumbling little single family dwelling. His shoulder and arms had gone numb by the time he reached the back door and kicked.

The Able Team leader entered a laundry room piled high with dirty clothes. With Schwarz and Blancanales toting the fat man at his heels, he hurried through the room and down the hall wondering whose house he was invading, whether they were home and if they might be armed.

He soon found out.

The elderly couple in the living room were ninety years old if they were a day. They stood holding hands and watching the police lights through a dirty picture window. Both wore hearing aids in their ears, and neither turned as Lyons entered the room and dropped the man in the *gi* on the carpet.

Lyons shook his head in irritation as he heard Schwarz and Blancanales enter the room behind him. On one hand Able Team couldn't have asked for a better house in which to make a stopover during their escape from the cops. This elderly couple would offer no resistance—so far they didn't even know they had company.

But on the other hand Carl Lyons didn't like scaring innocent old people. And when the couple staring out the window at the action in front finally turned, they weren't going to be scared, they were going to be terrified.

Lyons glanced to Blancanales as the Able Team psy-op expert and Schwarz lowered their man to the ground. The study of psychological warfare naturally entailed the study of general psychology, and Lyons nodded to Blancanales, then looked at the old couple at the window.

Blancanales nodded back, knowing without being told what was expected of him. Lyons and Schwarz stood quietly as their partner moved carefully toward the window. When he was directly behind the elderly couple, he cleared his throat. "Hello?" he said.

The old man and woman continued to stare out the window.

"They're both deaf," Schwarz whispered. "Or close to it."

Blancanales reached out, gently placing a hand on the old man's shoulders. The elderly man turned to face him, smiling. The smile faded fast.

The old woman saw her husband turn and twisted slowly. Her face never smiled. Her mouth opened to scream, but no sound issued forth.

"Who are you? Why are you here?" the old man said in a tottering voice.

"Please," Blancanales said in his most soothing voice, "we have no intention of hurting you."

Lyons watched the old man and woman visibly relax, and noticed something else about the elderly couple. Both had stared intently at Blancanales's mouth as he spoke. As Schwarz had said, they were either stone deaf or so hearing impaired that they were close to it, and they were reading his lips.

"Please," Blancanales said, "could the three of us sit down and I'll explain everything to you?" He reached out and took both elderly people by the elbow, softly guiding them past an end table on which the framed photograph of a young man in a USAF uniform stood. They reached a threadbare couch just past the table, and Blancanales helped them sit, then knelt on the floor, facing them.

Lyons moved forward to the window where they had been. Through the greasy glass he could see the police cars in front of Balforth's house. Looking down the block the other way, he saw the van. He turned to Schwarz. "We can't stay here, Gadgets," he said. "As soon as the cops realize someone left through the back, they'll start a door-to-door." He reached up, scratching his chin as he thought. "Go get the van. Make it look like you're on your way to work or something. Then circle the block. Pol and I will carry these guys—" he pointed down to the men on the floor "—and join you as soon as we can."

Schwarz nodded. He reached up, straightened his tie, then moved to the front door and onto the porch.

Blancanales continued to assure the elderly couple that everything was all right as Lyons watched Schwarz descend the steps to the sidewalk. By now clumps of curious onlookers had gathered up and down the street. The Able Team electronics expert gawked and rubbernecked at Casey Balforth's house with the best of them, blending in with the ghoulish crowd perfectly as he slid behind the wheel of the van and sped away.

Lyons took a final glance at the police cars across the street. The two black-and-whites and the unmarked vehicle had been abandoned as their occupants raced to cover the house. For a moment he was tempted to take his teammates and their sleeping captives and race for one of the vehicles. But through the partially tinted windows of the Voyager parked with the marked units, the Able Team leader could see the shadowy outlines of men. He nodded. The sight reconfirmed his suspicion that the Voyager was an undercover vehicle that just happened to be near Balforth's house when the "shots fired" call went out on the radio. The men inside would provide backup only if they were needed; there was no reason to get out and blow their covers in the area if they weren't.

But five men attempting to steal a police car from under their noses would mean they'd break cover, all right, and put holes in Able Team as Lyons, Blancanales and Schwarz attempted to throw their prisoners into the vehicle.

Turning back to the room, Lyons saw the old man holding the photograph of the Air Force officer from the end table. "Our son, Jeffrey," he said in his feeble, world-worn voice. "He was shot down in Vietnam."

Tears filled the eyes of both elderly people. Then a moan from the floor turned Lyons's attention back to the man he had carried into the house. Both prisoners were beginning to stir as they regained consciousness.

Blancanales heard the sounds and glanced over his shoulder. He saw the problem as fast as Lyons did. All hell could break loose if the men regained consciousness in the living room. But neither Lyons nor Blancanales wanted to upset the old people further by knocking the cult men out again in front of them.

The elderly woman solved the problem for them. Lyons heard her speak in a voice so low he couldn't make out the words. But Blancanales evidently did, because a moment later he said, "Why, yes, Mrs. Dempkowski, I would love to see your thimble collection." Holding the old woman's hand, he rose from his kneeling position, helped both her and her husband to their feet, then led them out of the living room and down a hall.

Lyons pivoted and rapped the toe of a shoe against the temple of both men on the floor. They went back to sleep without complaint. The Able Team leader walked back to the window. The same cars were out front, including the undercover vehicle. But by now several more marked units had joined them. In a few moments, the Able Team leader knew, they would begin a house-to-house search for anyone involved in the carnage they had found at Balforth's place.

It was time to leave.

Lyons heard Blancanales and the elderly couple coming back down the hall as he looked to the men on the floor. He wondered if one of them was Casey Balforth, and wondered again if their brains had been washed too clean by the cult to be of any good to Able Team now. If so, trying to get them to Schwarz on the other side of the block was worse than a waste of time—it increased the chances of the cops spotting them.

Yet there was a shred of a chance that they'd provide information about the upcoming nerve-gas attack in New York. And as long as even that shred remained, Lyons knew he and Blancanales would have to risk taking them along.

Blancanales and the elderly couple stopped in the middle of the living-room floor. The old man looked down at the cult men, evidently noticing them for the first time. "Where did they come from?" he asked shakily.

"They're friends of ours," Pol said. "They drink too much."

The old woman's face tightened. "My brother Clifford," she said. "He was like that."

Lyons nodded to Blancanales to get the man in the *gi*. With Schwarz gone, it would be up to him to carry the fat man. He bent and began lifting the deadweight to his shoulder. "Tell them thanks but we have to go now," he told Blancanales.

He did as Lyons instructed.

"Wouldn't you boys like some iced tea first?" the old woman asked.

"I wish we had time, Mrs. Dempkowski," Blancanales said as Lyons balanced the fat man precariously on his shoulder and headed back through the laundry room. Puffing with what had to be a good three hundred pounds, the Able Team leader opened the door and peered outside. All looked clear.

A moment later he and his teammates were hurrying across the backyard and across the alley to the next block. They lifted the unconscious men over one fence, then miraculously found a gate leading out the other side.

Schwarz was waiting for them two houses down from where they emerged. He slid the door open and helped them load their captives, then jumped back behind the wheel.

Lyons tried to catch his breath as the van slipped away from the neighborhood. "Find an out-of-the-way motel where we can talk to these guys," he said between gasps for air.

Schwarz nodded. "The old people all right?" he asked. Like all the operatives who worked out of Stony Man Farm, he was concerned about any innocents whose lives occasionally had to be interrupted for a greater good.

"They're fine," Blancanales replied. "By now they probably don't even remember we were there."

Schwarz nodded. "Then I take it everything went smoothly and I didn't miss anything exciting?" he asked.

"You sure did," Blancanales said.

Schwarz frowned behind the wheel. "Huh?"

"You missed a very nice thimble collection," Blancanales quipped, laughing.

CHAPTER TEN

Sierra Leone

The Executioner kicked with his legs, pulling himself along the underwater tunnel with his free hand, the Crossada knife gripped in the other. The blackened passageway had been fairly narrow at first, then widened to the point where he could easily maneuver. His movements were slow and steady, his objective to cover the most territory possible and use the least air in his lungs.

But already he could feel his chest starting to tighten.

Bolan swam on, reminding himself that there had to be oxygen at the other end. The RUF bandit had made it, which meant he could, too. But he'd have to pay attention, keep his wits about him. There was always the chance that the tunnel moved on past the exit, dead-ending somewhere beneath the mountain.

If that was the case, and the Executioner overshot the exit for the false lead, it would become his watery tomb. He'd very likely be out of air before he realized his mistake.

Gradually the passage began to narrow again. Bolan sensed it first, then felt the underwater outcroppings occasionally brush his shoulder. Then the passageway closed to the point where he slid against both sides as he swam along, both the Crossada and his free hand extended in front of him. A feeling of claustrophobia threatened him, but he pushed the emotion to the side. He moved on, hoping the rock walls narrowed no farther, yet knowing he would have to proceed even if they did.

Finally the watery shaft closed in so much he was forced to halt. Unable to see, he felt the area ahead. Just as he had feared, it was still large enough for an average-sized man to proceed. But too small for a man of the Executioner's stature.

Bolan paused, forcing himself to consider the situation. If he wriggled and wormed just right, there was just the chance that he could force himself through the narrow area. He would leave a good deal of shoulder skin and blood behind to feed the fish but he might make it.

In any case, he knew he had to try.

The Executioner started to move forward, then his chest told him not to. His blind pilgrimage down the underwater corridor had taken too long, and he would need more air before he attempted what he had in mind.

As quickly as he could manage, the Executioner pushed himself backward the way he had come. When the tunnel widened sufficiently, he turned and swam forward, the fingers of his left hand tracing the rocky wall as a guide. His lungs burned, feeling as if someone had injected an air pump into his chest and began pumping. After what seemed an eternity he emerged into the pool in the center of the cavern and swam to the top.

Bolan gasped for air as his head broke the surface, his arms shooting out to catch the side of the pool. His chest heaved up and down, his throat burning as his starved lungs drew in oxygen. He stayed in that position for perhaps three minutes, using the time to think and plan, as well as let his body replenish itself.

The Executioner sheathed the Crossada. He now knew what lay ahead—at least for a ways—and it didn't include the RUF bandit. His fight would be with the tunnel itself, and the large knife would only be in the way. He would leave it, and the Desert Eagle, at his sides until they prevented him from moving on, then shove them down the front of his shorts or abandon them altogether if necessary.

Still holding on to the rocky side of the pool, Bolan leaned forward and rested his face on his forearms in the black underground cavern. There was a distinct possibility that he would get stuck at the spot where he'd turned around. And even if he didn't, there was every chance that the passage narrowed even more farther along. If so, he would never be able to push himself back through the first constricted area again—not backward. He would run out of air between the two bottlenecks and die.

Continuing to breathe steadily and build up his endurance again, Bolan opened his eyes in the darkness. The fact that he might die didn't bother him. He had come to terms with his own mortality many years before when he had first dedicated his life to fighting the evils and injustices the law seemed impotent to correct. Since that moment he had considered himself living on borrowed time. Like the Japanese samurai warriors of old, he had thought of himself as already dead and therefore unable to be killed.

But what worried him was that if he perished in this underwater grave, what had happened to Spencer Kiethley might never be discovered. The mystery of how Kiethley's death tied into the events in Japan and Somalia might go unsolved until it was too late.

Something big was brewing. Bolan didn't know what, but his gut told him it was of earthshaking proportions.

He raised his head. His breathing was steady again now, and he felt as strong and rested as he was going to feel. Without further thought he dived once more.

Bolan entered the tunnel, swimming along through the wider areas and pulling himself through those that were more constricted. He made considerably better time now that he knew the route. Reaching the first area that had scraped against his shoulders, he wriggled through, then came to the spot where he had been forced to turn. Remembering the Crossada and Desert Eagle on his hips, he unthreaded both from his belt and shoved them down the front of his shorts where they would be less obtrusive.

Arms extended in front of him, the Executioner

stuck his head into the opening and began to inch on. His shoulders were the big problem, and he came to a dead stop as his deltoids hit stone. Shrugging his shoulders as close to his ears as he could, he gained another inch, then another. A few moments later he was free to his ribs, and then to his waist. Below his belly, the rock caught on the Desert Eagle and Crossada for a moment and stopped him once more. Bolan reached down, jerked the two weapons from the front of his waistband and extended them in front of his head. Their removal was just enough to enable him to move on.

The tunnel widened dramatically again, meaning that he would be able to turn and move headfirst if forced to turn back. He knew he would never have squeezed through the narrow area backward. Had he been able to do so, the Executioner would have taken in a deep breath of relief as he moved on through the tunnel. As it was, he had to settle for a small exhalation.

Bolan's relief was short-lived. Ahead he felt only solid rock. Ignoring the consternation that threatened to cloud his judgment, he let his hands search up and down, back and forth. He wasn't one to panic, no matter how harrowing the situation in which he found himself.

Bolan felt upward across the rock, then to both sides again. Again he hit solid rock. He turned, look-ing back at the blackness toward the direction he had come. Had he missed a fork in the tunnel? He didn't think so. For the first time he realized his chest was burning. Could he make it all the way back to the pool in the cavern? It was impossible to tell for sure, but his gut level reaction was no.

The Executioner turned back to the solid wall of rock. No, he hadn't missed a fork in the underwater passageway. The tunnel had been too narrow to overlook another route. That meant that somewhere, right here where he was, there was a way out. If not, he would have encountered the RUF hardman's body along the way, and he hadn't.

Feeling the rock ahead again, Bolan's hand traced down. He found the narrow hole almost at his feet.

He closed his eyes as his hand traced the circumference of the hole, estimating its size compared to his own magnitude. It would be a close squeeze. The opening was slotlike, perhaps two feet across and a little over a foot high by feel—narrower than he was, which meant the loss of more skin, at best.

But he had no choice.

Bolan knew he could afford no obstacles that might add to his circumference. Quickly he slipped out of the tank top and abandoned it. The cargo shorts came off next and he wrapped them tightly around the Crossada and Desert Eagle, which he held in his left hand. Dressed only in his undershorts, he pulled himself down to the opening with his left hand, stuck both arms through the narrow slot and began wedging himself forward.

The Executioner's chin was the first body part to donate skin as he squeezed into the tight opening. He felt the burn as if he'd cut himself shaving as he pressed on. His chest scraped the bottom of the slot, his back the top. More skin tore away. His shoulders stopped him again.

This time Bolan knew that there would be no shrugging himself through. The rock hit high on his trapezius muscles—too high to compensate. He pushed himself back and searched with his fingers for something to grab on to. He found nothing. He knew he didn't have enough time to make it back to the cavern; forward was the only way.

For a moment he wondered if this was how it was all to end. After so many years of facing the gun, the knife, the grenade—was he to die at the hands of nature rather than those of an enemy?

Bolan didn't know. But if this were indeed his time, he wouldn't go out with idle thoughts on his mind. He wouldn't die thinking but acting.

The Executioner would go out fighting.

His chest feeling as if a thick steel band encircled it, Bolan dug into the shorts in front of him and pulled out the Desert Eagle. Flipping off the safety with his thumb, he extended the weapon in front of him then shoved the barrel into a small fissure that ran along one side of the hole in front of him. He'd have one shot, one chance to move forward.

Bolan turned his head away. The concussion under water would be severe, and he opened his mouth to help equalize the pressure. Water rushed in as he fought to hold his breath and pulled the trigger.

Even with his mouth open, the underwater blast threatened to deafen him. He felt the concussion throughout his body as the pressure of the charge rippled through the water.

Bolan transferred the Desert Eagle to his left hand and seized the Crossada with his right hand. He drove the blade into the crevice with all of his might.

His chest felt as if he'd eaten fire as he strained to open the fissure wider. He felt the rock move slightly, and drove the blade in deeper. Placing the Desert Eagle in front of him, he twisted to get both hands on the giant fighting knife's micarta handle and pushed with every ounce of strength that remained in his tortured arms and shoulders.

Suddenly the rock gave way. A boulder the size of a man's head broke away, and the Executioner shot through the hole.

Bolan's brain was clouding now from lack of oxygen. He knew it was only a matter of seconds before he blacked out. When that happened, instinct would take over and he would open his mouth to gasp for air. Instead, water would rush into his lungs and he would drown.

Grabbing his shorts and the Desert Eagle as he swam past them, the Executioner realized he was no longer in the narrow tunnel. His arms shot out to both sides but met no resistance. He was in another pool like the one through which he'd entered the tunnel— he had to be. Which meant he could surface.

In any case he had no choice but to try. He had only seconds left before the air rushed out of his lungs and he involuntarily gasped for more.

Bolan shot straight up toward the surface, his oxygen-robbed brain only half-aware that the water was lightening as he neared the top. Black turned to gray, then gray became blue in the Executioner's eyes, and then suddenly he could see the top.

His chest heaved in and out, convulsing now as he struggled on. Two feet below the surface, Bolan looked through the clear water to see the moon high in the sky. He realized suddenly that the tunnel opened outside the mountain. He was two feet from the surface. Two feet from air.

Two feet from life.

Too late, the Executioner saw the dark shadowy form of the RUF hardman he had pursued through the underwater tunnel. The bandit knelt on the rocks just to the side of the pool with some dark object— a club of some type—held high over his head in both hands.

Bolan's head broke the surface, and at long last his mouth opened wide for air. He gasped both for oxygen and in surprise as he felt the bludgeon come down hard on the top of his skull.

The bright moon danced crazily in the sky for a moment.

Then the clear, moon-filled night went black again.

Somalia

THE GRAVEL ROAD WAS no smoother heading back into Mogadishu than it had been on the way to the equipment site. McCarter, Captain Jack and the other men of Phoenix Force, seated in the Wagoneer, rose and fell with each bump or ditch the vehicle hit.

Jack was quiet as they neared Somalia's capital city, but finally he said, "When will you let me go?"

"As soon as we're in town," McCarter replied. "You don't want to walk the rest of the way in, do you?"

"Now that you mention it, no."

The Wagoneer rounded a curve in the rough road, and Encizo hit the brake, slowing. "Uh oh," the Cuban said.

McCarter rolled down his window and stuck his head out. Down the road perhaps a hundred yards, several Somalian military vehicles blocked their path. Two automobiles had been stopped ahead of the Wagoneer, and uniformed men with rifles leaned against the cars talking to the drivers.

The Phoenix Force leader tapped Captain Jack on the shoulder and pointed for him to look between Encizo and James. James leaned away, toward Hawkins, to give the warlord a better line of vision.

"Any idea what's going on?" McCarter asked.

Captain Jack shook his head. "Any number of things," he said, pulling the red bandanna off the top of his head. "Perhaps they are looking for me. As you must know, I'm a wanted man and if they recognize me..." His voice trailed off as he slid the cutlass and sheath off his belt and jammed them beneath his feet on the floor. The gold earring came next, then Captain Jack reached up with both hands and untied the eye patch from around his head.

When it came away, McCarter saw a perfectly good, functioning eye.

The warlord looked at him and shrugged. "Image."

Encizo was still slowing. "Want me to cut a U?" he asked.

"No," McCarter said. "It's too late now. They've seen us, and they'll just send cars after us. Besides, there's no reason they should be looking for us. But get the weapons and anything else suspicious out of sight." Even as he said it, McCarter knew he might be wrong. Captain Berber had said little when they'd left his office-gym, but the man had looked like a time bomb ready to explode. The muscular customs captain didn't like losing the bench-press contest to Manning, and it was more than just possible that he'd decided to renege on his promise.

Encizo slowed further as the lead car that had stopped got the okay wave and moved through the roadblock. He pulled in behind a twenty-year-old GMC El Camino and stopped.

McCarter eyed the roadblock. Two military jeeps were parked on the right side of the road with a pair of rifle-bearing soldiers in each. On the other side of the road was a dark government sedan bearing the white-star-on-blue Somalian flag. Several soldiers in worn-out olive-drab fatigues stood around the vehicles bearing an assortment of weapons. None of the young men looked to be more than eighteen years old, and all looked frightened.

Not much of a blockade. Whoever had set it up

wasn't expecting to catch whomever they were looking for. And they weren't expecting much resistance if they happened to get lucky.

The Briton turned his attention to a young private who had just waved the other car on. The youth had holes in the knees of his pants and even bigger ones in the mustache he was doing his best to grow. It looked more like someone had glued coffee grounds to his upper lip. He tapped the hood of the car in front of Phoenix Force, waved it on and walked toward the Wagoneer.

McCarter studied the youth's eyes. The youngster appeared unsure of himself. If it was Phoenix Force they were looking for he could be bluffed.

A gut feeling suddenly overpowered McCarter. "Don't show him your passport, Rafael," McCarter told Encizo quickly. "Tell him you left it at the hotel."

"You sure, David?" Encizo asked as the young private approached. "It might be that—" By then the young man was at the window and there was no more time for talking.

Encizo rolled down the window and smiled. "Good day, Private," he said.

"Passport," he demanded.

"Gee, sir," Encizo said, "they kept it back at the hotel. Kept all of our passports." He chuckled. "Guess they were afraid we might walk on the bill. Can you imagine that?"

McCarter nodded silent approval at the way Encizo was handling the situation. It wasn't unusual for hotels to keep the passports of their guests who were traveling abroad. An American who stole the sheets from a Somalian hotel was a little hard to track down later when he'd made it back to Figure Five, Arkansas. It was easier to see that he never left the country.

"What is your business in Somalia?" the private asked.

Encizo had snapped to McCarter's suspicions. Instead of using the journalist story they'd cooked up, he said, "We're businessmen looking for potential investment opportunities. When all the shooting finally settles down, of course."

The young man outside the window looked at him suspiciously. "Do you have any form of identification?" he asked.

"No, I'm sorry," Encizo said. "Just the passport."

"No press card?" the private asked quickly.

Encizo saw the obvious attempt at trickery and frowned. "Press card? he asked. "Why on earth would I have a press card?"

The young private nodded. Leaning down farther, he rested his forearms on the open window and stared into the back seat. McCarter got only a glance. But Captain Jack rated a long and intense examination before the young man moved on to take a quick look at Manning. "Please wait," he finally said, then walked swiftly to a dark sedan. Opening the front door, he reached in and pulled a radio microphone from the vehicle.

McCarter watched him speak into the microphone.

"He's calling Captain Berber," he said. "That's what the deal about the press cards was all about. Berber's told them we entered the country as journalists."

Encizo nodded. "It seems our bench-pressing captain is still angry about the contest and has gone back on his promise."

Manning chuckled. "Maybe I should have let him win."

"If you had, we'd never have gotten away in the first place," Encizo said.

He turned his attention back to McCarter as they waited. "What do you want me to do, David?"

"Hang on," McCarter replied. "Let's see how it goes first. I'd still like to operate on the level while we're in country." He paused. "As long as we can, anyway."

"I don't think it is you who has drawn his suspicion," Captain Jack said. "He has recognized me."

McCarter glanced to his side. Captain Jack looked like a completely different man without his "pirate" accoutrements. Still, that might be the case. He shrugged. "Maybe."

The private finished speaking and stuck an ear back into the car, evidently listening to his answer over the radio. McCarter watched him look back to the Wagoneer, unconsciously nodding and shaking his head as he spoke again, as if the party on the other end of the airwaves could see him. His face took on a grim countenance as he spoke.

"He's beginning to look serious," Encizo stated.

"Agreed," McCarter said. "Get ready to roll if we have to."

"Does that mean only if they are after you?" Captain Jack asked nervously. "What if it is *me* they want. Will you hand me over to them?"

McCarter hesitated for a moment. If they had to "go outlaw" while in Somalia, it would help to have someone who knew the ropes like Captain Jack. A simple no right now might buy his loyalty.

"No," McCarter said.

"No? You will not give me to them?"

"Not if you'll agree to stick with us until we've accomplished what we're here in Somalia to do," McCarter said. "We could use a guide."

The warlord grinned. "You have found a guide. And made a friend."

The private dropped the radio microphone on the car seat and left the door open as he started back to the Wagoneer. His face was even more serious now, and his hand had dropped to the grips of the pistol on his belt.

"If I'm any judge of body language at all," Calvin James said, "I'd say we're about to leave." He paused. "*Fast*, without permission from the principal."

The private didn't lean down onto the window this time but stood at attention. "You will all exit the vehicle," he ordered.

"Sure thing, Private," Encizo said. "But could I ask you what this is all about first?"

The young man hesitated. "You fit the descriptions of several men who entered the country illegally," he finally stated. "There is a customs captain on his way. If he does not identify you as those men, you will be free to go."

"I see," Encizo said. "Could I ask one more favor?"

The young man was growing restless. "What?"

"Could you tell Captain Berber that if he'd beef up his bench press a little, this kind of thing wouldn't happen?"

As the words left his mouth, Encizo threw the Wagoneer into Drive and stomped the accelerator. Gravel and dirt flew from beneath the tires, showering the private and the other men standing near the Wagoneer as it skidded away from the roadblock.

"Well," Hawkins said as the first shots burst from the soldier's rifles behind them. "It's official."

"What's that?" Manning asked, looking over his shoulder through the rear windshield.

"We're wanted men."

Captain Jack smiled widely. "Welcome to the club," he said. "You are in good company."

New York

THE YELLOW BRICK MOTEL was built of exactly what the name implied. The white trim, shutters and doors, and the white picket fence that encircled the property gave it a homy effect. A yellow brick sidewalk led from the parking lot to the office, and a sign featuring Dorothy and Toto, the Cowardly Lion,

Scarecrow and Tin Man screamed at patrons to Follow The Yellow Brick Road To Comfort!

Schwarz pulled the van into the parking lot. Lyons got out and started toward the office.

Blancanales rolled down his window. "Ironman?"

Lyons turned back.

"Watch out for witches." Blancanales grinned. "The wicked ones, at least."

"And those winged-monkey things," Schwarz added. He blew air through his closed lips, making them flutter. "Those things still give me nightmares."

Lyons couldn't help smiling himself. But he turned before his teammates could catch him at it.

The office inside was as colorful as the motel's exterior. Photos and promotional posters of the *Wizard of Oz* covered the walls, and full-size cardboard cutouts of the major characters stood around the lobby. The Wicked Witch of the West sat on her broom, pointing toward the front desk. A speech balloon shooting out of her mouth said, "This way, dearie!"

Lyons walked up and rang the bell. A high, squeaky voice called out, "Yes, sir?"

The Able Team leader looked up and down the counter but saw no one. He rang the bell again.

A tiny head suddenly appeared behind the desk as a little person hopped up on some unseen stool or platform. "I said, *yes, sir?*" the little man repeated angrily. The stench of stale alcohol shot from his mouth as if propelled by a flamethrower.

The little man's face was vaguely familiar. Lyons looked up on the back wall and saw a picture of him—much younger of course—talking to Dorothy. He'd been one of the Munchkins in the movie.

"Sorry, I didn't see you," Lyons said. "I need a room."

"How many, sir?"

"Just one room."

The man turned red in the face with anger once more. "How many in your party?" he asked sarcastically. "Are you alone? Do you have your wife with you? Your girlfriend? Your...whatever?" He paused and glared up at Lyons. "Do you understand the question now? I'll give you a moment to think about it." He disappeared for a moment behind the counter again, and when he returned, fresh waves of bourbon drifted through the air.

"There'll be five of us," he said. "We'll only be here a few hours for a meeting."

The little man's face twisted into a lewd grin. "One of those, are you." He closed his eyes and shook his head. "God forgive you. But I suppose it's not for me to judge—as long as you pay." His hand shot out, palm up. "By the way, you pay in advance."

Lyons considered setting him straight, then decided it wasn't worth his time. Let the little man think what he wanted. His life had evidently taken a downhill turn since the movie was made and if wild fantasies helped him get through the day, so be it.

The Able Team leader scribbled the name Ralph

Murphy on a registration card, made up an address in Detroit and handed the man a fifty-dollar bill. "Keep the change," he said, took the key extended in the hand and walked back out of the office.

The two cultists had awakened by the time Lyons got back to the van. They had made no effort to escape, and sat preaching their philosophy and doing their best to save Schwarz's and Blancanales's souls.

Room 16 was located on the other side of the building away from the street. Schwarz pulled up in front, and the five men got out.

Lyons led the way, opening the door and standing back for the others to enter. He glanced at Blancanales for a moment. They were in the psy-op expert's domain again, and the big ex-cop would step back and take a back seat to Blancanales. But he had an idea this interrogation would be much different than that of Ira Rook.

Lyons was right.

Blancanales took charge as soon as all five men had entered the room. The Able Team psychological-warfare expert was grateful that the interior of the room was simple and plain. He had already learned that in many ways the brainwashed cultists were like children, and the *Wizard of Oz* motif of the Yellow Brick Motel had been distracting to them.

He had also learned the names of two cult members while Lyons was inside the motel office. The overweight man was George. The man wearing the *gi* was Casey Balforth.

Blancanales spoke to the two men now as if they

were all old friends. "Casey, why don't you, George and I take a seat at the table?" He pointed to the bare wood table next to the front window. "Are you guys hungry?"

The two men looked at each other quizzically.

"Yes," George replied, "but Hikari will provide for us when we need sustenance."

Balforth nodded. "Hikari will provide."

"That's fine," Blancanales said. "Just fine. But in the meantime Hikari has instructed me to help provide for you, and I feel like a pizza. How about you?"

Both men looked at each other again.

"You are a follower of the Great Hikari?" Balforth asked.

"He has spoken to you?" George asked in awe.

Blancanales hesitated. He had to establish common ground with these men if he was to gain their confidence and pick what was left of their brains. But one of the best ways to lose a subject's confidence was to get caught in a lie. If he proclaimed to follow Hikari, they might well ask him a question that cult members could answer but he couldn't. Any bond of trust established up to that point would then be irreparably broken.

"No. I'm not a follower, but I'm interested. I guess what I said was a poor choice of words. I just meant that since I want to learn more about the Followers of the Truth it didn't make sense that Hikari would mind me buying you a pizza. Sausage? Double cheese? What kind do you want?"

A dim light lit in the back of George's eyes. "Everything," he said. "Make it a combo."

Balforth gave him a dirty look, then turned back to Blancanales. "We are instructed to avoid meat," he said. "Cheese only for me."

Blancanales wasn't surprised at the part about avoiding meat. Diet was a big part in brainwashing and protein deprivation rendered people more pliant and receptive to suggestion. It was a technique used by both religious and political brainwashers.

The psy-op man looked up at Lyons. "Ironman, you and Gadgets want to go pick up the pizza?" Blancanales needed time alone with the two men if the intimacy he desired was to be established.

Lyons's face reflected his understanding. He nodded to Schwarz, and the two men left.

Blancanales turned back to the two cult members across the table from him. The bottom line was that he wanted to know all they could tell him about the plan to gas the New York subway. But he had to be careful not to alienate them. And there was another area of concern, as well. The men had not only been brainwashed into being subservient followers of Hikari, but they had also been trained as killers, mindless, conscienceless killers. Blancanales knew if he wasn't careful he might pull the wrong strings, which would set them off. If that happened, he might have to kill them to protect himself.

The psy-op expert needed to start off slow and relaxed. He would get around to the subway thing when the time seemed right. "You are wearing a martial-arts uniform, Casey," he said. "Can you tell me why?"

"Many American followers wear Japanese clothing," Balforth replied. "It is to show our allegiance to the Great Hikari and the Followers of the Truth."

Blancanales nodded. "Tell me more about the Followers of the Truth."

"It is the path to salvation," Casey said,

"It is the road to eternity," George added.

"Really? How do you achieve salvation?" Blancanales asked.

"There are several paths," George stated. "To drink the master's blood is the one I chose."

Blancanales fought the revulsion that shot through him. "Where did you get this blood?" he asked.

"I purchased it for the equivalent of one million yen."

"I see." Blancanales wasn't surprised. Such rip-offs were common in cults. "But you said there were other ways to salvation."

"Yes," Balforth said. "I drank the master's bathwater." He glanced down at the floor in shame. "I couldn't afford the blood."

"He is saved, but he won't have the seat of honor in the kingdom to come that I will have," George added.

"Are there any other ways to be saved?" Blancanales asked.

"For women, there is Hikari himself," Balforth replied. "They may partake of the master's flesh.

They may unite with him. Only a chosen few are given the privilege of that path to salvation."

And Blancanales knew that not one of them would be ugly. Again, taking advantage of their followers sexually was standard fare for cult leaders. "Tell me about Hikari," Blancanales said.

"Hikari is good," George recited.

"Hikari is all-knowing," Balforth parroted.

"Okay, that's all fine and good, but tell me about Hikari the man."

"Hikari is good. Hikari is—"

Blancanales cut off the litany. "Have you ever met Hikari?"

"Oh, no," Balforth said. "Hikari is in Japan."

"Only the chosen may meet the master face-to-face," George declared. "We haven't yet proved ourselves to be worthy."

"But then who sold you the blood, George? Who provided the bathwater, Casey?"

Before either of the men could answer the door opened. Lyons and Blancanales walked in, each carrying a large pizza. They set them down on the table between Balforth, George and Blancanales, then moved to take seats on the bed on the far side of the room.

Blancanales opened both pizzas boxes. Without looking directly at them he watched the men's reactions.

George looked like a starving man who had stumbled into the finest restaurant in town. Balforth was less obvious, but it was more than evident he hadn't eaten well for a while, either.

"Dig in," Blancanales said, scooping up a slice of the combination pizza and taking a bite. "But be careful. It's still hot."

George's hand shot forward to grab the biggest piece on the circular piece of corrugated cardboard. Again, Balforth showed less enthusiasm. But he took a piece of the cheese pizza.

The men ate in silence for a few minutes. Blancanales watched Balforth out of the corner of his eye. The man would be a little harder to crack than George. He had bought into the cult's philosophy even more than his overweight friend. And he didn't have the craving for food that George did. He had already confessed that the cult members were instructed not to eat meat. What he didn't realize was that protein itself was what the Great Hikari didn't want them to have. Blancanales hoped the cheese would provide enough of the muscle-building fuel to get Balforth started thinking for himself again.

After they'd each had three pieces of pizza, Blancanales repeated the question he'd asked before Lyons and Schwarz had arrived. "I'm interested in your salvation," he said. "Where did you get the bathwater and blood of the guru?"

"From the archangel," George said around a mouthful of pizza. "When he visited."

"Yes, from the archangel," Balforth added. "The archangel sent by the Great Hikari to watch over us and our lesser angel."

"Your lesser angel?"

"Yes, the lesser angel is with us always."

Lyons stood, crossed the room quickly and whispered into Blancanales's ear. "I think I shot him back at the house," the Able Team leader said. "Ask what he was wearing."

"What was your angel wearing today?"

Balforth thought for a moment. "A camel-colored sport coat and blue slacks," he said.

Lyons nodded as he sat back down.

Blancanales continued to eat with the men, watching them closely. Both were far more relaxed and talkative. They were a far cry from being deprogrammed, but at least they were beginning to speak their own words rather than simply reiterate programmed answers as if they were mantras.

It was time to start getting closer to the real reason for the interview.

"Tell me, guys," Blancanales said. "What else does the archangel or lesser angel do?" He saw a questioning look come over Balforth's face and backpedaled for a moment. "I really want to know about all this. Do they give you instructions? Order you to do things?"

George was happily finishing the last piece of his combo and beginning to cast glances at what remained of Balforth's cheese pizza. He was also less apprehensive than his partner. "Yes," he said. "The archangel gives the lesser angel instructions. The lesser angel passes them on to us. They both look over us, and keep us safe from outsiders who do not follow the Great Hikari. We obey the angels.'' He swallowed, and said, ''Casey, are you going to eat the rest of your pizza?''

Balforth shook his head.

George reached over and grabbed a piece of cheese pizza.

''What instructions did the angels give you?'' Blancanales asked. ''Do the angels have names?''

Balforth stiffened visibly at the question, and even George balked now, realizing he was talking too much as he shoved half the slice of pizza into his mouth and bit it off. ''We aren't allowed to speak of such things with outsiders.''

Blancanales knew it was time to play his hole card, time to go for broke. What he had planned would either work or it wouldn't, but he'd gotten all he was going to get out of the men without playing it. ''But Casey, George,'' he said, ''I'm *not* an outsider.''

The two men looked up at him, again puzzled.

''Congratulations,'' Blancanales said. ''You have both passed the test the Great Hikari sent me to administer. I was to attempt to persuade you to speak of that which you were instructed to keep secret.'' He smiled broadly. ''But you didn't.''

George fairly beamed.

Balforth wasn't as easily led away from the matter at hand. ''With all due respect, if you are telling the truth, how are we to know that the Great Hikari sent you?''

Blancanales smiled. He had that base covered. ''I'll tell you something you'll recognize that only

Hikari himself could have told me." He paused. "You were instructed by the angel to put sarin gas in a New York subway."

"Praise Hikari, you are telling the truth!" Balforth fairly shouted. "The master *has* sent you!"

"Praise Hikari!" George echoed, long strings of mozzarella cheese hanging from his open mouth. "Hikari the Great."

"Hikari the all-knowing," Balforth added. "And then you must be aware that all who die to the sarin will immediately reawaken in heaven."

"Sure," Blancanales said. The Great Hikari had covered all the bases himself. If George and Balforth were sending souls straight to heaven by gassing the subway, how could they question their actions?

Both men fell to the floor before Blancanales and bowed their heads low to the ground. From that point on, whether they knew it or not, Balforth's and George's hearts, souls and brains no longer belonged to the Great Hikari. They belonged to a psychological-warfare expert by the name of Rosario Blancanales. And the two cult members' brains were in far safer hands than they had been before.

"So," Blancanales said, "I will ask you once more. What are the angels' names? The ones who instructed you to put gas in the subway?"

Neither man seemed to wonder why this messenger from the Great Hikari wouldn't already have this information.

"The lesser angel is called Daniel," George stated.

"And the archangel is Carver," Balforth added.

"Yes," George agreed, "Archangel Carver."

CHAPTER ELEVEN

Japan

Toshiro Ohara took a seat at the head of the long conference table and looked to the man seated to his right. The rest of the table, and the forty folding chairs that had been arranged theater style behind it in the large room, were vacant.

"Are you listening to me, Toshi?" Ichiro Murai asked in the voice of a father scolding his son. "Have you heard a word I have said?"

Ohara sighed wearily. "Again, as you do every day, Ichiro," he said. "You have been preaching to me about the fact that I like women too much." In truth he had been only half listening. The rest of his mind had been on Yoshiko's breasts.

"No, I was not telling you you *like* women too much," Murai said. "I told you that you *trust* these new women too much. Particularly the one."

"Which one?"

Murai slammed a hand down on the table in disgust. "You know which one, Toshi!"

His tone irritated Ohara. "Do you realize, Ichiro," he said, "that if any of my other followers—"

"I am not one of your followers," Murai practically screamed.

"If anyone else spoke to me like this, they would be killed."

"Do not threaten me, Toshiro Ohara," Murai continued. "I remember before you called yourself the Great Hikari. I remember when you were a mere street criminal picking pockets and hustling small-time con games. I remember because I was there, doing it with you."

"So what is your point, Ichiro?" he asked.

"The point is, as I have told you over and over, you are going to slip and let one of these women who fascinates you so hear something she should not hear."

"Ichiro, I do not talk business around them. It is all 'love and harmony and spiritual salvation.'"

"But you now have Yoshiko retained as a servant here in the palace," Murai said. "How do you know when she will hear something she shouldn't?"

As if to prove his point, the door to the conference room opened and Yoshiko walked in carrying a silver tea service. She smiled sweetly as she placed it on the conference table.

"Do you no longer knock when you enter the Great Hikari's presence?" Murai asked angrily.

Yoshiko's face darkened, and she looked down at her feet. "I am sorry. I—"

"I pardon you," Ohara stated, raising his hand and

bringing it down on her shoulder in a gesture of forgiveness. "Now, please go. You are so lovely, I find you distracting when I must discuss business matters with Murai."

Yoshiko beamed the joy of the delivered as she walked out of the conference room.

Ohara watched her, then turned back to his second-in-command. "I grow bored being a god," he said. "Sometimes I must be a man." He chuckled. "Do not worry, Ichiro. I will not let things get out of hand."

"I hope not," Murai replied in disgust. "I have said all I will say on the matter for now."

Ohara cleared his head. "The archangels and angels will arrive soon. Have we encountered any problems?"

"Only in New York," Murai said. "Someone attacked the home of Casey Balforth. Angel Daniel Thomas was killed."

"Do you know who is responsible?"

Murai shook his head. He lifted the silver teapot and poured a cup of tea for Ohara, then slid it in front of the cult leader. "No. It is confusing. But we do not think the house was attacked by police or U.S. government agents." Pouring a cup for himself, he continued. "They would have proceeded differently."

"Who, then?" Ohara wondered aloud.

Murai shrugged. "Perhaps one of the youthful street gangs for which America is becoming famous," he said. "Carver thinks they may have learned that there were weapons in the house.'' He took a sip of tea and shrugged again. "In any case it is not important. The sarin gas is stored at the base house in Wichita, Kansas, and will be distributed to the subbases from there.''

Ohara nodded. "And what of the classified documents still in Somalia?''

"The search teams are still looking,'' Murai said. "There is still time. But if we do not find them, we will proceed with the sarin.''

Ohara nodded absentmindedly, his mind drifting back to Yoshiko and Reiko and the sexual acts in which he had engaged with the two of them the night before. One of the things he loved about them both was how creative they had become. Perhaps tonight—

Murai cut into his thoughts. "Toshi, are you with me?'' he said in irritation.

"Yes,'' Ohara answered. "My mind drifted for a moment.''

"Well, let it drift on this,'' Murai said. "We do not know if we will use sarin again or the new gas, but otherwise things are progressing as planned. You must remember, however, that your followers are just that—followers. When we take away their free will, we also take away their ability to lead. They do not plan well, and they must be pointed in the right direction.'' He paused. "That is why it has been necessary to employ men like Carver. But do not forget that these 'angels' are nothing more than criminals. I do not trust any single one of them.''

Ohara nodded. "It is a necessary evil."

The phone on the conference table between the two men buzzed, and Murai lifted the receiver from its cradle. "Yes?" he said. He listened for a moment, his face becoming angry again. "Wait."

Turning to Ohara, he covered the mouthpiece. "You have Reiko working as a secretary now?" he asked.

Ohara shrugged. "She was a typist before coming to me."

Murai turned back to the phone. "What do you want?" he ask in a surly voice.

A moment later he turned back to Ohara and said, "Carver and the others have arrived. They are downstairs waiting. Are you ready for them?"

Ohara nodded.

"Send them up," Murai said, and half slammed the phone back down. "Another foolish move, Toshiro," he said. "Reiko will be privy to too many things."

Ohara sighed for what seemed like the thousandth time. He knew Murai was probably right, but he seemed to have no will to get rid of the women anymore. The truth was, it was lonely being a god, and he was tired of it.

Two minutes later the door opened and a brawny black man wearing a cheap, ill-fitting suit walked into the room. Behind him came a short man in Arabic robes and a kaffiyeh. The third man wore a European-cut suit that fit as poorly as the clothes of the black man.

Ohara waved them toward the table. Murai stood, met the fourth man to enter the room and directed him toward the chairs. The men kept coming until all but one of the forty chairs were filled.

Carver, the black man in the bad suit, dropped into the chair to Ohara's left as Murai returned to the seat on the Great Hikari's right. Muhammad Araba and Jean-Marc LeForce took seats next to Carver and Murai across the table from each other.

Ohara watched Murai out of the corner of his eye. The expression of mild disgust on his old friend's face told him that even though Murai had traveled the world handpicking these men himself, he didn't approve of them. And there was little reason he should. Although they were competent to perform the duties for which they had been hired, they were far from admirable as human beings.

Carver, the American, had a criminal record that began the day after his eighteenth birthday when he had been arrested for trafficking heroin. The arrests, which were spliced in between prison terms, paroles and suspended sentences and included everything from petty larceny to murder, had continued for more than thirty years. He had even contracted to do hits for the Mob on several occasions.

Muhammad Araba and Jean-Marc LeForce were nothing more than Saudi and French versions of Carver. All three men were career criminals who had spent their lives breaking the law and, for the most part, getting away with it. They represented three different continents. They were his three archangels, and they supervised the lesser angels on each of their respective continents—the men who were now moving toward the chairs in the back.

The Great Hikari suppressed a smile. Archangels, lesser angels—how pliable his followers were. How they wanted to believe in something, anything. It had been no problem to convince the men and women who made up the cells of the Followers of the Truth scattered throughout the world that these three men, and the thirty-nine seated behind them, were superhuman beings from heaven.

Ohara watched the thirty-nine men behind the table settle into their seats. His mind drifted briefly to the lesser angel who had been killed at Casey Balforth's house. It didn't matter. The New York gassing could be scrubbed, and he would still have thirty-nine cities around the world covered.

Ohara looked back to the lesser angels. Some of them served as security forces here at the castle, but these thirty-nine would lead their individual cult cells in planting and detonating the gas in their respective cities. The bombs would all go off at once, and to put it mildly, should "rock the world." If they used sarin, and each bomb was the same size and as successful as the one in the Tokyo subway, Toshiro Ohara could count on more than ten thousand dead and around eighty thousand injured. But if his men in Somalia were able to locate the rest of the classified documents that the American Spencer Kiethley had hidden, they would then have the formula to make the gas the Americans called Nerve Ending,

and the damage would be tenfold. The easily manufactured Nerve Ending had an effective range ten
times that of sarin and caused almost instantaneous
death. Sarin and other such gases could be dumped
into the ocean as obsolete. Ohara would kill hundreds
of thousands and hold the entire planet hostage.

The thrill of it all overwhelmed him. He suddenly
felt drunk on the power he now held, and even more
intoxicated at the thought of what was to come.

The Great Hikari waited until all of the men were
seated, then said, "I have called you together to go
over the last-minute arrangements. But before I begin, are there any questions?"

Toshiro Ohara waited silently. No hands went up.
He cleared his throat in preparation to speak. "Then,
gentleman," he said, beginning his final address, "as
you know, we will begin distributing the bombs two
nights from now—either those already stored at the
central bases or the new ones we make should we
get the technology in time." He smiled graciously.
"In any case, once the bombs have been distributed
to the subbases, there will be no chance of stopping
us."

Sierra Leone

THE EXECUTIONER FELT as if an anvil had fallen off
the top floor of the World Trade Center and landed
on his skull. But as his vision cleared, he saw the
real root of the pain searing through his brain. A six-

foot-long tree branch lay beside the man squatting next to a campfire.

As his vision continued to focus, Bolan took in his surroundings. He was outside the tunnel, outside the mountain under which the underwater passage had been located. He was in a small clearing, next to the side of the mountain on one side and a row of trees on the other. He remembered emerging to see the RUF bandit, and then the branch had come down on his head to knock him unconscious.

The Executioner kept his eyes half-closed as he turned his attention back to the man next to the fire. He wanted to ascertain just where he was and what his position might be before the bandit realized he was awake. He was certain it was the same man he'd seen run into the cave, then pursued through the underground tunnel. The man's clothes looked damp, and he wore the leather vest and ragged blue jeans Bolan remembered from earlier. On his right hip was a holstered revolver.

Bolan tried to move. He couldn't, and he realized his hands were bound behind his back with what felt like leather strips. His legs extended straight out from him, and he could see more leather securing his feet at the ankles. He felt something hard against his spine and, looking overhead, saw the boughs of a tall tree. The RUF hardman had to have run more restraints through those on his wrists and secured him to the tree trunk.

The Executioner took in the rest of his surroundings. He was still in the mountains, and a pool of water could be seen ten feet to his left. The pool from which he had emerged from the tunnel? Probably. He didn't know how long he had been out of the passageway, but it couldn't have been long. His cargo shorts had been dropped next to him. Along with the underwear he still wore, they were soaking wet.

The RUF hardman was roughly ten feet in front of him, and as Bolan watched, he twisted a rabbit skewered over a spit he had fashioned from sticks. The roasting meat smelled good, and the Executioner was reminded that while it was still dark, it had to be almost breakfast time.

The RUF hardman sat back on his haunches, and for the first time Bolan noticed his Crossada knife strapped to the man's left leg. As he waited for the rabbit to cook, the bandit drew the huge knife and held it up in the firelight for examination, smiling as he ran his thumb along one side of the blade to test the edge. The smile suddenly vanished, and he cursed as blood shot from his thumb.

The bandit shoved the blade into the dirt and wrapped his thumb with a rag he pulled from his pocket. The fire had died down, and he grabbed the branch with which he'd struck Bolan and poked at the glowing embers beneath the rabbit. When the flames failed to return, he cursed again and rose.

Bolan watched the man walk into the trees and begin to gather more limbs to put on the fire. He looked back at the knife thrust in the ground. It was less than a foot from the soles of his hiking boots.

He glanced back at his captor in the trees as the man bent to pick up another dried branch. The man might turn and see him at any moment, and it wouldn't take him long to gather enough wood to get the fire going again. On the other hand the Executioner might not get another chance. And if he couldn't free himself before the man returned, at least he could get the process started.

Sliding down the tree as far as he could, Bolan stretched his legs toward the knife embedded in the soft earth. His boots still a good two inches from the blade, he strained against the restraints that held him to the tree, hoping they'd break or at least stretch. They didn't break, but they did stretch.

Bolan cast a quick glance to the trees. The man was still collecting firewood, but he wouldn't be much longer.

The Executioner stretched again, feeling the leather bite into his wrists. He ignored the pain. He felt a tiny jolt as the leather stretched once more, then his right boot sole struck the knife.

The movement tilted the knife away from the Executioner, but the blade remained upright. There was no question that he had to finish freeing himself before the RUF hardman came back. The awkward angle of the blade to the ground would be proof it had been tampered with.

Bolan shifted slightly so the leather strip between his boots made contact with the blade. Careful not to tip the knife over farther, he began sawing up and down the sharp edge. A moment later, the leather snapped and his feet were free.

But that had been the easy part.

The Executioner glanced into the trees. He could see the bandit leaning over for more wood, his arms almost full. Even if he planned to gather more, he would have to return in a moment with this load.

Which meant the Executioner had to work fast.

Bolan stretched farther, trying to work enough of his feet around the sides of the Crossada to trap the blade between his boots. Again the leather behind his back cut into his flesh. Blood began to drip over his hands, and all feeling below the wrists went numb.

Getting the knife between his boots, the Executioner snapped them together, trapping the blade. Now would come the tricky part.

Bolan pulled his knees to his chest, then straightened his legs upward. With the Crossada held over his head, he paused. He had to rock backward slightly, then drop the huge knife directly behind him—between his back and the tree. If he underestimated the force necessary to accomplish this, the blade would come down on top of his head. If he overestimated, it would rebound against the tree trunk and again drop on top of him or go spinning off to the side where it would be of no use.

But worrying about what might happen would do no good. The Executioner took a deep breath, rocked slightly back and pulled his feet apart.

The twelve-inch blade fell straight down, shaving

a small swatch of skin from Bolan's back. Rather than stick in the ground as he'd hoped it would do, the knife fell sideways, lodging between his hip and the base of the tree trunk.

Bolan leaned to the side, twisting his hands horizontally behind his back. He pulled hard, trying to expose as much of the leather restraint as he could. While the razor-sharp Crossada would easily sever the leather, he was working blind, and it could also cut through the veins in his wrists if he positioned the edge incorrectly.

The Executioner took another look into the trees and saw the RUF hardman heading back toward the fire, his arms loaded with dried branches. So far he hadn't noticed that the knife was missing.

Bolan placed his wrists at the angle he wanted and hoped he was right. Bringing the leather into contact with the blade, he began to saw back and forth.

His captor dropped the wood next to the fire, stirred the coals with one of the limbs, then began to toss the wood onto the embers.

The leather restraint behind Bolan's back snapped at the same instant the bandit's eyes fell on the spot where he'd thrust the knife into the earth.

The RUF hardman went for the gun on his hip as Bolan propelled himself away from the tree trunk to his feet. The bandit's gun had cleared leather by the time the Executioner was on him. Bolan caught a brief glimpse of the .44-caliber hole in the end of the revolver's barrel as he swept the weapon to the side.

The gun fired, the bullet speeding past the Executioner's side, so close he felt the burn on his bare ribs. He grasped the barrel of the weapon and twisted. A loud cracking sound echoed though the night as the explosion from the gunshot died down and the bandit's index finger snapped inside the trigger guard.

The RUF bandit screamed.

Bolan jerked the revolver from his hand and slammed it against the man's temple. The bandit froze in place for a moment, then his knees buckled and he fell forward, unconscious, his arm flying out and coming to rest in the fire.

The big American leaned down and jerked the man away from the fire before the burn could become serious. Returning to the tree, he found the leather restraints that had bound him, and, after tying the severed ends together, used them to tie the RUF man's hands behind his back. Bolan wanted the man able to walk when he came to, so rather than bind his legs together he hobbled the man's ankles with a length that would allow only short, choppy steps.

As soon as the bandit was secured, the Executioner slid into his cargo shorts once more, slipped the knife's sheath from the bandit's belt and onto his own. He dried the Desert Eagle as best he could, then he pulled a fresh magazine from the pocket of his shorts, rammed it into the butt and replaced the gun on his right side. As soon as he had the chance, he would properly strip and oil the weapon.

Bolan reexamined the man on the ground. The burn on his arm wasn't bad, but he was still out cold, and he looked like he'd remain that way a little longer. Dropping to a cross-legged position on the ground in front of the fire, the Executioner pulled the rabbit off the spit, drew the knife and cut a small piece. He tasted it. It was done. As he waited for the RUF man to wake up, Bolan began to eat.

The Executioner's head still throbbed from the blow he'd taken. He looked up at the sky. There was no way he'd make it back to the training camp by morning. He'd be lucky to even locate Buchanan by then. No, the cover of training officer was over. From now on, he'd be on his own.

The RUF hardman was just coming around when the Executioner heard the noise on the other side of the fire. The Desert Eagle leaped into his hand and the safety flew off.

"Hey, don't shoot. It's me." Buchanan's voice was unmistakable. The soldier-journalist stepped out to the side of the fire where Bolan could see him. He had Margai tied and hobbled much the way Bolan had done the RUF man next to the fire.

"We'll have to hurry," Buchanan said. "That is, if we want to stash these two somewhere and get back on time."

Bolan shook his head. "No way it can be done," he said. He held out the rabbit at arm's length. "Want some?"

"Yeah, but I'll eat on the way. You can drive?"

"Yeah, but do you know something I don't?"

Buchanan grinned. "There's a path that leads back

to the main road just around the bend there." He pointed back in the direction he had come.

"So what do we drive?" the Executioner asked.

"How about this guy's Jeep?" Buchanan suggested, nudging the awakening bandit with a toe. "It's parked over there and ready to go."

Bolan chuckled as he stood. Several times since they'd met, Buchanan had said he not only trusted, but liked, the Executioner.

Now the Executioner was beginning to like him.

Somalia

IN THE REARVIEW MIRROR, McCarter saw the young private leap into the passenger's seat of the sedan bearing the Somalian flag on the door. The vehicle made a fast U-turn and, followed by the two jeeps, took up pursuit.

McCarter floored the accelerator, coaxing as much speed from the Wagoneer as he could. It was enough to outdistance the jeeps, but the sedan soon began to gain ground. The Phoenix Force leader squinted, trying to see inside the sedan as it grew larger in the mirror. The windows were tinted, and all he could make out was movement.

The road bent sharply, and McCarter gripped the wheel, doing his best to keep the top-heavy Wagoneer on all four wheels. Another quick glance into the mirror told him the lower-slung government sedan hadn't had as much trouble negotiating the curve. It had gained more ground.

Finally, what McCarter had dreaded but known
was inevitable, happened. The passenger's window
on the sedan rolled down and the barrel of a carbine
was poked through the aperture. The Briton squinted
into the mirror. The weapon was a SANNA 77, a
version of the Czech Model 25 submachine designed
as a personal-defense weapon for residents of South
Africa's rural areas. It was modified to fire semiauto
only.

But semiauto could kill as fast as full rock-and-
roll.

McCarter stood on the accelerator, knowing he had
already coaxed all the speed he was going to get out
of the Wagoneer. In the mirror he saw a head, shoulders and arms join the carbine and aim the weapon
at the Wagoneer.

The former SAS commando swerved to the side,
sending gravel flying as the first few rounds blasted
from the weapon. The bullets flew wide as he corrected the steering wheel, then swung back the other
way as a fresh semiauto burst sailed by on the Wagoneer's other side.

In the back seat McCarter heard movement and
glanced over his seat to see that Gary Manning had
drawn his Beretta 92 and was twisting toward the
rear of the Wagoneer as he rolled down the window.

"They're just scared kids doing their job,"
McCarter directed. "Don't hurt them."

"I'll do my best," Manning replied. He leaned out
the window, dropped the sights just over the sedan
and pulled the trigger three times.

All three rounds hit the roof of the sedan and skimmed across like flat stones skipping across the water. It was the government vehicle's turn to swerve. The man firing the carbine disappeared back inside the window as the vehicle fishtailed down the road in a new storm of dirt and gravel.

The sedan slowed, then sped out again. McCarter cursed under his breath. He looked ahead and saw an abandoned sod farmhouse appear on the side of the road. He remembered it from the trip out. They were only a few miles from Mogadishu now.

Manning fired again, this time taking out a headlight on the government car. The sedan swerved once more but kept coming. The SANNA 9 mm carbine reappeared. A long string of semiauto fire blasted away at the Wagoneer, one of the rounds striking the rear bumper.

Gravel shot from the rear tires as if propelled from a pistol. McCarter zigzagged down the road, hoping to present a difficult target. They neared the crumbling sod house—the marker that had reminded him how near they now were to Mogadishu—and the Phoenix Force leader knew he couldn't allow the government car to follow them into the city. Once there, they would have access to police and other military backup.

McCarter had a decision to make. He took a deep breath and made it. "Take out a tire, Gary."

Manning twisted to look at him. "You sure, David?" he asked. "They could wreck."

"We've got no choice. We'll just have to hope for the best."

Manning nodded. "You got it, boss," he said, and leaned back out the window.

In the side mirror McCarter watched Manning take aim. He pulled the trigger once, but the Wagoneer hit a bump and the round went wild. His second shot was more accurate.

A loud pop, not unlike another round being fired—drifted up to meet McCarter's ears. It was replaced by a short hissing sound. In the mirror he watched the sedan's right front tire drop to the rim, and the sedan skidded off the road and out of control.

McCarter braked to a halt as the government vehicle crashed into the sod house. Dirt and grass flew up in the air, forming a cloud of dust that all but concealed the sedan. The vehicle burst through the other side of the house.

The Phoenix Force leader waited warily as the government car stalled and stopped. As he'd told Manning, and as Manning and the other commandos of Phoenix Force already knew, those youths in fatigues weren't the enemy. They were scared, honest young men trying to do their jobs as soldiers. If there were injuries, Phoenix Force would have to treat them or get them to medical help. If there were deaths...

McCarter didn't want to think about it, but he had no choice. He had been forced to make a decision, and that decision had been to take a chance. If his decision had been wrong he would have to live with it.

He felt a wave of relief wash over him as the driver's door opened and a man wearing dust-covered green fatigues got out. A moment later the young private who had questioned them exited the passenger's seat. Both men were coughing as they opened the back door and pulled a third man from the seat.

McCarter could see into the car, and there were no more Somalian soldiers inside. Twisting the wheel, he pulled back onto the gravel road.

Captain Jack had been silent throughout the chase. McCarter glanced at him in the rearview mirror and saw he had put his earring back in and was slipping on the phony eye patch. The man might have a flair for the dramatic, but he was no wimp when the chips were down. His face was as calm as those of the Phoenix Force commandos.

Captain Jack was a warlord. He was as accustomed to violence as the men from Stony Man Farm.

Now he spoke up. "It was *not* me they were looking for, was it." The words came out more statement than question.

McCarter paused before answering, wondering just how straightforward he should be with the man. They could use his help, particularly as a guide to get around the war-torn nation. But Captain Jack had his own political agenda, and the Phoenix Force leader knew that would be his primary loyalty. The bottom line was that the warlord would help them only as long as he shared Phoenix Force's goals. After that, he would give them up in a heartbeat if it would further his own ambitions.

On the other hand the man wasn't likely to help at all if he thought McCarter and the others were being less than honest with him. The Briton decided that he would be honest—as honest as necessary—in answering the warlord's questions but volunteering nothing.

"No, they were after us," McCarter finally said.

"Why?"

McCarter didn't hesitate to answer this time. "I'll tell you what I can," he said, "and nothing more. We're here to find out about the classified U.S. documents the UN abandoned when they moved out."

"Who do you represent?" Captain Jack asked. "You do not sound American."

"I'm not," McCarter said. "Think of us more as a sort of international task force. A task force that has the best interests of Somalia, as well as our own individual countries, at heart."

"Why should I believe you?" the warlord asked.

"Because we can help you, Jack."

"Oh? How?" Captain Jack wasn't convinced.

Mogadishu appeared on the road ahead. "You wanted the weapons and equipment we brought, right?"

"Of course."

"Well, you help us and when we leave the country, we'll leave all the hardware with you."

Captain Jack sat back against the seat and frowned

as the Wagoneer passed the Mogadishu airport and ministry of tourism. "This does not make sense," he said. "You may not all be Americans but you are all Westerners, and therefore it is America you serve."

"That's a very debatable issue," McCarter replied. "But for the sake of argument go ahead."

"All warlords are wanted men. Not just by the Somalian government but by the West, as well. Surely whatever government or organization you represent has intelligence to this fact."

"We go beyond the normal intelligence, Jack," McCarter told him. "That intel says you're a little different than the other warlords."

Again McCarter saw Captain Jack frown in the mirror.

"That intel says you rob and you kill when you have to, but you're discriminate about it. And we know that lining your own pockets isn't your prime objective." He paused, looking at the street ahead. "You know where the UN building is?"

Captain Jack leaned forward. "Turn here, onto Shire Warsme," he said. "What else do your intelligence sources tell you?"

McCarter made the turn. "Exactly what you told us a few minutes ago. That you want to be president, and you're working toward that goal by playing Robin Hood. You're already gaining the support of the people, people who will eventually be voters." He glanced over his shoulder at the pirate-looking man in the back seat. "We can help you," he said, "but only if you help us. Where do I turn?"

"Keep going straight. Shire Warsme runs into Jamhuuriyadda Avenue. The UN building is on that street." He leaned forward again. "Although I cannot imagine why you want to go there. It has been abandoned, and whoever you are seeking will not be there."

"You didn't answer my question," McCarter said. "Will you help us?"

"There...ahead on your left," Captain Jack directed.

McCarter pulled the Wagoneer to the curb in front of a three-story office building that had obviously been abandoned. Many of the windows had been broken. Some had been patched with cardboard and plywood; others still gaped empty. Here and there graffiti unflattering to Americans and the West in general had been spray painted on the brick walls. Broken glass and other rubble led the way up the sidewalk to the front doors, which stood wide open.

"Well?" McCarter prompted as he threw the Wagoneer into neutral. "Will you help?"

Captain Jack smiled. "I guided you here. It appears that I already am."

McCarter twisted in his seat to face the warlord. "Then it's a deal? You stick with us until we accomplish our mission, then we leave the guns, ammo and other equipment with you?"

"It is a deal," Captain Jack said.

The two men shook hands.

Which was what they were doing when a sudden barrage of automatic-rifle fire took out the Wagoneer's windshield and side windows.

CHAPTER TWELVE

Stony Man Farm, Virginia

The man in the white lab coat shook his head in disgust as the kanji letters lit up once more on the computer screen. Rather than go to the trouble of linking up his Quick-Cross translation program for just two words, he had called Akira Tokaido to his workstation to interpret the first time they had appeared. The young Japanese American had told him exactly what he'd suspected the letters meant.

"Access denied," Tokaido had said. Though not thoroughly versed in kanji, the young man was striving to learn all he could of his heritage. This one was easy.

. Kurtzman ignored the impulse to bring his fist down on the keyboard. Instead, he cleared the monitor and started again. He had hacked his way into the Japanese police and military-intelligence files the night before when he'd been trying to identify the Great Hikari. The Japanese computer coders were among the best in the world, and gaining entry had not been easy. Then, once he'd finally broken the code, he'd still come up empty on Hikari. It appeared that the government in Tokyo knew no more about the Followers of the Truth cult leader than anyone else.

So Kurtzman had decided to go after the identity of the man who had been with Hikari in the news tape, the man with the clear eyes that said he wasn't a follower. And during the brief few seconds during which he was changing his entry, the Japanese had changed their access codes.

Kurtzman tapped another entry attempt onto the keyboard and sat back waiting for the information to be processed. He wondered what were the odds of both police and military records and intelligence departments performing periodic computer-file security-code changes at exactly that time. If he had time, he could use his probability program to find out. But he didn't have time. Whatever the odds against such a thing happening, they had come through. Both codes had been changed, he'd been automatically cut off from the files and he'd been trying to get back in ever since.

Footsteps came up the ramp behind the computer genius. Kurtzman turned, not sure who he expected to see as he looked up.

But whomever it was he expected, it wasn't Carl Lyons.

Kurtzman sat back in his chair. Past the Able Team leader, on the other side of the glass divider, he could see Schwarz, Blancanales and a Stony Man pilot trainee talking to Barbara Price in the communications room. That meant that Able Team had to have just returned from New York. The pilot was standing by to take them out again as soon as they learned whatever it was they needed to know from Kurtzman.

When a mission was in progress, greetings were swift and simple, if not dispensed with altogether around the Farm. The first words out of Lyons's mouth were "We need you to run down a name, Bear. The name is Carver."

Kurtzman waited for more. When he didn't get it, he said, "Go ahead."

"That's it," Lyons said. "I know it's not much."

"Carver isn't quite as bad as Smith or Jones, but it isn't too far off, either. I'm sorry, Carl, you'll need to give me something to narrow it down."

"My hunch is that he's working for the cult but not one of the Great Hikari's anesthetized craniums," Lyons said.

Kurtzman thought of the man in the news clip again. "That's nice, but it does nothing to narrow down the field."

Lyons blew air out between his pursed lips. "Okay, let me run the details by you and see if we can think of something." He leaned back against the rail. "This Carver has some position of authority in the cult. The spaced-out wackos of the cult think he's an archangel. I've got a pair of brain-dead bozos stashed downstairs in the east office with a couple of security guys if you'd like to hear it from the horse's mouth."

"You brought them here to the Farm?" Kurtzman asked.

Lyons nodded. "Don't get your hemorrhoids in an uproar. They were blindfolded."

"They're cooperating?" Kurtzman asked.

The Able Team leader nodded again. "I don't know what all they've been through, but I think these guys have had weirder things done to them than getting blindfolded. Anyway, I didn't know what else to do with them. They're almost like children. Children who will kill on command, granted, but sometimes like regular children, too. Our pilot knows some guy who's a cult deprogrammer. He and Barb are trying to contact him now."

Kurtzman glanced back through the glass divider and saw Jock Reno, the pilot, on Barbara Price's phone. "Where does this Carver come in?"

"George and Casey—they're the cult guys downstairs—they think he's this archangel the Great Hikari sent to watch over them. Evidently the cult has lesser angels, too. Carver is also the one who told them they're going to let sarin loose in a subway." He paused for a breath, then answered the obvious questions without being asked. "They don't know when or where yet."

Kurtzman shook his head. "Carl, it can't be done. Carver is too common a name. There are thousands of people named Carver in this country alone. And there will be thousands of others from Canada, Great Britain, Australia—any English-speaking nation." He turned and lifted his coffee cup to his lips. "And to make things worse, it could always be an alias. It might even be a nickname." Kurtzman set his cup back down on the console. "Are you sure Carver is his real name?"

"No." Lyons frowned. "I know it's a long shot, Bear, but I'm at a dead end. The cult members downstairs—Pol picked what was left of their brains clean. They don't have anything else to offer. Can you give it a try?"

"I'm trying to ID the Great Hikari through his sidekick right now," Kurtzman said, "and I'm not having much luck."

"How about one of your people?" Lyons asked. He glanced down the bank of computers. "How about Akira?"

Kurtzman followed his gaze. "He's wrapped up in computer research." He frowned. "Go ask Carmen. It won't hurt for her to pull off the serial killer for a little while."

Lyons grinned. "Thanks, Bear."

"You're welcome," Kurtzman said. He turned back to his keyboard as Lyons headed toward the redhead on the other side of Akira Tokaido. There was a way back into the Japanese police and military computer files, a way past the new security codes. He just had to find it.

And he would.

CARL LYONS HAD an uneasy feeling as he left Kurtzman's computer console. Something the man in the wheelchair had mentioned, or maybe something he himself had said or maybe just some passing thought he'd had in the past few minutes had settled in his unconscious mind. Right now, whatever it was, was trying to surface. But it wasn't having any more luck than Kurtzman had so far trying to break the new Japanese computer codes.

Lyons tried to clear his mind. The thought would come when it was ready. There was no sense pushing it. That never worked.

The Able Team leader looked down the bank of computers and saw the vivacious redhead seated between Tokaido and Hunt Wethers. He had always liked Carmen Delahunt. She was a cop at heart, just like him. She came from an old-line FBI background, a period in the history of the Bureau when J. Edgar Hoover might not still have been running the show but when his ghost still hovered over the organization. Delahunt had received her baptism of fire during the days when the special agents were cops rather than the politicians they had become in the past few years. Which was one of the reasons Lyons suspected Hal Brognola had stolen her away from the FBI for Stony Man Farm.

Delahunt had been engrossed in whatever it was she was working on ever since Lyons had entered the computer room. Now, as he moved away from Kurtzman's work area past that of Akira Tokaido, the Able Team leader saw her glance his way. She looked immediately back to the screen.

"Carmen," Lyons said as he walked up behind the woman.

"Just a minute, Carl," the woman said. "Let me get to a stopping point." She continued to type.

Moments later Delahunt stopped what she was doing and swiveled to face him. "What can I do for you?" she asked, her smile vibrant and intoxicating.

"I'm in a situation where I need some help with religious crazies. Can you break away and give me a hand?"

"Sure. What do you need?"

Lyons told her about Carver.

Delahunt expressed the same doubts that Kurtzman had.

"We've got to start somewhere," Lyons said. "How many Carvers are there in the United States?"

Delahunt turned back to her computer and typed. A few seconds later a number appeared in yellow.

Lyons didn't even want to look at it.

"It's only an estimate," Delahunt said with mock cheerfulness. "There might be a few thousand less. Or more."

"Okay," Lyons replied. "I see your point. There's too many to start checking them all out one by one."

"Too many for this lifetime," Delahunt agreed. "I can always get started and try but—good night, Carl—I'd *rather* look for that needle in the haystack."

"Damn!" Akira Tokaido said to Lyons's side. "I cut myself trying to fish a paperclip out of my printer."

Lyons turned to see the young man clutching his hand.

"You okay?" Delahunt asked. She had already pulled a small bottle of disinfectant and a plastic adhesive strip from her purse.

"Yes, I'll survive," Tokaido said in disgust. "But it's embarrassing to cut myself up as if I were the Christmas turkey."

Lyons's subconscious mind suddenly went wild. What was it Tokaido had just said? It was linked to whatever it was that had bothered him as he was leaving Kurtzman's computer area. Cut himself up like a Christmas turkey?

People sometimes got adages and expressions a little twisted, especially when excited, in pain or in shock.

You didn't *cut* a Christmas turkey. You *carved* it.

Cut. Carve. Carver. Someone who carved the turkey could be called a carver, but that wouldn't be their real name. It would be a nickname.

Like Kurtzman had said. Carver might be a nickname.

And that narrowed things down considerably.

"Carmen, let's assume that Carver is a nickname. Can you check that out?" Lyons asked.

"Sure. I can scan files for the name Carver as either an a.k.a. or nickname." She turned back to the keyboard. "There are far fewer people who actually use aliases than there are real people named Carver, and as a nickname there should be even less. I'll go FBI first. It'll take a minute or two."

"Want me to get us some coffee?"

"Hey, I'm a cop, aren't I?" She began to type.

Lyons watched her for a second, then descended the ramp and opened the door into the communications room. Reno was still on the phone as the Able Team leader crossed the room to the coffee maker.

"Jock's gotten hold of the deprogrammer he knows," Schwarz said. "Guy's in Tennessee. Barb's sending the security guys to deliver George and Casey to him."

Lyons nodded. He poured two cups of black coffee, turned and hurried back to the computer room.

Delahunt swiveled in her chair to face Lyons as he mounted the ramp once more. A smile covered the woman's face as she smoothed the pleats in her skirt with both hands, then took the coffee cup from the Able Team leader. "Sometimes you get lucky," she said. She pointed to the screen, then took a sip.

Lyons stared at the monitor. There were at least two hundred names on the screen, each having gone by an alias of Carver or having had Carver as a nickname at one time or another.

"That's still too many names to run down," Lyons said.

Delahunt took another sip of coffee and shook her hair out of her eyes. "Look closer," she said. "Where I left the curser."

Lyons's eyes traveled to the name next to the small blinking rectangle. "Wayman, Eugene Freeman, a.k.a. Willie Freeman, a.k.a. Gene Freeman, a.k.a. Finley Porter. Nicknames: Bo, Slash, Carver."

"Okay," the Able Team leader said. "He's used

the name. What makes him different than the other 199?''

"How many of them currently live in Brooklyn less than a block from where you found this Casey Balforth?" Delahunt asked.

Lyons set his coffee cup on Delahunt's console as his eyes flew to the address on the screen. It had to be one of the brownstones they had passed as they'd walked toward Balforth's house from the van.

Lyons jotted the numbers down on a piece of scratch paper. "Carmen, thanks," he said.

"One cop to another," Delahunt replied. "Don't mention it." She wasn't sure Lyons heard her. By the time the words left her mouth, he was down the ramp and heading through the door to the communications room.

Sierra Leone

DAWN BROKE SWIFTLY over the Loma Mountains in northeastern Sierra Leone. Tropical birds sang their morning songs from the treetops. Unseen in the bushes and rocks, daytime animals rose and stretched while nocturnal creatures hurried home to their nests.

A mile from the training camp, Bolan sat on the edge of an outcropping waiting for Bobcat Buchanan to return. Loko—the RUF bandit the Executioner had pursued through the underwater tunnel—and Margai sat on the ground at his sides, their hands bound behind their backs. Certain bits of intelligence gained from the two men during the ride back to camp had changed the Executioner's and Buchanan's plans.

In true criminal form, both Margai and Loko had been more than ready to snitch on others to further their own position. First Bolan had learned that, as he'd suspected, Margai was a bandit posing as a Sierra Leone commando candidate in order to obtain intel on the government's plans to wipe out the RUF. That had come as no shock after what the Executioner had already seen. What *had* surprised him to some extent was what both men had told him about Spencer Kiethley. Since no one had actually seen Kiethley die, Bolan had known there was a chance, however slight, that the man might still be alive.

The Executioner smiled slightly as he waited in the early-morning light. Both Margai and Loko swore Kiethley had been taken prisoner rather than killed.

Bolan heard the sound of the Jeep CJ-5's engine coming up the road and stood, stretching. Buchanan had gone on into camp to get things started for the day and pick up certain items of equipment they would need before the day was out—among them, Bolan's Beretta 93-R. The soldier-journalist would leave the unit's training in the hands of the Gurkhas, with Dax in charge of the camp.

According to Loko and Margai, RUF bandits had taken Kiethley prisoner, learned that he was an American journalist and planned to hold him for ransom. Then an Arab had approached the Front through a contact in Freetown with an offer to buy Kiethley from them. Since the amount offered was more than the RUF had planned to ask from Kiethley's *Retained Warrior* associates in America, the bandits had taken the offer with no questions asked.

The bottom line was that Margai and Loko knew where Kiethley was being held, and they would take Bolan and Buchanan there in exchange for their own freedom.

The CJ-5 rounded a curve in the road, and Buchanan pulled the vehicle to a halt. Bolan saw the barrels of two AK-47s sticking up in the air, their stocks jammed between the front seats. Buchanan had changed from his shorts and tank top into khakis and an OD T-shirt. He left the engine running as Bolan jerked the two RUF bandits to their feet and half helped, half threw them into the back seat of the Jeep. He climbed over the side into the front, shifting a duffel bag—extra clothing for him and Buchanan—out of the way.

Buchanan reached under the front seat and came up with Bolan's Beretta, still in the shoulder rig. He handed it to the Executioner, threw the Jeep into gear and took off down the mountain road.

It was late morning when they reached the outskirts of Freetown. Bolan had changed into his own khakis during the drive and wore a light, short-sleeved safari jacket that covered the Beretta, Desert Eagle and Crossada knife. Buchanan had donned a tropical-weight shirt over his T-shirt that hid his .45, spare magazines and the subhilt fighting knife. The AK-47s had been stashed in the duffel bag.

The Executioner drew an all-purpose multitool from his pocket and flipped out the small knife blade. Twisting to the back seat, he said, "Turn around. Both of you."

The RUF men did as ordered.

Bolan sliced through the leather strips that bound their hands. "Remember this, though," he said. "Make one funny move, and I'll cut more than the restraints." He tapped the Crossada through his jacket.

Both bandits had seen the huge blade, and both knew what it could do. They nodded.

"Now point out the way," the Executioner said.

Margai gave most of the directions, guiding the vehicle on into the central area of town on the deeply potholed road. They passed several old colonial wooden buildings. The streets were crowded with people and cars, and sewage flowed with the traffic along the open drains.

Freetown had been built on a series of hills, and the nose of the Jeep was constantly heading up or down. They entered the Basket Market at the bottom of Lamina Sankoh Street and passed stands and stalls selling not only basketware but also spoons, gourds, rattles and other juju medicine. Cutting west, Margai directed Buchanan to the suburb of Aberdeen. They passed several expensive hotels along the beach, then drove a mile or so into the countryside.

"I would pull to the side of the road at this point," Margai said. "We are close and should talk."

Buchanan stopped on the narrow shoulder.

The bandit pointed to the top of a hill a quarter mile ahead. The tops of several houses were barely visible on the horizon. "It is an exclusive new housing addition," he said. "We delivered your Mr. Kiethley to one of the houses."

"To the Arab?" Bolan asked.

"To the Arab," Margai confirmed. "But he had Oriental men with him."

Bolan nodded. Japanese again. It *had* to be the Followers of the Truth. He pulled a set of binoculars from the duffel bag and held them to his eyes. He could see the tops of the houses better but nothing else. Dropping the binoculars, he looked across the road and saw a thickly forested area. "Bobcat," he said, "pull the Jeep into those trees and out of sight. You stay here with Loko." The Executioner got out of the vehicle. "Margai and I are going to recon the house. Wait for us."

Buchanan nodded.

Bolan let Margai lead the way up the side of the hill using patches of trees as sporadic cover. When they reached the crest of the hill, they stopped inside a clump of knotted scrub trees. Bolan dropped to his belly, and Margai followed suit. Below, on the other side of the hill, the Executioner could see several acres of development. He wasn't familiar with the Sierra Leone real-estate market, but none of the houses he saw below could have been built anywhere in the U.S. for less than half a million dollars. There was money behind whoever had purchased the house where Kiethley was being kept, big money.

Bolan pressed the binoculars against his eyes, turned them toward the lone entrance-exit that led from the road into the residential area, then aimed them back at the houses. "Which one is it?" he asked.

Margai pointed out a large white two-story structure three blocks from the entrance to the addition. Bolan studied it through the binoculars. Several vehicles were parked in the circular driveway out front, which meant the house could be heavily guarded.

The Executioner lowered the binoculars and studied the neighborhood. The approach to the house would be open, and if guards were posted—and they most certainly would be—he'd be spotted. He glanced to Margai at his side, then back toward where Buchanan and Loko waited. What would be the best plan of attack? He didn't trust either one of the bandits. At least not enough to take them along when he went after Kiethley. He could use Buchanan's gun, but that would mean no one was left to guard the RUF hardmen. And if he took the two bandits into the house, they might turn on him and Buchanan in the middle of the firefight.

Bolan knew he couldn't risk that, knew he and Buchanan couldn't baby-sit the RUF men and fight the Arab and his henchmen at the same time. Letting the bandits go at this point was equally out of the question—the story about Kiethley being alive might be a complete fabrication created simply to assure the RUF men's freedom. Margai could have pointed out the house in the distance at random for all Bolan knew.

As he contemplated the dilemma, Bolan watched a truck drive down the road and pull through the entrance to the neighborhood. It stopped at the mailbox in front of the first house. A hand snaked out the window to deposit mail, and suddenly the Executioner had the answer to both of his problems.

He knew how he would approach the house without being seen. And he knew what he would do with the bandits while he and Buchanan attacked.

Bolan reached over and grabbed a handful of Margai's shirt.

The startled bandit turned to face him.

"Listen to me," the Executioner said. "Listen good and listen fast, because we don't have much time. We're going down there and hijack that mail truck. I want you with me the whole way. Every time I look to my side, I want to see you. You understand?"

Margai nodded.

"Good," Bolan said, nodding back. "Because if I don't, I'll kill you."

The Executioner scrambled to his feet and pulled the bandit up with him. They sprinted down the side of the hill as the mail truck moved to the next house. Bolan knew he had to grab it before it got close to the house where Kiethley was being held. If curious eyes spotted him taking it, the truck would lose all value.

Bolan and Margai got to the vehicle just as it

pulled up to the box in front of the second house. The Executioner grabbed the wrist of the hand holding the mail as it came through the window. With his other hand he thrust the Beretta into the truck and shoved it under the startled driver's nose.

"Put the truck in neutral," Bolan commanded.

"What?"

"Put it in neutral!"

The man's hand shook as if he had palsy as he took the stick out of gear.

"Now put the parking brake on," Bolan directed.

This time the man didn't have to be told twice.

Bolan jerked the Beretta back out of the truck and hooked a hard left through the window. His knuckles cracked against the driver's chin, and the man's eyelids closed.

The Executioner opened the door, lifted the driver out of the seat and shoved him to the floor between the seats. He stepped up, scooted across the steering wheel and lifted the man's limp body again. Motioning for Margai to follow, Bolan carried the mailman back into the cargo area and laid him gently on the ground.

"Lie down next to him," Bolan ordered Margai.

The bandit shrugged and did as he'd been told.

Bolan drew the Crossada knife and cut the cord from several stacks of mail. Jamming the fighting knife back in its sheath, he used the cords to bind both men. Returning to the cab area, he took a seat, threw the mail truck in gear and cut a U-turn out of the residential area.

Buchanan was a little surprised to see a postal-service vehicle enter the wooded area. But the wisecracking soldier-journalist wasn't without words for long. "What, you don't like the Jeep?" he asked, grinning. But he sensed what was happening and didn't have to be told what he should do next. He handed Bolan the duffel bag with the rifles.

Bolan waited as Buchanan pushed Loko up into the truck and took him into the cargo area, then started back toward the residential area. He heard the sounds of more cord being cut, and a moment later Buchanan returned and took the passenger's seat as Bolan turned into the housing area's entrance.

The Executioner drove moderately as he entered the exclusive housing area, turning the corner onto the street where the house Margai had pointed out was located. "Get the AKs ready," he told Buchanan.

Buchanan opened the duffel bag, produced the rifles and jammed a 30-round magazine up each one. He handed Bolan several extra mags and jammed more into his pants pockets.

Three houses away Bolan stomped the accelerator and shot the mail truck forward. He drove up into the circular driveway, navigated the vehicle between a Mercedes and a Lincoln and onto the grass in front of the porch.

The next-to-last thing the Executioner saw before the mail truck hit the front door was a startled face in the window next to it.

The very last thing was a rifle barrel breaking the glass and poking through the hole.

Somalia

McCARTER DUCKED instinctively behind the wheel of the Wagoneer as the bullets flew through the windshield and windows like angry bees. The other Phoenix Force commandos and Captain Jack did the same.

"Get out and take cover!" McCarter yelled as he fumbled for the door latch with one hand and drew the .40 S&W Browning Hi-Power with the other. He heard the back doors open as he dived from the vehicle.

The attack came from across the street. McCarter crawled behind the Wagoneer's engine block as more rounds exploded. He paused for a deep breath as James, Encizo and Captain Jack moved in next to him. Manning and Hawkins had exited the vehicle on the other side and taken refuge behind an aged Ford F-100 pickup parked directly behind the Wagoneer.

McCarter drew the other Browning—the 9 mm— with his left hand. Peering over the hood of the Wagoneer, he saw another abandoned building. A sign in the front yard proclaimed it to be the United Nations Annex.

Several people shooting rifles were visible in the windows of the annex. McCarter picked one and lined up the Browning's sights. As he pulled the trigger, he noted that the eyes at which he fired were almond shaped; the man was Oriental.

The Phoenix Force leader fired a double-tap of .40-caliber slugs into the window and heard a groan. The shooter disappeared below the windowsill and a Howa Type 64 7.62 mm automatic rifle fell out of the building onto the grass.

McCarter frowned. The face in the window had been Oriental. The Howa was a Japanese rifle, and an unusual weapon to find here in Somalia. Again there was the Japanese connection.

More rounds blew from the building into the Wagoneer. At least one struck the radiator, and a hiss of steam erupted from the hood as water drained to the pavement. The other men of Phoenix Force returned fire, rising over the Wagoneer and pickup long enough to pump off a round or two, then dropping back to cover as 7.62 mm rounds answered their shots.

McCarter scanned the area across the street and quickly evaluated the situation. The enemy, concentrated in the UN Annex building, had Phoenix Force effectively pinned down. That had to change. Someone had to get to the side or behind the annex to divert fire.

The Briton studied the layout on the other side of the street. To the right of the annex was a landscaped wooded area. If he could make it across the street to the trees, he'd have a fair chance of darting from trunk to trunk and circling the building without taking a bullet.

As he considered the possibilities, McCarter felt a tug on his sleeve and he turned to see Captain Jack. "Give me a gun," the warlord said.

The Phoenix Force leader considered it. He had made a deal with the man, but he still didn't know how far to trust him. On the other hand the team could use all the help they could get. The warlord wasn't likely to turn on them now—not while their objectives still coincided.

A hard smile crept across the Phoenix Force leader's face. Right now the objectives of Captain Jack and Phoenix Force not only coincided, but were also identical. They were all trying to stay alive.

McCarter handed him the 9 mm Browning, then leaned past him. "T.J.! Gary!" he yelled at the men behind the pickup.

Both men turned to face him.

The Briton lowered his voice. "I'm going to circle," he said just loud enough for the other men to hear. "As soon as I move, hit them hard. I'll need cover."

The two men nodded. James and Encizo, on just the other side of Captain Jack, also heard. "I'll go with you," James said.

"As will I," Captain Jack added.

Again McCarter hesitated, but only for a moment. He had given the man a weapon. He might as well make use of him. And if he, James and the warlord could all make it to the rear of the building, they would have the enemy in an equal cross fire—three in the front and three in the back. He nodded. "Let's go, then."

McCarter rose suddenly, sprinting past the gap between the Wagoneer and the pickup. The men in the UN Annex saw him move and fired several bursts that hit the pavement around his feet, sending chips of concrete and white dust dancing into the air. Encizo, Manning and Hawkins opened up with cover fire. Directly behind him, barely audible over the gunfire, McCarter could hear the running footsteps of Calvin James and Captain Jack.

The Phoenix Force leader dived headfirst behind the pickup, sliding to a halt between Manning and Hawkins. James and Captain Jack crowded in next to him and the gunfire from both sides continued. McCarter looked under the truck. The trees stood on the other side of the street approximately fifteen yards from the pickup. That meant fifteen yards in the open. Fifteen yards that wouldn't be a lot different than being a duck in a shooting gallery, but he could see no other option.

Turning to Manning, the Briton whispered, "On three." Manning told Hawkins, who passed the word on to Encizo, still behind the Wagoneer.

"One," McCarter said, inching toward the front bumper of the pickup. Right behind him, James duck-walked along the side of the pickup. Captain Jack followed. "Two," the Briton whispered. With the .40-caliber S&W in his right hand he reached out and grabbed the bumper with his left. "Three!"

McCarter pulled hard on the bumper and shoved

off with his legs, darting around the hood of the pickup and into the street. Once more he heard the footsteps of Captain Jack and James right behind him.

A barrage of fire from behind the two vehicles crossed the street, splattering the face of the UN Annex and slowing the response from the men in the building. The Phoenix Force leader was halfway to the trees before the return fire started. And even then, it was hurried. The assault thrown out by Manning, Hawkins and Encizo kept the men in the annex off balance, and their rounds flew high past McCarter and the others.

McCarter made it safely into the trees, taking refuge behind a thick trunk. By now the men in the annex had corrected their aim and round after round thumped into the wood at the Phoenix Force leader's back. More bullets flew past to cut leaves and twigs from the branches of other trees.

Turning to his side, McCarter saw that both Captain Jack and Calvin James had made it to safety behind their own tree trunks. But that was only the first step. Spotting another thick trunk ten yards deeper into the wooded area, the Briton took a deep breath and darted from cover. Rounds flew through the trees again, whizzing past his ear like enraged hornets. Reaching the tree, the Phoenix Force leader took refuge once more.

One by one, tree by tree, McCarter, James and Captain Jack hopscotched their way farther into the woods and along the side of the UN Annex building.

The gunfire from Encizo, Hawkins and Manning continued across the street.

The Phoenix Force leader cast a glance around the sides of a tree. By now he and the others had worked past the point where anyone at the front of the annex would have a shot at them. But rounds continued to strike the trees. That could only mean that some of the enemy had abandoned the front windows for locations along the side of the building. The Orientals were following them toward the annex's rear, which was exactly what he'd hoped they would do. The enemy was dividing, no longer able to focus an assault in one direction.

The trees curved around the rear of the annex, and McCarter led the way, again darting from cover to cover until he, James and Captain Jack were at the rear of the building. He and the others had held their fire during the trip through the trees, but now they opened up with all they had.

McCarter saw two more heads drop as he and James each took out one. The Phoenix Force leader shook his head. Every man he had seen so far was Oriental. Sure there were Orientals in Africa, but this many together as a team? McCarter knew there was a Somalian connection to the cult through Kiethley. But what was it?

McCarter stared out from the trees at the back of the annex building. Two entrances led into the building, one to his left, the other to the right. Both doors were a good ten yards from the trees, which meant another precarious sprint under fire. He, James and

Captain Jack would have no cover at all until they reached the short concrete entryway walls that shot out two feet on both sides of the doors. Even then cover would be minimal, as the walls had decorative holes the size of volleyballs cut into them, making them look like the honeycombs of giant bees.

What worried McCarter was the time it would take to open the doors. They would have to slow down and be almost-stationary targets, which meant anyone on the second floor above could simply lean out the windows and shoot down.

But McCarter could see no other alternative. If they didn't go in the enemy could hole up inside the building until Somalian authorities arrived to arrest anyone on either side who hadn't been shot.

McCarter maneuvered to a tree where both Captain Jack and James could hear him. "We go on three again," he said. "Calvin, take the door to the right. Jack, you and I will go left. We've got to hit them hard and fast, then we've got to get out of here before the cops come."

James had been thinking along the same lines. "I've been expecting to see our buddy Captain Berber for the last ten minutes," he said, then frowned. "But what bothers me even more are those doors, David. They open out. It's not like we can sprint up and just push our way through. We'll have to come to a complete stop and—"

"And hope we don't catch a few bullets in the top of the head." McCarter nodded. "I know. If you have a better idea, I'm ready to hear it."

James shook his head.

"Then get ready," McCarter said. He turned back to face the rear of the UN Annex. Then, with another countdown he was leading the way under a storm of rounds toward the back door.

The Phoenix Force leader snapped two quick rounds up at the second-story windows as he sprinted toward the blue steel door. Out of the corner of his eye he could see James heading across the grass to the door on the right. Behind him McCarter heard Captain Jack's heavy breaths as the warlord followed.

McCarter was ten feet away from the blue steel door, close enough to see the steel security mesh in the window in the upper half, when the cold, lonely thought struck him.

The door might be locked.

But by then there was no turning back. McCarter sprinted on under the gunfire from the second floor. He reached the hole-ridden concrete entryway wall, slammed into the blue steel door, grasped the handle and pulled, again wondering if the bolt might be locked.

It was.

CHAPTER THIRTEEN

New York

The van was still parked in the small airport parking lot when Jock Reno dropped off Able Team in the Harrier. Schwarz commandeered the steering wheel. Blancanales slid the side door open and got in back, and Lyons took the shotgun seat. Ten minutes later they had left the area and were cruising through the Brooklyn Polish district of Greenpoint.

On the fringes of Park Slope, Schwarz turned the van into the Jamaican and Dominican neighborhoods. They passed brownstones, limestones and row houses built a hundred years earlier and entered a Victorian area that dated from the turn of the century. Turning onto a road paralleling the Brooklyn Bridge, they entered the villagelike atmosphere of Brooklyn Heights.

Wayman Eugene Freeman lived on the fourth flour of a renovated mansion facing the East River. What at the turn of the century had been a single-family dwelling suitable for a king had gone to ruin by the

1950s and sold cheap to young speculators in the 1970s. Remodeled into fashionable condominiums, each individual unit now sold for perhaps ten times what the owner had paid.

Schwarz pulled the van to a halt down the block and killed the engine. "So, Ironman, we just go in, say, 'Good day, Mr. Freeman, we'd like to ask you a few questions about all the people you and your little Japanese potentate friend are planning to gas in the subway'?"

Basically it was the same question Lyons had asked himself during the flight back to Brooklyn. Kurtzman had run him a hard copy of Freeman's rap sheet, and he had studied it while they were in the air. Violence was no stranger to Wayman Freeman; he'd been arrested for strong-arm robbery, murder conspiracy and most everything else in between.

Lyons needed to talk to the man, not kill him. And an up-front assault stood a good chance of forcing Freeman into a fight. The former LAPD detective glanced at the date of birth listed on the page. He knew from experience that Freeman had reached an age when many career criminals make a decision to die fighting rather than return to prison. They'd decided they'd done all the time they intended to do and preferred death to incarceration.

"Let's go scout it out first," the Able Team leader finally said. "Then we'll decide."

"Suits me," Schwarz said.

Blancanales nodded his agreement.

Able Team got out of the van. They had changed out of their suits and sport coats during the flight in order to blend in better in Brooklyn Heights. All three now wore jeans, T-shirts and athletic shoes. Blancanales had donned a faded leather bomber jacket, Lyons wore a khaki bush jacket and Schwarz had gone with a jean jacket.

There was more reason for the outerwear than fashion or weather. The jackets covered the team's weapons.

Lyons looked out over the East River as they walked along the crowded sidewalk past painters, street musicians and vendors selling pretzels and bagels. The Manhattan skyline was the prominent attraction, and the Able Team leader saw tourists snapping photos as they emitted oohs and ahhs. The trio passed a short shopping strip that housed a butcher's shop, a bakery and a hardware outlet that all looked as if they'd been run by families for generations.

Able Team came to the restored mansion and walked up the sidewalk. Two men and a woman walked out of the front entrance, none of them stopping to give Lyons, Schwarz or Blancanales a second look. Lyons led the way inside the building and up the steps.

The renovators had kept the Victorian flavor of the house. What had once been the mansion's entryway and living room had been converted into a common sitting area. The decor included ornately carved chairs and love seats, velvet curtains drawn back from the windows and fringed lamp shades. Lyons walked to the black registry on the wall.

Freeman's apartment was just off the stairs on the fourth floor. The team climbed the stairs warily, their hands close to their guns. There was no reason Freeman should expect them, but he was getting close to a major operation—gassing a subway. He might be wary anyway.

On the fourth floor they walked down the hall, waiting as an elderly woman carrying a newspaper in one hand and a leashed poodle in the other came out and hurried past them toward the stairs.

As soon as she was out of sight, Lyons took up position to the left of Freeman's door, his back against the wall. Schwarz and Blancanales took the right. The Able Team leader rapped backhanded several times on the door with his left hand, his right curled around the rubber grips on the Colt Python.

He got no response.

Lyons knocked again, then again. Glancing across the door, he saw Schwarz shrug, then nod at the door with a questioning look.

Lyons nodded.

Schwarz fished into the breast pocket of his jean jacket and came out with a leather case not unlike those that accommodate manicure sets. But unzipping it, he revealed a set of professional lock picks rather than nail files and cuticle trimmers. Kneeling on the floor in front of the door, Schwarz went to work, and thirty seconds later the tumblers rolled into line.

Thirty-one seconds later the door opened.

Lyons went in first, the Python up and leading. He found himself inside a large living room bare of furniture. Odds and ends scattered the soiled carpet: a discarded magazine here, an empty can of cleaning solvent there. Trash of all types indicated that someone had just moved out. Hurriedly.

The Able Team leader stuck his head around the corner into a small kitchen and saw a similar story with abandoned utensils and dirty dishes. Blancanales and Schwarz had left the kitchen to him and moved to the hall on the other side of the living room. Lyons saw Blancanales in the bathroom halfway down the hall. Schwarz had gone on into the bedroom.

Blancanales was reading the label on a prescription-medicine bottle as Lyons passed. "The script's for Gene Freeman, Ironman," he said. "It's the right place. At least it was the right place."

Lyons nodded, shoved the Python back into his holster and joined Schwarz in the bedroom. It was the same story there with the forsaken items consisting primarily of worn-out clothing. The place had obviously been deserted, fast.

Lyons thought back to dishes in the kitchen. There had been food left on some of them, but it hadn't rotted badly yet. Freeman—or at least someone—had been here within the past day or two.

"Hey, Ironman," Schwarz said suddenly, dropping to a squatting position on the carpet. He dug through a cigar box filled with junk jewelry and other odds and ends and came up with several photographs. As he shuffled through the pictures, Lyons saw a grin break out on his face. "Oh, baby," Schwarz said.

"What's that?" Blancanales asked as he entered the room.

"Take a look." Schwarz held out one of the photos.

Blancanales looked at the picture, then turned his smile up to Lyons, as well. "Well, I've got the answer to why my interrogation of Ira Rook left me feeling uneasy," he said. "He *was* holding out on me."

Lyons held out his hand, and Blancanales handed the picture to him.

The big ex-cop looked down at the photo and saw a Caucasian man wearing a kimono. Kneeling in front of the man the world knew as the Great Hikari, the Caucasian was obviously receiving some sort of blessing.

"Recognize the guy on his knees?" Schwarz asked.

Lyons nodded. "And I'd say Rook was holding out even more than you thought." He stuck the photo in his pocket and started for the door.

"This could turn out to be even more fun than last time," Blancanales said.

"It could," Schwarz agreed as they stepped out into the hall. "That smile on Ironman's face—I saw it in a cartoon one time. The cat had just captured the mouse and was sharpening his knife on his fork."

Blancanales laughed. "He does look happy," he said as they tried to keep up with their leader going down the steps. "But then, how many times do you get to slap around an old enemy like Ira Rook twice in one mission?"

Sierra Leone

THE FRONT DOOR, the trim around it and most of the door frame crashed inward as Bolan guided the mail truck across the porch and into the house. Wood splintered, and wallboard burst into dusty chunks.

The Executioner dived from the driver's side of the truck, Buchanan from the other. Bolan readied the AK-47 as he hit the ground in the house's antechamber. An Oriental—the same man he had seen in the window only seconds before driving the truck into the house—now appeared nearby, holding a 7.62 mm Howa.

The Executioner's AK-47 beat the man to the punch, peppering the gunner's chest, leaving tiny red holes where the rounds entered. In the second that followed, the red circles doubled in size, as did the Oriental's shocked eyes. Dropping the Howa, the man fell forward onto his face, his eyes frozen wide for all eternity.

On the other side of the truck Bolan heard Buchanan open up with his own AK-47. The soldier-journalist held the trigger back, sending a full-auto blast into two more men who had entered the foyer. The men danced like the marionettes of some crazed puppet master as the rounds struck home, then collapsed to the tile floor next to a staircase leading to the second floor.

Bolan wondered at the preponderance of Orientals as he took a second to survey the surroundings. Margai and Loko had said that an Arab had "bought" Kiethley from them. But they hadn't mentioned Orientals. The cult had members on three continents now, but the majority were still Japanese. Was that the reason? Pushing the unanswered questions to the back burner for the time being, Bolan wondered briefly what room in the house held Spencer Kiethley. He had no idea, and the only way to find out was to conduct a systematic search.

Before the Executioner could organize his thoughts further, a short squat man toting another of the Howas suddenly appeared in a side door to the entryway. He held the Japanese rifle against his shoulder and took aim at Bolan.

The Executioner cut him down with a 3-round burst. The shooter was thrown back against the wall of the foyer, then slid down to a sitting position in a pool of his own blood.

To the left of the staircase Bolan saw a formal dining room. A long dining table, chairs, buffets and other items carefully carved from dark mahogany furnished the room. The door through which the squatty man had come led into a hall.

To the right of the stairs the Executioner saw the living room. Beyond that a glass wall led to a conservatory, stocked with plants. Through the glass wall he could see the long picture window that formed the back wall to the house and, through it, the backyard.

"Take the dining room!" Bolan ordered Buchanan, then hurried into the living room. Behind him he heard Buchanan immediately open fire, and was turning to assist when three more men carrying Howas lunged into the living room from the conservatory.

Bolan dropped to one knee, letting a swarm of rounds fly over his head. He braced the stock of the AK-47 on his shoulder and held the trigger back. A figure eight of bullets cut through the trio of attackers.

The Executioner walked cautiously toward the conservatory, stepping over the bodies of the three men as he went. He stepped off the carpet of the living room onto the multicolored tile that held the potted plants, and stopped. He could see the backyard clearly now through the plate-glass window. It looked as clear as the conservatory.

Glancing left down the long narrow room, the Executioner saw a door he knew had to lead back into the area of the house where Buchanan had gone; through it he could hear gunfire. At the other end of the room was a single step leading downward to a thick wooden door. The door stood open, and from where he stood Bolan could see what looked like part of a den. The AK-47 aimed ahead of him, he started that way.

The Executioner had taken only two steps when a sudden flash of movement in the backyard through the plate-glass window caught his attention. He whirled, and the glass shattered as a man in the back-yard pulled the trigger of his rifle. The rounds burst into the conservatory in a flurry of sparkling glass slivers to strike the wall just to one side of Bolan.

The Executioner returned fire, his own rounds shattering more of the plate glass before drilling into the gunner's face, punching him out of sight below the windows.

Buchanan's AK-47 continued to chatter from the other end of the house as Bolan hurried to the step in front of the thick wooden door. Taking up a po-sition against the wall, he shoved a fresh magazine into the rifle. Risking a quick look around the corner, the Executioner saw no one in the den. Cautiously he took the single step down and moved into the room.

The den was large and comfortably furnished with overstuffed couches and armchairs, and its walls were paneled with knotty pine. A wet bar with a slotted swinging half door in the counter sat just in-side the room to the Executioner's right.

Bolan saw another quick flurry of movement through the slats as he passed. Twisting at the hips, he fired the AK-47 through the door, the slats exploding as if they'd been struck by a sledgehammer. Short slivers of wood blew through the air like twigs in a windstorm. The door fell from its hinges.

The big American cleared the rest of the den. Finding nothing, he retraced his steps into the conservatory. Moving past the living room, he took the door at the other end and emerged into a short hallway. From where he stood, he could see the front door again to his left. The kitchen stood directly ahead.

The Executioner entered the kitchen to find two dead Japanese on the floor. He pushed through a swing door set in the opposite wall, looked through and saw the dining room. Buchanan had left his mark with another dead man staining the carpet with his blood.

Bolan entered the dining room, carefully stepping over Buchanan's handiwork. He wondered where the soldier-journalist had gone—he could hear no more firing from anywhere in the house. Returning to the front entryway, the Executioner turned his attention up the staircase.

And none too soon. As he looked up, a muscular Oriental wearing a black tank top aimed a rifle down the steps.

Bolan angled the AK upward, hip-shooting a 3-round burst that struck low in the assailant's groin. The man dropped his weapon, screamed and toppled down the steps, both hands cupping his bloody crotch. The Executioner put three more rounds in his chest as the man passed.

His battle senses on high alert, the Executioner

hurried up the staircase, pausing at the top of the steps. White marble statues sat on stands against the wall opposite the rail. He moved forward toward a door that led into a hallway, passing what he recognized as a representation of Amaterasu-o-mi-Kami, the Shinto sun goddess. He drew the Desert Eagle and eased past a statue of a dog, then a fox— also Shinto *kami,* or gods. Glancing at the wall, he was surprised to see a crucifix, a Star of David and a framed pen-and-ink sketch of Muhammad.

Bolan thought back to what he had read of the Japanese cult in the Stony Man intelligence file. No specifics had been cited, but it appeared that the Great Hikari had mixed many aspects of the different world religions to come up with his cult.

Reaching the door, the Executioner paused, then started down the hall. He had heard no gunfire since leaving the first floor, but now he heard a voice. An angry voice. With a Mideastern accent.

The Executioner's instincts told him to hurry.

Breaking into a sprint, Bolan reached the open door at the end of the hall and burst into a bedroom in time to see a man wearing a European-cut suit and a black-and-white-striped kaffiyeh cock the hammer on a S&W Model 66 .357 Magnum pistol. The man was slight of stature and had a ferret look to his face.

The Arab that Margai and Loko had spoken of, the one who had bought Kiethley? Maybe.

But this was hardly the time to ask questions. Buchanan sat on the edge of the bed, the four-inch barrel of the Smith & Wesson in the Arab's hand pressed against his forehead.

Bolan leveled the Desert Eagle on the stainless steel of the Model 66, lining the sights up on the trigger guard. He squeezed the trigger, and the huge .44 exploded.

The man in the kaffiyeh screamed as the revolver went spinning from his hand. He turned toward Bolan, drew a long dagger from beneath the jacket of his suit and lunged forward.

Another .44 Magnum hollowpoint round roared from the Desert Eagle's barrel and added a third eye in the center of the attacker's forehead. His other two eyes rolled back into his head as he sunk first to his knees, then fell forward onto his face.

Bolan walked forward and patted the man's suit until he felt a wallet. Pulling it from the Arab's blood-soaked slacks, he opened it to find several credit cards and an international driver's license in the name of Muhammad Araba. The name meant nothing to the Executioner.

"Saving my ass is getting to be a habit of yours, Pollock," Buchanan said. "Not a *bad* habit though— don't try to break it or anything." When Bolan didn't respond, he added, "Thanks. Our Arab friend—whoever he was—was getting tired of me refusing to tell him who we were."

Bolan nodded, sticking the driver's license and credit cards back in the billfold. He dropped it into his pocket, making a mental note to have Kurtzman run down the name.

Buchanan stood, lifted his AK-47 from the floor, then grinned at Bolan. "By the way," he said, crooking his neck toward a door on the other side of the bedroom.

Bolan followed him into a small private office. Bound and gagged and sitting in a straight-backed wooden chair in the center of the room was Spencer Kiethley.

Bolan drew his fighting knife, then hurried forward to cut the ropes around Kiethley's chest.

Somalia

McCARTER JERKED again on the steel door handle, muttering a flurry of curses under his breath. Close at his heels, he heard Captain Jack grind to a halt.

"What's wrong?" the warlord said. "What's wrong!"

"It's locked," McCarter said, angry at himself for not thinking of the possibility before he sprinted out of the trees. He turned his eyes to the other rear door in time to see it swinging slowly shut. He caught a fleeting glimpse of Calvin James's legs as the commando sprinted through the door and into the UN Annex.

A round from somewhere struck the concrete wall to McCarter's right, then went zinging away. A second round zipped through one of the decorative holes to strike the concrete on the Phoenix Force leader's other side. This time the bullet bounced back at him, missing his shoulder by inches and striking the opposite wall. It continued to ricochet back and forth against the walls like a steel ball on a roulette wheel.

McCarter looked through one of the holes in the direction from which the bullet had come. In a second-story window halfway between where he stood and the door through which James had entered, he saw a man changing magazines in his Howa rifle. The Phoenix Force leader aimed the Browning through the hole and pulled the trigger.

The rifleman dropped his weapon and dropped out of sight below the window.

McCarter took a step back and looked up at the other windows overhead. The barrel of an automatic rifle appeared in the open window directly above the door. Then the rest of the rifle poked through the opening. An Oriental man became visible.

As if in slow motion, McCarter watched as the Howa was aimed toward him.

The Briton raised the Browning and sighted on the man in the window. He fired a lone .40 S&W round that took off the top of the rifleman's head as neatly as if McCarter had scalped the man. The gunman's eyes rolled up as he tried to see what had happened.

McCarter's next round drilled between those eyes. The man pitched forward out of the window, performing a somersault in the air before he hit the ground behind both McCarter and Captain Jack.

The Phoenix Force leader glanced quickly along the rest of the windows on the building's second floor. Seeing no immediate threat, he looked back through the wall at the door where James had entered the building. For a moment he considered leading Captain Jack on a sprint across the yard to that door. But that would mean leaving even the little cover the hole-ridden wall provided.

McCarter looked back at the door in front of him. There might be a better way.

"Jack! Cover the second floor!" McCarter yelled. Through the tiny squares formed by the steel mesh between the double window panes he could see a brightly lighted hallway. He jammed the muzzle of the Browning against the glass and crisscrossed steel bands and pulled the trigger repeatedly, shattering the glass. Reaching up, he tried to pull the steel away.

The mesh showed the wear the .40-caliber rounds had caused, but it didn't move.

McCarter heard two pops behind him and glanced up in time to see another man in the window. Captain Jack had fired twice. Both rounds had missed the man but had been close enough that he jerked back into the window. As McCarter watched, he leaned back out again and tried to aim his rifle.

McCarter didn't let him. He raised his pistol.

Captain Jack fired again a split second before the Phoenix Force leader pulled the trigger. Once more the warlord's round missed its target, striking the building next to the window and chipping off a nugget of brick the size of a golf ball.

McCarter's aim was more true. His .40-caliber round punctured the gunman's throat, and another of the Japanese attackers plunged from the window, belly-flopping on the ground.

The Briton pressed the Browning against the window again and emptied the weapon with rapid semi-auto fire. He dumped the empty magazine and rammed a fresh box into the grips. Then he reached up, trying to move the steel mesh away, and get to the bar handle that ran the width of the door on the inside.

Again the steel stayed in place.

McCarter heard Captain Jack firing behind him and glanced overhead to see the warlord's rounds drive another man back inside the building. But the head and rifle returned, and once more the Briton had to postpone his assault on the door to take the man out with two more rounds to the upper chest.

Blood rained on both McCarter and Captain Jack as the man plummeted to the ground.

The Phoenix Force leader turned back to the door. By now all the glass over the steel mesh had shattered. McCarter aimed the Browning carefully at the bottom left-hand corner of the steel and fired. A round hole appeared. Moving the sights slightly, he fired again. The second hole struck just to one side of the first, the round edge barely overlapping. McCarter readjusted his aim and pulled the trigger a third time.

On and on the Phoenix Force leader went, cutting a .40-caliber line through the steel across the bottom of the window.

Again McCarter emptied the Browning, dropped the empty mag and shoved a fresh one into the grips. This time when he pushed on the steel, it swung in.

Not much. But enough. With the Browning in his right hand, McCarter stuck his left arm through the window, reached down and grasped the cross bar.

"Jack!" the Phoenix Force leader shouted. "Get ready!"

The steel mesh had closed back over McCarter's arm after he'd stuck it through the hole, trapping him against the door. The angle was awkward; he had to press in on the bar, at the same time pulling the door toward him. He would have no way of aiming accurately until after he'd freed his arm and entered the hallway. He watched the hall through what remained of the mesh as the steel door slowly swung outward.

The door was halfway open when the man with the submachine gun stepped into the hallway.

"Jack!" McCarter shouted. He swung the door all the way open and against the wall in the hopes that the warlord could shoot past him trapped between the door and the wall of the entryway, unable to quickly withdraw his arm and get into position.

Captain Jack took the shot, all right. The only problem was he missed again.

The Oriental with the subgun—a Japanese Type 100 McCarter could see now—took his time aiming. The Briton tried to pry his arm free from the window as he heard Captain Jack fire again. Once more the warlord choked and missed.

The man with the subgun opened fire, sending a steady stream of rounds within an inch of McCarter's exposed left arm and on through the open door.

Behind him, Captain Jack kept firing, too. Both men kept missing.

McCarter closed the door slightly and leaned to his right, allowing himself enough room to maneuver his right arm around the door and aim the Browning. He squeezed the trigger, sending a .40-caliber round down the hall. The bullet went high over the left shoulder of the enemy gunner. McCarter corrected his aim and hammered another pair of rounds from the weapon.

The first of the pair caught the subgunner squarely in the chest. The second drilled through his nose and out the back of his head.

With a moment to breathe now, McCarter braced his gun hand against the door and pried his other arm back out of the window. He turned quickly to Captain Jack. The man had almost emptied the Browning and had yet to hit a man. Pulling the warlord's Ruger Vaquero from his belt, McCarter handed it to him. Maybe he'd do better with his own gun. "Follow me," he ordered, and hurried on down the hall.

McCarter filed two items in the back of his mind as he made his way over the dead subgunner to a cross hall. First Captain Jack had stood fearlessly beside him, firing away at the enemy. But second, and equally important, the Phoenix Force leader didn't want to forget that the warlord's accuracy left a lot to be desired.

The bottom line was that Captain Jack couldn't shoot worth a damn.

McCarter heard running footsteps as he neared the

intersecting hallway. He stopped, the Browning held tight to his side. A second later a black man carrying another of the Type 100 weapons rounded the corner.

The Briton jammed the Browning into the man's belly and pulled the trigger twice. The gunner jerked both times, looking more like a boxer taking a pair of uppercuts to the abdomen than a man being shot. He dropped to the ground.

McCarter led Captain Jack on. Rounding the corner, he saw a door leading to the stairs at the end of the hall. He sprinted toward it with the warlord at his heels. With a quick glance through the glass, he shoved the door open, held it until Jack caught it and hurried through.

The former SAS commando took the steps three at a time as he made his way to the second floor. He paused again before stepping into the open. This time he heard nothing.

But this time something heard *him*.

The Phoenix Force leader sensed his mistake as he stepped out of the stairwell and tried to turn, bringing up the Browning. Before he could do so, a pistol jammed into his temple. For a moment nothing happened.

Then McCarter heard a low chuckle in the still hallway.

The pistol lowered, and the Briton turned to see Calvin James. "Sorry, boss," James whispered.

"Think nothing of it."

Sporadic fire sounded at the other end of the second-floor hall. James motioned that way with his head. "I don't think there are many left," he whispered, "and they're all down at that end—still firing across the street. I don't think they know they're alone yet, or that we're in the building."

McCarter frowned. He hadn't heard any fire that sounded as if it came from James's Beretta since he and Captain Jack had made it into the building. But several bodies littered the hall in the direction James had indicated. "They haven't heard you?" he asked.

The Phoenix Force commando grinned, and for the first time McCarter noticed what the former SEAL held in his other hand—a SOG Trident knife with a razor-edged six-and-one-quarter-inch blade.

"Lead the way," McCarter instructed him.

James turned and started down the hall. McCarter and Captain Jack followed, stepping over the knife-fighting SEAL's handiwork as they went. Calvin James had learned his blade techniques as a wayward youth on the streets of South Side Chicago. He had refined them in the Navy, and the man knew a thousand and one ways to employ the silent edged weapon.

By the time they were halfway down the hall, McCarter had heard enough gunfire to know that three of the enemy remained. Two were firing the Howas. The third kept up chatter with another of the Type 100 subguns. The Phoenix Force leader grabbed James's sleeve as they neared the room from which the gunshots came. "We need at least one of them alive," he whispered. "I want to know why this many Japanese are in Somalia."

James nodded.

McCarter and James edged toward the open door. When Captain Jack started to follow, the Phoenix Force leader stopped him. "Cover our backs, Jack," he said, remembering the man's poor marksmanship. He pointed back down the hall.

The warlord turned, both the Browning and Vaquero aimed that way.

McCarter held up his index finger, and James nodded.

The Phoenix Force leader added his middle finger, and James nodded again.

As the third finger went into the air, both men turned the corner into the office.

Three men knelt in front of the windows, still pouring fire down on Hawkins, Manning and Encizo. The one on the far left was a black man, and he turned as the men from Stony Man Farm entered the room.

McCarter raised his weapon and squeezed the trigger, sending a lone .40-caliber round into the man's eye as he sprinted forward.

The gunner at the window to the right was also black. James caught him with a double-tap of 9 mm rounds as he, too, tried to turn.

By then McCarter had left his feet and was sailing through the air. His flying tackle ended with his arms around the neck of the third man at the center window. James joined his teammate, driving a shoulder into the Oriental's spine.

The man grunted in both pain and surprise.

McCarter brought the Browning around and knocked him cold. Wasting no time, he looked back toward the door. "Jack!" he called out.

The warlord ducked into the room.

"Give me a hand with this guy," McCarter ordered. He had already grabbed the unconscious man under the arms.

Looking up at James, he added, "Calvin, you cover us. Yell down first and tell the others we're coming out."

James hurried to the window. "Hold your fire!" he yelled down to Manning, Hawkins and Encizo.

The gunfire ceased immediately.

McCarter and Captain Jack lugged their prisoner out of the room and into the hall. James joined them, then hurried past, his Beretta held in both hands and ready to answer any threat that presented itself.

By the time the men reached the first floor, they could hear the sirens. By the time they had made it out the front door, they could see the cars. Some of the vehicles bore the logo of the Somalian police. Others displayed that of the customs department.

McCarter and Captain Jack carried the Oriental across the street as James fired several rounds in the general direction of the flashing lights and screaming sirens. The commando had no intention of hitting them. He merely wanted to slow them.

With the Wagoneer's radiator punctured, Hawkins, Manning and Encizo had commandeered the Ford F-100 parked next to it, and Hawkins was already hot-wiring the aging pickup. Manning and Encizo helped

throw the unconscious Oriental into the bed of the
pickup, then jumped into the cab next to Hawkins.
McCarter, James and Captain Jack leaped over the
sides of the Ford next to the unconscious man.

As Hawkins pulled away from the curb, rifle
rounds flew past the vehicle like a sudden swarm of
locusts.

CHAPTER FOURTEEN

Alexandria, Virginia

Ira Rook might work in Washington, D.C., but he wasn't about to live there. In spite of his raging editorials about how the American rich became wealthy at the expense of the poor, in the face of his printed diatribes that America was the most racist nation on the planet and regardless of how many times he held a martini glass in one hand and preached the morality of a more socialistic redistribution of wealth in the United States, Ira Rook wasn't stupid.

He knew it was just too dangerous to live in Washington, D.C., proper. And besides, it was so dirty....

The night was approaching as Lyons pulled the rented Lumina APV off the bridge and entered Alexandria, Virginia, just across the river from Washington. Along with all of his other hypocrisies, Ira Rook had an unlisted phone number and address. Kurtzman had put Huntington Wethers to work locating the man. It had taken the cybernetics expert all of thirty seconds to crack the phone company's unlisted file and find both the house and number of the Able Team leader's old nemesis.

Lyons turned onto Fairfax Street and cruised past Carlyle House, a restored 1752 Virginia mansion. He shook his head. He would never have guessed that Rook was a follower of the Great Hikari, but the picture appeared to be proof. The unscrupulous editor couldn't have been a member of the cult very long, however, or he'd have been talked into giving up his worldly possessions like other converts. Insider information gained through the newspaper business had meant that Rook had done well financially with investments; he had far more wealth than the average Follower of the Truth convert. Which meant that the Great Hikari might not have gotten around to going after his money yet, but he would soon.

The Lumina cruised past the eighteenth-century Stabler-Leadbetter Apothecary, now a pharmaceutical museum.

"He was playing both sides of the fence," Blancanales said from the seat next to Lyons, breaking into the Able Team leader's thoughts. "He had to be."

Lyons glanced toward him. "Sorry, I was thinking about something else. What did you mean?

"Rook, playing both sides of the fence. He took the information from Spencer Kiethley and printed the story." The Able Team psy-op expert shook his head in disgust at the treachery. "Then he turned around and told his cult buddies where they could find Kiethley in Sierra Leone.''

"Yeah, but Kiethley fooled them all in the end," Schwarz said from the back seat.

Blancanales turned toward him. "How's that?"

"He went and got killed by the RUF before the cult flunkies could find him," Schwarz said cynically.

"That's if he *was* killed," Lyons said. "No one actually saw him die. Striker had his doubts about it. So do I."

"What I don't get," Schwarz went on, "is how Rook held out when you questioned him, Pol."

Blancanales shrugged, remembering the strange interrogation to which he had subjected the editor in the storage garage. "I never asked him anything about the cult," he said. "At least not directly. It never dawned on me that he might be connected to them. I was just trying to find out what he knew about Kiethley."

Lyons drove on, twisting and turning through the historical city and finally turning onto North Royal Street. They cruised past the famous Gadsby's Tavern, where George Washington had recruited men for the French and Indian wars, and later for the revolution. Leaving the historic district, the Lumina entered a modern light-commercial area, then a lower-middle-income residential neighborhood. Gradually the houses became larger, turning to mansions that could belong only to the rich and famous.

"What was the address?" Blancanales asked.

"It's 14 Natural Chimneys," Lyons said.

Blancanales frowned. "Weird name for a street."

"It must be named after the Natural Chimneys near Staunton," Schwarz said from the back seat. "They're odd-looking stone towers about a hundred feet high and pierced with tunnels."

"Thank you, Professor," Blancanales said, grinning. "Will that be on the test?"

Lyons turned onto the street they were discussing. "All right, knock it off," he said. "We're almost there." He drove for another mile, and the houses and lots became even larger. The Able Team leader felt another surge of anger at Rook's duplicity.

But a reckoning was at hand. Lyons intended to find out what else Ira Rook knew about the cult and the upcoming subway gassing. And if Rook had to get bruised a little in the process, well, that was just his tough luck.

By the time the men of Able Team saw Rook's house, dusk had fallen, and they had entered a small lake area. The houses faced the road, but each had a huge deck that faced the water. Although it was an embarrassment of wealth, Rook's wasn't the biggest.

Lyons pulled the Lumina to a halt a quarter mile from Rook's house and lifted a pair of binoculars to his eyes. Through the quickly fading light he saw a Colonial-style house with steeply pitched dormers and a deep columned front porch. A massive double chimney rose from one side of the house, and small windows—traditional to the simple "farmhouse" architectural style—had been arranged in a contemporary way to light the interior.

The Able Team leader shifted the binoculars to the rear of the house. A long pier led from the shore to a boathouse on the lake. Both a small rowboat and a larger motorboat were tied to posts under the roof. A stone breakwater and marsh grass ran under the pier twenty yards from the shoreline.

"It looks to me like running you down in the newspaper is a profitable activity, Ironman," Blancanales said.

"Maybe we should try it." Schwarz grinned. "We've got some good stories we could tell."

Lyons ignored their ribbing, shifting the binoculars back to the circular driveway in the front of the house and the variety of vehicles parked on the curved pavement. A scan along the windows showed lights on in several areas of the house.

Rook wasn't alone.

Lyons dropped the binoculars. "Get the Calicos, Gadgets."

Schwarz reached into the storage area behind him and pulled three hard plastic gun cases over the seat, keeping one for himself and handing one each to the men in the front seat. "You looking forward to this, Ironman?" he asked.

"What's that?" Lyons asked as he opened his case.

"When we talked to Rook before, we just thought

he was a hypocritical liar,'' Schwarz said. ''Now we find out he's not only a cult member, he betrayed Spencer Kiethley and may be responsible for his death. He's a righteous bad guy.''

Lyons pulled the Calico 960 submachine pistol from its case. ''Yeah? So what's your point?'' he asked.

Schwarz glanced to Blancanales and grinned. ''He's not just a citizen you don't agree with anymore,'' he said. ''He's a scumbag criminal like all the rest. You won't have to treat him with kid gloves anymore.''

Lyons slipped into the Calico's shoulder sling and adjusted the straps. ''I do my job, Gadgets,'' he said. ''No more, no less.''

Blancanales had been getting into his own Calico rig. ''Yeah, but sometimes our jobs are more fun than others.''

Lyons glanced at the sky. In another two minutes it would be dark.

The men of Able Team waited, then they got out of the Lumina and started for Ira Rook's house, prepared for battle.

Sierra Leone

THE JEEP CJ-5 was too small to transport Bolan, Buchanan, Kiethley and their two RUF prisoners back to the training camp. The mail truck would soon be missed, and it would be far too easy for authorities to spot on the road.

They needed another vehicle.

The French-run Lagon Bleu Hotel was located just on the other side of the bridge that connected Freetown and Aberdeen Creek. Bolan guided the mail truck across it into the parking lot and killed the engine.

In the bucket seat against the opposite window of the cab sat Spencer Kiethley. The man had been beaten severely, and systematically, since falling into the hands of the cult. It was all Kiethley could do to move his tortured limbs enough to eat a little of the food Bolan found in the kitchen of the house in which he'd been held prisoner. Once Kiethley had something in his stomach, the Executioner had also given the battered man a healthy dose of aspirin. That seemed to have helped the pain, but full recovery would take time. He was unable to walk, and Bolan and Buchanan had been forced to carry him from the house. Kiethley had told them the bizarre story of how the events in Somalia, Japan, Sierra Leone and the U.S. all fit together, and then fallen asleep in the truck.

Bolan paused, sorting it all through his mind. It seemed that the abandonment of the classified U.S. documents that had started the whole show hadn't been simple carelessness on the part of UN staffers as had been originally thought. The boxes of top secret material had been purposely discarded. The Followers of the Truth had infiltrated the United

Nations, and their spy had hidden the documents when the UN had pulled out of the building.

Another cult member had been on his way to retrieve them when Kiethley, who had been hired as part of a security team to assist in the withdrawal, stumbled onto the boxes. He had turned some of the classified files over to U.S. forces but hidden others.

"Why?" Bolan had asked the beaten man. But by then an exhausted Kiethley had fallen asleep.

Buchanan squatted in the open area between Bolan and Kiethley. In the rear of the truck, still tied up, were Margai, Loko and a very confused Sierra Leone mailman.

Bolan glanced at the Lagon Bleu, then began to scan the parking lot. The hotel was medium priced, and the lot contained the same medium-priced, nondescript type of vehicle that the Executioner was looking for. He wanted something that would get them all back to the training camp without drawing attention.

The Executioner's eyes passed over a Chevy Suburban Silverado, a Toyota pickup, then a Ford Bronco II.

"How about the Jimmy?" Buchanan asked, pointing to the left.

Bolan followed Buchanan's finger toward a white two-door 4×4 two rows from where they sat. It looked to be in good shape, and it would get them back to camp as well as anything else he saw. The Executioner nodded. "Stay here," he said. "I'll drive back and pick you up as soon as I've wired it.''

Buchanan nodded.

The Executioner opened the door and dropped down from the mail truck, glancing toward the hotel, then around the parking lot as he made his way casually toward the Jimmy. The restaurant was open and looked to be frequented by a mixture of locals and tourists. Men and women, some in shorts with cameras around their necks and others wearing more-traditional native dress, had come and gone ever since he'd pulled into the lot. No one seemed to have noticed the truck.

The Jimmy was locked when the Executioner reached it. Not caring to take the time to pick it open, he glanced quickly around, then drove an elbow through the glass. The shattering made little noise, and a second later Bolan had unlocked the door, swept the glass off the seat and slipped behind the wheel. A second later he had cracked the steering column and had the Jimmy's engine purring.

He backed the vehicle out of the parking place, drove to the end of the row of parked cars and turned back toward the mail truck. He stopped next to the vehicle, looked up into the cab and saw a fully awake and frantic Spencer Kiethley waving at him.

Buchanan was nowhere to be seen.

The amber ''caution light'' that was always on in the Executioner's brain flashed red.

Leaping from the Jimmy, Bolan looked up again to see that Kiethley was now missing, too. He jerked open the mail truck's door and pulled himself into the cab to see that Kiethley had fallen between the seats. The beaten man was trying to pull himself along the floor to the back of the truck.

Drawing the sound-suppressed Beretta, the Executioner stepped over the man, threw the dividing curtain back and saw why.

The Executioner looked into the cargo area in time to see Buchanan jerk his subhilt fighting knife out of Loko's chest. The RUF bandit, his eyes open wide but sightless in death, slithered to the floor.

The soldier-journalist had already dealt with Margai. The RUF man lay on the floor, both hands clutching the puncture in his chest. The mailman was still tied, gagged and watching everything with wild eyes.

Buchanan turned to Bolan, blood covering the blade of his knife and dripping to the floor. "Sons of bitches got loose," he said. "They reached through the curtain, jerked me into the back and this one—" he nodded at Loko "— damn near strangled me."

Only then did Bolan notice that the cord with which Loko had been bound was still wrapped around Buchanan's neck. He also saw the red line on Buchanan's skin where the makeshift garrote had been. He stood over Margai. "Why?" he asked. "Why did you do it? You took us to Kiethley. We were about to let you go like we promised."

Margai struggled for air. When he spoke, blood

poured out with the words. "We...didn't...believe you," he whispered. They were his dying words.

"You should have," Buchanan said simply as he wiped the subhilt on Margai's shirt and then sheathed the blade.

In the wake of everything that had happened, Bolan had temporarily forgotten Spencer Kiethley. Now he saw the man struggling to get off the floor and back into his seat. The Executioner grabbed him under the arms and lifted him to a sitting position, then turned back to the rear of the truck. "Bobcat, leave what's left of Loko and Margai here. The mailman, too—he'll work himself free eventually or else someone will find the truck. Help me with Kiethley."

Bolan and Buchanan lifted Kiethley and got him out of the mail truck and into the back seat of the Jimmy. Buchanan took the passenger's seat next to the Executioner, who then pulled out of the parking lot and started back into Freetown proper.

Kiethley was full awake now and, even after his fall trying to help Buchanan, seemed to be doing much better. He wouldn't be running any marathons for a while, but he looked as if he was up to a little more talk.

"Kiethley, how come you turned some of the classified documents back over to the UN but hid others?" the Executioner asked over his shoulder as they drove back across the bridge into the city.

Kiethley glanced up at Buchanan, then to Bolan, then back to Buchanan. "Look, Bobcat," he said. "I've known you for more years than I tell young girls I'm old," he said. "And after all I've been through, you may just be the only human being I still trust." He looked back to the Executioner. "So even though you guys saved my ass back there, I got to ask, okay?" He looked back at Bolan. "Can I trust this guy?"

Buchanan laughed. "So far he's saved my ass even more times than he's saved yours."

"Okay," Kiethley said. "Point made. You ever heard of Nerve Ending? I don't mean the usual way, like the nerve endings in your body. I mean in reference to chemical warfare."

Both Bolan and Buchanan shook their heads.

"I hadn't, either," Kiethley said. "Until I came across those boxes of classified documents. "It's new stuff, Nerve Ending is. But it's aptly named—a nerve gas that puts an end to anything it reaches."

Bolan guided the Jimmy through the city toward the road to the training camp. "Tell me more," he said.

"It's got a range roughly ten times that of sarin, and it makes Tabun and VX symptoms seem like a mild allergy," Kiethley said. "It kills fast, and it's easy and fast to manufacture. You just have to know the formula." He paused. "That's what was in one of the boxes of classified documents. The formula for Nerve Ending."

Bolan felt a cold chill run up his spine as the components of the mission that had so far seemed unrelated began to take shape in his mind. "I'm assuming that's the box you hid?"

In the rearview mirror he saw Kiethley nod. "The other boxes contain innocuous stuff, at least compared to Nerve Ending. I figure the cult member working for the UN just left them out so the whole thing would be chalked up to incompetence, which it was."

The Jimmy left the city and started down the road to the commando training camp. Bolan kept one eye on the sides of the road for bandits as he listened to Kiethley's story continue to unfold. "And so you turned the less important stuff back over to the UN to see what would happen?"

"Right. Call it a hunch or whatever you want. Some little voice in the back of my head just told me to be careful."

"And what happened?"

"The UN security officer who took the stuff kept asking me questions about whether there was more. He asked enough times that I began to realize he already knew there was more."

"This security officer," Buchanan said. "A Follower of the Truth member, too?"

Kiethley shrugged. "That was my guess. All I know is that after I left the boxes with him I picked up a tail. They tried to nab me twice—not kill me, that would have been easy. They were trying to take me alive, which tells me they wanted to know where the missing box was stashed."

Bolan guided the Jimmy on down the road, seeing no sign of RUF bandits this time. "So you figured it was the Great Hikari's boys trying to get their hands on the formula so their little subway parties would be even more fun than with sarin?" he asked.

"You got it," Kiethley said. "I needed to split Somalia fast anyway, what with them trying to grab me, so I headed for Japan." He looked down at his feet and shook his head in frustration. "I made an appointment with one of the Japanese detectives familiar with the subway-gassing cases and guess what?"

"You began to suspect he was affiliated with the cult, too," Bolan said.

Kiethley's head jerked up in surprise. "How'd you know that?"

"Because you went to Ira Rook in Washington at that point," Bolan stated. "If you'd been satisfied with what you'd done in Japan there would have been no need to do that."

"Right," Kiethley said. He turned to Buchanan and grinned through the bruises that covered his face. "Your new partner's pretty sharp, Bobcat," he said, then looked back to Bolan. "By the way, what do I call you?"

"Pollock," Bolan said.

"All right, Pollock, I haven't officially thanked you for getting me away from our blood-and-bathwater-imbibing friends. So thanks."

"You're welcome," Bolan said. "One more question."

"Shoot."

"Where is the Nerve Ending formula now?"

Kiethley shrugged. "Unless somebody's found them, still back where I hid it in Mogadishu."

The Executioner stomped the brakes, skidding the Jimmy into a U-turn on the rugged road. The other men in the vehicle groped for handholds as they slid through the 180 degrees. Suddenly they were heading back in the direction from which they had come.

For a moment there was silence, then Buchanan said, "I take it our tour of duty as Sierra Leone commando trainers has ended."

Bolan nodded.

Buchanan shrugged. "The Gurkhas can take it from here as well as we could," he said. "And what the hell, I haven't been to Somalia for a while."

Bolan shook his head.

"What? We're not going to Somalia to recover the Nerve Ending box?" Buchanan asked.

"I've got some friends already there. Kiethley can tell them where it is, and they'll pick it up."

"Then where *are* we going?" Buchanan asked. "If making a phone call is all we need to do, there's a secure line back at camp."

"We can use a phone here," Bolan said. "The call can be scrambled from the other end. And besides, making the call isn't all we need to do."

"What then?" Kiethley asked. "We going somewhere?"

"Japan," the Executioner said. "We're going to find the Great Hikari and put an end to all this once and for all."

"Kill him?" Spencer Kiethley asked.

Bolan didn't bother to answer.

Kiethley raised a hand and gingerly felt his battered face. "I just got one request."

Bolan looked at the man in the rearview mirror. His face wouldn't heal for some time, and some of the scars would remain to remind him of the Great Hikari and his cult from now on. "What is it?" the Executioner asked.

"Let *me* do it," Kiethley stated grimly.

Somalia

TWO SOMALIAN POLICE CARS, led by a Ford Bronco marked with the seal of the customs department, took after the F-100 pickup carrying the men of Phoenix Force away from the UN building.

McCarter sat with his back against the cab. The Japanese man they had brought out of the UN Annex lay at his feet in the bed of the pickup, still unconscious. Captain Jack sat next to the Phoenix Force leader with Calvin James on the other side of the warlord. All three men faced the oncoming convoy of law enforcement.

Hawkins swerved periodically, dodging the bullets that flew from the police vehicles. McCarter and the others gripped whatever handholds they could find, fighting valiantly to keep from being thrown from the truck. In between being bounced back and forth across the pickup bed, McCarter squinted at the man in the passenger's seat of the Bronco: broad shoulders, barrel chest, full black beard above a Somalian customs uniform tunic.

It was Manning's old bench-pressing buddy, Captain Berber.

Hawkins swerved suddenly, and McCarter saw an old woman dive for the pavement to the side. She was frightened but unhurt, and McCarter watched her shake her fist at the passing vehicles as she got back to her feet. She'd been lucky.

The next person not paying attention might not be.

McCarter turned to James as they hit a straightaway past a pair of mosques, then a Roman Catholic cathedral next to the al-Aruba Hotel. They were nearing the market where pedestrian traffic would be thick and a stray bullet or bumper could easily take out innocents. "Calvin," McCarter said, "think you can hit a tire?"

"Think I better at least try." Pulling his knees almost up to his chin, James drew his Beretta and extended it between his legs. The black Phoenix Force warrior's thighs clamped tight around his wrists, bracing the weapon. McCarter watched him sight down the barrel, then take a deep breath as they bumped through a series of dips. As soon as the dips ended and the ride evened out, he pulled the trigger.

The explosions from pistol and rubber sounded like one as a 9 mm round struck the right front tire of the Bronco. The customs vehicle skidded, then began to fishtail.

McCarter watched Captain Berber reach out and brace both of his arms on the dash as his driver fought to keep control of the vehicle. For a second it looked as if the man would succeed, then the front fender skimmed against a parked car. The Bronco slowed, quit fishtailing and began to whirl in circles.

The police car right behind it smashed into the side, ending the revolutions. The second police car struck the first. The force shoved all three vehicles down the street another thirty yards in an orgy of screaming metal, then they all came to a halt in the center of the road.

McCarter watched a shaky Captain Berber get out of the Bronco and dust himself off as the F-100 continued on away from the scene.

"Nice shot," McCarter said.

A tap sounded on the rear windshield of the pickup behind them, and McCarter, Captain Jack and James all turned.

Manning and Encizo faced them, their fists extended with the thumb pointing upward.

The pickup slowed as it entered the market area by the main bus station. Hawkins chauffeured them past booths and stalls where vendors hawked cloth, carved pipes and other objects, and jewelry. The livestock market appeared, and with it came all the accompanying sounds, sights and odors.

McCarter glanced at the unconscious Oriental as the man began to stir, then twisted and stuck his head over the side of the pickup and toward the cab so Hawkins could hear him. "We need some place private to talk to this guy," he shouted against the wind. "Head for the beach area."

Hawkins nodded. McCarter shifted to the rear of the pickup bed, braced his back against the tailgate and faced the front. They passed the Lido Club, the Djibouti embassy, the Anglo-American Club and then a line of craft shops advertising exotic fabrics and camel-bone carvings. Traffic thinned as they left the city proper. A sign pointed them on toward Gezira Beach and the F-100 rolled along, the waves of the Indian Ocean lapping at the sands. A hotel appeared along the beach with a sign that promised a shark-protected beach.

An idea struck the Briton.

Short dirt roads that led into coves began to shoot off the roadway. Some had crude hand-painted signs that announced their names. Other grottoes were too small to be designated. A mile or so past the hotel, McCarter saw another sign, this one with a bright red arrow pointing toward the water. Shark's Cove, it announced, which sounded like just what he wanted.

The Phoenix Force leader tapped the glass. Manning turned to face him. McCarter pointed toward the sign, then hooked a thumb off the road toward the cove. He watched Manning translate his pantomime to Hawkins, and a moment later the young Phoenix Force commando was slowing at the turn.

The bumpy road led to the edge of the water fifty yards off the highway. McCarter looked out over the gentle waves and saw a shark-shaped coral formation jumping out of the water. For a moment he wondered if that was what had given the cove its name, then he saw the dorsal fin sliding along the surface of the water to the right of the coral.

The coral might have been one reason Shark's Cove got its name, but it wasn't the only one.

The Japanese man had come around by the time Hawkins ground the pickup to a halt on the sand. James had already taken over as baby-sitter, moving the man to a sitting position on the open tailgate and shoving his Beretta up under his chin. McCarter took the opportunity to scout around for the type of terrain he wanted for what he was planning.

He found it twenty yards away. Just to the right of the pickup, a hard finger of rocky shore jutted off the bank and over the water. McCarter walked out onto the solid extension, squatted and looked down into the water. Warm waves washed gently against the bottom of the outcropping.

The Phoenix Force leader looked out over the water and saw the dorsal fin passing the coral formation again. Where there was one, he knew there would be others close by.

McCarter rose and walked back to the pickup. Manning, Hawkins, Encizo and Captain Jack had all gathered around the Oriental.

McCarter walked up and stood in front of the man, looking down. "Are you a follower of the Great Hikari?" he asked.

Slowly the man nodded. "Praise Hikari!" he said. "The Great Hikari!"

"What were you doing back at the UN building?"

The man's lips clamped shut.

McCarter looked him in the eye. "What is your name?"

"Haki," the man said.

"You're Japanese?"

The man nodded.

"What were you doing back at the UN?"

Again the man wouldn't answer.

McCarter sighed. "Haki," he said, "we can do this the hard way if we have to. I'd rather not, but we can."

The Japanese didn't respond.

McCarter looked at the man. He was small, most likely weighing less than 120 pounds. The Phoenix Force leader reached out and grabbed Haki's left arm. He nodded to Manning, who grabbed the right. Together they lifted the man off the tailgate and into the air.

McCarter and Manning marched the surprised Oriental out to the end of the rock finger, setting him on his feet on the edge. The Phoenix Force leader pulled the Spyderco Delica knife from his pocket and thumbed it open. He held the knife in his right hand, grabbed Haki's arm with his left and extended the man's limb over the water. McCarter flicked the tip of the blade lightly across Haki's wrist, and several drops of blood dropped into the waves.

Fifty yards away the dorsal fin gliding along the top of the water turned toward them.

Haki had already figured out what was up and tried to turn. Manning grabbed him by the scruff of the neck and lifted him into the air again. "Don't run off, Haki," the big Canadian said pleasantly. "We're just starting to have fun."

McCarter and Manning each grabbed an arm again and lifted the man over the water.

"No...please, no..." His legs kicked ferociously in the air as if he were riding a bicycle.

"Sorry, my friend," McCarter said. "If you don't want to answer our questions, you have to pay the price." Slowly he and Manning lowered their captive until the man's kicking feet churned the water.

The dorsal fin swam steadily closer until McCarter could see the distinctive snout of a hammerhead shark. He and Manning waited until the hammerhead was three feet away before jerking Haki back onto the rock.

The shark followed the movement, rising up out of the water, its teeth snapping the air an inch from Haki's knee.

The man screamed.

The shark splashed back down into the water and disappeared beneath the gentle waves.

"Now, what was it you said you were doing back at the UN?" McCarter asked.

Tears streamed down Haki's cheeks, and McCarter almost felt sorry for him. The Phoenix Force leader had to remind himself that only a few minutes earlier Haki had been doing his best to kill them and, if given half a chance, he would try again.

The shark reappeared thirty yards from the rock formation. It slid along the water, back and forth in front of the men, as if its tiny brain somehow sensed that the "bait" would be lowered into the water again.

McCarter decided to try a stronger approach and add to their captive's fear. "What were you doing at the UN!" he yelled in Haki's ear at the top of his lungs.

"I cannot tell you!" Haki shouted back. "Praise the name Hikari! I cannot tell you!"

Manning and McCarter lifted the Japanese into the air again. As they lowered him toward the water, Manning said, "I'd try not to kick if I were you, Haki. Fluttering the water will just attract our fine finned friend."

Haki tried to follow the advice, his whole body going rigid. But as soon as the toes of his shoes touched the surface of the water, instinctive fear overrode common sense. His feet began to run in place and churn the water like an outboard motor.

The wild rippling didn't escape the Hammerhead and several of his friends. Across the water twenty yards away, McCarter saw four more sharks headed toward them.

"Look, David," Manning said. "Looks like a family reunion headed our way."

"Yes," McCarter said, "it does."

The four new dorsal fins joined the original shark and swam toward them.

"You know, when my family gets together," Manning said, "we always have a big dinner to celebrate."

"Mine, too," McCarter agreed. "Everybody brings something. Salad, or potatoes, or whatever."

"Spanish rice," Manning said. "My grandmother used to always bring Spanish rice."

The five sharks were now within ten feet of Haki's feet.

"Well, I don't know what *they* brought," McCarter said, nodding toward the sharks. "But we're providing the main course."

"The meat," Manning agreed.

A second later he and Manning jerked Haki out of the water. This time five sharks rose, bit the air, then dived back under the gentle waves.

Haki was crying uncontrollably now.

"You ready to talk?" McCarter asked.

The man didn't answer.

"All right, I've had it," McCarter said in disgust. He pulled Haki's arm over the edge of the water and pinched the small cut he'd opened on the man earlier. More blood dripped into the waves.

The sharks had stayed by the rock formation this time and were circling in anticipation. As the blood hit the water, they went wild, jerking and snapping their long teeth. A large shark sunk his teeth into a smaller one, and more blood seeped into the water.

Suddenly the cove was a whirlwind of crunching teeth, swirling water and flying blood as the hammerheads attacked one another.

"This is your last chance, Haki," McCarter warned, lifting the Japanese off his feet again and dangling him over the water. "You've got to the count of three to start talking. If you haven't told us what your were doing at the UN by then I'm simply going to drop you in.'' He paused. ''One...''

''No! In the name of the Great Hikari—''

''Two...'' McCarter said.

Haki closed his eyes in prayer. ''O, Great Hikari, all-knowing protector, O Great—''

''Three!'' McCarter shouted. He let his grip loosen on the Japanese.

''Hikari forgive me for what I am about to do!'' Haki screamed. ''We were looking for the box!''

McCarter tightened his grip again. ''What box?'' he demanded.

''The box that contains the formula for manufacturing Nerve Ending!''

''Nerve ending?'' McCarter asked, puzzled.

''Yes, Nerve Ending! Put me down on the ground! Please, put me down! I will tell you all about it!''

The Japanese did as he had promised, and when he was done, David McCarter wondered if his face looked as white as those of the other men of Phoenix Force.

CHAPTER FIFTEEN

Stony Man Farm

Aaron Kurtzman couldn't help thinking of the old jokes that used to begin with "I've got some good news and some bad news...."

The good news was that five minutes earlier he'd finally broken the new computer codes for the Japanese police records and intelligence divisions, and tapped into the files. From the records division he had identified the man in the news clip with the Great Hikari—a small-time criminal named Ichiro Murai. Murai had a long series of arrests, but few convictions.

Switching to police intelligence files, Kurtzman had found little hard intel concerning Murai but a great deal of speculation in the reports. Officers had even suggested that Murai had to have had a partner in many of his confidence games and other crimes. The police didn't know who that partner was.

Neither did Kurtzman. But the Stony Man Farm

computer ace suspected that whoever it was now called himself the Great Hikari.

The bad news? That was where things stopped. Murai and the Great Hikari were in hiding, and until Bolan or McCarter or Lyons called in with some new bit of evidence, Kurtzman had nowhere else to go on his magic machines. The old computer adage "garbage in, garbage out" didn't really apply; it was more like nothing in nothing out. Which could drive a man like Aaron Kurtzman crazy. He might be confined to a wheelchair, but in his own way he was as much a man of action as any of the Stony Man Farm personnel. He knew that every mission involved a blend of computer and legwork but downtime irritated him. If this went on too long...

It didn't. "Boss man!" Akira Tokaido suddenly shouted.

"Look."

Kurtzman, already picking up on some of the young man's excitement, quickly cleared his screen and tapped in the necessary information to link him to Tokaido's computer.

"Look!" Tokaido said again, pointing to his monitor.

It didn't take Kurtzman long to see why his young assistant was excited.

The computer man had the telephone receiver in his hand and was about to tap Barbara Price's intercom button when Price called him instead. "Aaron," she said, "I've got David on the line. I think you'd better listen to what he has to say." She paused. "Hal just landed. He's on his way upstairs to his office phone right now."

Kurtzman heard a click, then McCarter's voice said, "Aaron?"

The computer man said, "Yeah, David, where are you?"

"Place called the Lido Club just outside Mogadishu," McCarter replied. "Don't worry—Barb's scrambling the call." He cleared his throat and went on to explain to Kurtzman what Haki had told the men of Phoenix Force about Nerve Ending.

"You ever heard of it before?" McCarter asked.

"Rumors of a supergas, yeah," the computer man said. "But never anything concrete, and never a name."

"Kiethley hid the documents pertaining to the gas's manufacture and dispersion somewhere in Somalia. My guess is he suspected the Followers of the Truth had men inside the UN."

As he listened, Kurtzman heard another line ring in the mission control room. Through the glass he saw Price pick up the phone again.

"We know the box is here," McCarter told Kurtzman, "but we don't know where. The cult hardman we grabbed and his friends were looking for it. They'd already searched the UN building and the annex and were about to leave when we showed up."

"Then at least the Followers of the Truth don't

have Nerve Ending," Kurtzman said. "They didn't find it."

"*They* didn't find it. But our friend Haki says there are other search teams looking other places, so by now, who knows? Too bad Spencer Kiethley's not still around. He's the only one who could have told us where it is—or was."

McCarter went on to explain a few of the details, but for all practical purposes he was finished when Price cut back in. "Aaron? David?" she said. "Striker is on the other line. He's with Spencer Kiethley."

"Put him on!" McCarter said.

A click sounded over the line, then Kurtzman heard Bolan's familiar voice. "David," he began, "Barb tells me you already know about Nerve Ending. Let me put Kiethley on, and he'll tell you where to find the box."

Yet another line began ringing in the mission control room as they all waited for Kiethley. Kurtzman watched Price answer it through the glass again.

A moment later a weak voice got on the line. "Mr. McCarter," Kiethley said, "where are you right now?"

"Just outside Mogadishu at a place called the Lido Club. You know it?"

"Damn!" Kiethley said. "You're right across the road! Go across to the Anglo-American Club—men's locker room, locker number 412. You got it?"

"We're on our way," McCarter said. "I'll call

back from there in a couple of minutes." Another click sounded as he hung up.

Bolan got back on in place of Kiethley and said, "What else, Aaron?"

Before Kurtzman could answer, they heard another line being picked up. "Aaron? Striker? Who am I talking to?" The voice was Brognola's.

Kurtzman and Bolan both filled in the director from their points of view, teaming up to include the intel McCarter had from Somalia. As they were winding it down, Price came back on. "Gentlemen," she said. "Hold the line for Able Team."

Carl Lyons was the next voice heard. "We're sitting here in Ira Rook's living room," he said, "and you aren't going to believe what he just told me."

"Does it happen to have to do with a new nerve gas called Nerve Ending?" Kurtzman asked.

For a moment Lyons was silent. Then he said, "How'd *you* know?"

Kurtzman told Lyons what the others had learned.

"So let me get this straight," the Able Team leader said. "Kiethley hid the box that has the Nerve Ending formula in it. He just told McCarter and his boys where it is so they can go pick it up?"

"Right," Kurtzman said. "Assuming that one of the other cult search teams hasn't found it yet."

"We don't know?"

"We don't know."

"Does anybody know what the cult has planned if they get the formula?" Lyons asked.

Now it was Kurtzman's turn to add to the barrage of intelligence that had suddenly come down from all ends of the mission. "To manufacture the gas and hit thirty-nine different sites around the world," Kurtzman said. "The Great Hikari, known until two years ago simply as Toshiro Ohara, is planning to have his angels and brain-dead disciples take out millions of people all over the globe."

For a moment all phone lines leading into Stony Man Farm were silent.

Then Bolan said, "Angels?"

"Toshiro Ohara?" Lyons said. "You've IDed the Great Hikari?"

"Wait a minute," Brognola said. "How do you know all this, Aaron?"

Kurtzman cleared his throat. "Akira has been monitoring the Japanese Defense Forces computers," he said. "Just a few seconds before you called in, he intercepted a phone call from an agent of theirs named Reiko Fukoto. Seems she's been sleeping with the Great Hikari."

"So she knows where he is?"

"Both of them—Ohara and Murai—are in an old castle in Okinawa. Fukoto informed her bosses that it was owned by one of Hikari's converts."

"Does this Reiko Fukoto have a list of the sites they plan to gas if they get the Nerve Ending formula?" Brognola asked.

The phone in mission control was ringing again and Kurtzman watched Price pick up the receiver as he answered. "Negative," Kurtzman said. "She says Ohara and Murai are playing that one close to the vest." He cleared his throat. "But keep in mind that the cult plans to carry out these thirty-nine attacks—it would have been forty, but Able Team already neutralized the one in Brooklyn—even if they don't get the formula for Nerve Ending. Fukoto's phone call claims they'll just substitute sarin."

The line clicked yet again. Kurtzman glanced at his watch. If Phoenix Force was right across the street from the formula as Kiethley claimed, they'd had time to get it and call back by now.

"What good news," Lyons said sarcastically. "If the Followers of the Truth have to use sarin, then millions of people won't die. Just hundreds of thousands."

David McCarter's voice was calm and clear when he said, "Count on the millions, Ironman." Again the lines went silent for a moment as every member of the Stony Man team digested exactly what that meant. Then McCarter confirmed it. "We just arrived here at the Anglo-American Club locker room. All the attendants are dead. Locker number 412 has been pried open." He paused, then everyone on the other lines of the conference call heard him take in a deep breath.

"It's empty," the Phoenix Force leader stated. "The Great Hikari and the Followers of the Truth have got Nerve Ending."

Okinawa

ICHIRO MURAI SLAMMED the door behind him and walked to the bed.

Reiko Fukoto opened her eyes and looked up.

Murai grabbed the woman by the throat and pulled her from the bed onto the floor. A quick kick to the temple rendered her unconscious again.

"What—?" Toshiro Ohara blurted out, sitting up in bed.

"She is a spy!" Murai shouted. "She is with the Japanese Defense Forces!" Looking at the floor, he shook his head angrily back and forth. "I warned you, Toshiro! I warned you!" He leaned over the bed and slapped the Great Hikari across the face.

Yoshiko, lying next to the cult leader, gasped.

The Great Hikari's hand went to his face, rubbing it. "I am sorry, Ichiro," he almost whined.

Such a statement in such a tone of voice from a god brought another gasp to the woman's lips.

Murai turned his attention to the woman with the big breasts. "Get her out of here before I kill both of you!" he roared.

Yoshiko looked to her god in horror.

"My dear, perhaps you should go out and—" Ohara started to say.

Murai slapped Ohara again, cutting him off. Reaching across the man in the bed, he grabbed Yoshiko by the hair and jerked the nude woman across Ohara and onto the floor. Still holding her hair, he began to drag her across the room. Yoshiko alternately panted for air and shrieked in pain as she struggled to keep up on all fours.

When Murai reached the door, he opened it. Moving behind the woman, who was still on her hands and knees, he placed a shoe between her buttocks and propelled her out into the hall where one of the lesser angels was waiting to take her away.

The man grabbed Yoshiko by the hair as Murai had done, and dragged her down the hall.

Murai slammed the door behind him again. He looked from Fukoto to Ohara and felt his stomach wrench—in anger toward the woman and disgust toward the man. At that moment in time he would have loved to have killed his old friend. But such a move would be counterproductive. If they could escape to another hiding place before the Japanese Defense Forces arrived, the gassings could go on. Even if they were captured here in Okinawa, the Nerve Ending gas was already on its way to the distribution bases and the attacks could be used as a bargaining tool.

In either case the Great Hikari was still needed as a figurehead for the Followers of the Truth. Damage control was what was called for rather than revenge. At least for the moment.

"What did she tell them?" Ohara asked, a weak, pitiful smile on his lips.

"Everything, you fool! What we have planned, where we are now. Everything except the list of sites we plan to gas."

"How did you catch her?" Ohara asked.

"She did not know that our phones have automatic

recorders on them. The call was made last night, but the recordings were not reviewed until this morning. Which means the Japanese Defense Forces have had her information for hours now.'' He lifted his wristwatch to his eyes. ''I should expect them to kick in our doors at any time.''

Ohara sat straighter up in bed. ''It is too late, Ichiro,'' he said. ''Carver and LeForce and Araba have already returned to the command bases on their respective continents. The Nerve Ending gas has already been manufactured. There is no way to stop us.''

Murai reached forward with both hands, closing his fingers around the Great Hikari's throat. ''You fool!'' he said again. ''While you lie in bed having sex with *spies,* some of us pay attention to the world outside!'' Ohara's eyes were bugging, and Murai forced himself to let go of the man's throat. He also lowered his voice, knowing he was still mad enough to kill his old friend if he didn't get a grip on himself.

''Let me explain the situation to you,'' he said. ''Carver is in America. LeForce is in Paris, and Araba *would have been* in Riyadh if he had not been killed in Sierra Leone.''

Ohara sat up straighter. ''Muhammad Araba is dead?''

''Yes. When he left the meeting here, I sent him to Freetown to take charge of Kiethley's interrogation himself. The others were getting nowhere. Then, late yesterday afternoon, someone drove a mail truck into the house, killed them all and freed Kiethley.''

Ohara shook his head in disbelief. "The Defense Forces?" he asked.

Murai shook his head. "I do not think so," he said. "Reiko had not yet made her call. And one of our lesser angels returned from an errand in time to see the mail truck leave the house. He said they looked like Americans." Murai turned toward the wall. "But without Araba, the thirteen Nerve Ending sites in the Mideast cannot go forward. We now have only twenty-six gas sites left."

The Great Hikari leaped from his bed and hurried toward the clothes closet. "Twenty-six is enough," he said as he opened the door and began rummaging through the contents. "Millions will still die, and we will still hold the world in terror and awe. We will be able to name whatever price we like. But we must leave here immediately." He grabbed a Western-style shirt and a pair of blue jeans. With sunglasses and his braid hidden under a baseball cap, he could travel without being recognized.

Another thought crossed Ohara's mind, and he turned to Murai. "We must destroy all evidence of what is about to happen," he said.

Murai nodded. "I have already given that order. The lesser angels are doing so," he said. "The gas has been manufactured, formed into time bombs and delivered to the primary sites in Paris and Wichita, Kansas. At the appointed time, they will go to the local sites throughout Europe and America to be planted. Once that has happened, there is no way we can be stopped."

AT ONE TIME, when security was a vital part of the castle's role in violent feudal Japan, the wooded area around the stone structure would have been kept cleared so the guards in the watch towers could see the enemy approach from a distance. But according to Reiko Fukoto's report to her superiors, the owners of the building during the past hundred years had liked the privacy and atmosphere the trees lent the castle and the forest had been allowed to grow up within feet of the walls.

Bolan silently thanked the owners for the cover they had provided as he sprinted from the trees to the wall. Combined with the dark night and Fukoto's intel that Toshiro Ohara, a.k.a. the Great Hikari, and Ichiro Murai were relying on a low profile rather than on a massive security force, he could be relatively sure of an unnoticed approach.

Behind him Bolan heard Buchanan and Kiethley. Kiethley was recovering quicker than Bolan had expected, and the Executioner had decided to grant his request to come along on the mission's grande finale. Kiethley had risked his life and been through hell— he deserved a shot at the Great Hikari.

Reaching up, Bolan grasped the rugged stones in the wall and began to climb. The wall wasn't tall by castle standards—no more than ten feet—and a moment later he rested on the ledge. Looking down, he saw Buchanan pushing Kiethley up. Bolan reached down, grabbed the man's outstretched arms and lifted him to the top. White faced and panting, Kiethley closed his eyes as Buchanan made the climb.

"You sure you're up to this?" Bolan whispered in the darkness.

Kiethley opened his eyes. "Wouldn't miss it for the world."

Bolan glanced across the open ground, seeing several small outbuildings he supposed had once been stables and soldiers quarters. Lights were on in the windows of the main building, and he dropped to the ground, then sprinted to the closest door. His eyes scanned the doorway for alarm wires as he waited for Buchanan and Kiethley to join him. Finding none, he drew the Beretta with one hand, the Crossada knife with the other.

Buchanan and Kiethley arrived at the Executioner's side. The journalist gripped the subhilt fighter in his left fist, a Colt Woodsman .22 with sound suppressor in his right. The Woodsman had come from the weapons locker on board the SR-71 in which Jack Grimaldi had whisked them from Sierra Leone to Okinawa, as had the identical pistol Kiethley carried and the Randall Model 13 Arkansas toothpick the beaten Buchanan had chosen.

The castle was ancient, but the doors leading into it were modern. Nine small windowpanes covered the top half of the door, and Bolan used the hilt of his knife to smash the glass in the one nearest the knob. Reaching through the hole, he unlocked the lock and led the other two men inside.

What had once been a dark hallway was now lighted by electric lamps and overhead lighting. The Executioner led the way past ornate paintings of dragons on the stone walls. Ahead he saw a cross hall. He was ten feet away when he heard the voices.

Bolan slowed, crept to the corner and leaned around the edge. An open doorway stood ten feet down the cross hall, and the voices came from there. Motioning Buchanan and Kiethley to follow, he rounded the corner, moved to the door, then peered around the opening.

Four men sat around a short table playing mah-jongg. One had a long drooping mustache and wore a black T-shirt. Seated next to him was a fat man with a shoulder holster. Facing the door, Bolan saw a young Japanese with a topknot, and the fourth man—the oldest—had short gray hair. None of them had the classic look of cult brainwashing in their eyes. The fact was each, in his own way, looked like a typical career criminal. Bolan guessed them to be a party of the "angels" used as security by the cult.

The Executioner stepped into the room with the Beretta.

A 3-round burst of quiet 9 mm rounds exited the barrel, taking out the man with the mustache as he looked up in surprise. Buchanan was right behind Bolan, sending a double-tap of quiet .22-caliber slugs into a fat man who was trying to draw a pistol from his shoulder rig.

Kiethley's turn came next, and he fired three times with his Woodsman, the weapon barely whispering as it spit .22-caliber Stingers into the face of the gray-haired "angel."

The man with the topknot evidently had no gun,

but Bolan saw the *wakazashi* short sword come out of the scabbard as the man rose from the table, screamed and lunged forward. The blade was halfway to the Executioner's head when Bolan fell to the floor in a classical *pasata soto*. The sword went over his head as he thrust the Crossada into the man's abdomen. Cutting upward as he returned to his feet, the Executioner angled the blade up into Topknot's heart.

Bolan followed the hall to the staircase and took the steps to the castle's second floor, the Beretta and Crossada both ready in front of him. As he reached the top of the steps, he spotted another man coming down the hall. The man was pulling a nude Oriental woman by the hair, forcing her to struggle along on hands and knees.

A 9 mm hollowpoint round drilled the man between the eyes. He released the woman's hair as he slithered to the ground.

Buchanan and Kiethley stopped next to his side as Bolan knelt by the woman. "Reiko?" he asked.

The woman shook her head, sobbing. "I am Yoshiko."

Bolan glanced over her body. She wasn't hurt. "Where's Reiko?" he asked.

Yoshiko pointed silently back in the direction she had come.

"Wait here," Bolan whispered. "We'll be back for you." He led the way on down the hall to a closed door. On the other side he could hear two voices—one angry, the other frightened.

Grasping the knob, he threw the door open.

The Executioner recognized Toshiro Ohara from Kurtzman's description of the news tape photo. The Great Hikari stood in front of an open closet door, changing clothes. Another nude woman, Reiko, Bolan assumed, lay unconscious on the floor.

The third person in the room had to be Ichiro Murai. The cult's second-in-command turned toward Bolan as the door hit the wall to the Executioner's side. Murai hesitated for a moment, then his hand shot inside his kimono and returned holding a .38-caliber Nambu revolver.

Bolan let the Beretta spit more lead. Two rounds took the Great Hikari's confederate in the chest, and the third rose to his face. The Executioner turned the weapon on Ohara, but there was little need.

The Great Hikari had fallen to his knees on the floor and was weeping. "Please!" he cried. "Do not hurt me!"

Bolan fought the revulsion in his belly. The Great Hikari didn't mind gassing millions to death but he didn't like pain himself. "I want a list of all gassing sites," he said. "I want them *now*."

The Great Hikari looked up from his knees, tears streaming down his eyes. "No," he whispered quietly. "That is the only bargaining tool I have left."

Bolan turned to Kiethley, then back to Ohara. "You know who this guy is?" he asked.

Ohara shook his head.

"Spencer Kiethley," Bolan said. "The bruises came from your 'angels.'" The Executioner gave it time to sink in, then turned back to Kiethley. "Spence," he said, "the Great Hikari is all yours."

Kiethley grinned as he walked forward. "You know what they say about paybacks, Ohara?" he asked.

When the Great Hikari didn't reply, the beaten American answered for him. "They're a bitch, Ohara," he said. "A real bitch."

Kansas

A MORE CENTRAL United States location might have been possible to find than Wichita, Kansas, but not much more central.

Lyons watched through the window of the C-17 Globemaster aircraft as Jock Reno lowered it through the sky toward the Wichita airport. Below he could see the Boeing and Cessna aircraft plants, an oil refinery and a huge field full of farm implements. Then the runway appeared, and parked along the sides of the grass he could see twenty-six Chevy vans with civilian license plates.

The Able Team leader was on his feet as soon as the wheels of the big transport plane touched the tarmac. Moving back into the cargo area, he saw Schwarz and Blancanales standing just inside the door. An even one hundred Stony Man Farm blacksuits sat on the floor behind them. Most were studying street maps of Kansas's largest metropolitan area.

"Okay, heads up!" Lyons called out. "We'll deploy alphabetically by team. Able will go first, then

Baker. You already have your drivers assigned. Take the closest van and move onto your preassigned location." He paused. "Check in by radio as soon as you're set up." He paused. "Any questions?"

No hands rose.

"Then there's just one other thing to remember," Lyons declared. "We don't want anyone getting through the perimeter defense. But remember what these cult freaks are holding. It's called Nerve Ending, and if even one of the canisters is pierced by a stray round, half of Wichita is going to die." He paused a final time, letting the gravity of the situation sink in, then said, "All right. Let's do it."

Without further ado the Able Team leader led Schwarz and Blancanales off the C-17 and into the closest van.

Lyons drove, entering the city proper and turning onto Kellogg, Wichita's main drag. Next to him in the shotgun seat, Blancanales kept a map open in his lap.

"Take the next right, Ironman," the psy-op expert said as they stopped at a red light. "Looks like two blocks, then a left."

The light turned green. Lyons guided the Chevy through the intersection to the next cross street and turned. The team found itself in an older middle-income housing area. Two blocks later the van turned left onto Barclay. The house they wanted, 1138, stood another two blocks down.

Lyons cruised past the address, seeing several cars parked outside. He knew they were there to pick up the Nerve Ending canister-bombs that would then be transported to the various sites around the country. Glancing into the rearview mirror as he passed the house, the big ex-cop saw one of the blacksuit vans pull in against the curb a block behind. The five-man teams would encircle the house, cutting off every possible avenue of escape. They were there as a precaution in the unlikely event that any of the cult members or angels slipped past Lyons, Schwarz and Blancanales.

The radio mounted on the dashboard of the van coughed static, then a voice said, "Charlie to Able. Come in Able."

In the back of the van Schwarz lifted a walkie-talkie to his mouth. "Roger, Charlie," he said. "We read you."

"Charlie Team in place," the voice stated.

"Affirmative, Charlie," Schwarz replied. In the mirror Lyons saw Schwarz make a mark on the clipboard in his lap.

The Able Team leader turned at the next corner and drove past another of the blacksuit vans. He saw the driver with a microphone to his lips and a moment later heard, "David Team to Able. David in place, Able."

"Roger, David." Schwarz made another mark.

Lyons cruised on, passing more vans and listening as the rest of the backup teams found their positions and called in. Returning to Kellogg, he saw a black-and-white Wichita PD car driving toward them. That didn't bother Lyons.

Brognola had used his Justice Department position to pull strings from Washington and ensure that local authorities would steer clear of the neighborhood.

The black-and-white moved on.

The Able Team van was still on Kellogg when the final team called in. "That's it, Ironman," Schwarz said.

Lyons turned back, driving slowly toward the house again. "You hear how Mack hit the house in Freetown?" he asked Schwarz and Blancanales as he turned the final corner.

"With the mail truck?" Blancanales asked.

Lyons's intentions suddenly dawned on both of the other Able Team commandos as he floored the accelerator and pulled up over the curb in front of the house. Both men braced themselves and grabbed their Calicos.

"Schwarz, with me," Lyons said. "Pol, take the rear." Then the front bumper of the Chevy hopped up the two short steps, smashed the front of the one-story wood-frame house and the time for talk was over.

Lyons dived from the van, bringing his Calico 960 into play as soon as he hit the hole in front of the van. Inside the living room, he saw roughly twenty faces look up in surprise. Some had the now familiar zombie look of the crazed Followers of the Truth devotee. Others had the dark look of the men the Great Hikari called his angels.

But no matter how they looked, the surprise on the

faces didn't last long. All of the men reached for weapons.

Lyons scanned the room, looking for signs of the Nerve Ending containers. Seeing none, he flipped the Calico to full-auto and sprayed the men before their guns came into play. Bodies flipped and flopped onto the living-room carpet as Schwarz stepped in at his side. A few return rounds went zinging past his ear as both Able Team commandos continued blanketing the living room with full-auto rounds.

Then, suddenly, only Lyons and Schwarz remained standing.

The Able Team leader motioned Schwarz to the right and moved to the left. Quickly he checked each man for a pulse, and, finding none, moved from the living room into the hall. The next order of business was to secure the canisters of Nerve Ending.

The Able Team leader found them in a bedroom halfway down the hall. The canisters stood roughly three feet tall. They were arranged in rows against the wall, three rows, four canisters to each row.

That made twelve.

But Lyons had been told that there were thirteen gassings planned.

The soft sound of shoes on carpet came from down the hall. Lyons aimed the Calico that way and followed the noise. He came to another bedroom and looked inside.

A tall black man stood in the center of the room next to the bed. "Don't move, motherfucker," he said.

Lyons froze. In one of the man's hands was a 1911 Government Model with the hammer cocked, the manual safety off. In the other hand was the missing Nerve Ending canister.

"Carver," Carl Lyons said under his breath. Without thinking, he switched the Calico's selector to semiauto.

Carver saw the movement and hugged the gas canister closer to his chest and face, covering his vital areas and making a snap shot from Lyons's Calico impossible. Peering around the side, he cackled. "*Archangel* Carver, if you don't mind," he said. "Don't try what you're thinking." He tapped the canister with the barrel of the .45. "Or I'll kill our friend here." He laughed hideously.

"What do you want?" Lyons said. "You can't—"

Running footsteps sounded behind him, then Schwarz ground to a halt at Lyons's side.

"Freeze!" Carver called out. "Both of you!" He jammed the barrel of his pistol tighter against the metal container. "Put down your weapons."

When Lyons and Schwarz didn't obey, Carver roared, "Now, dammit! Or I swear to God I'll blow this damn thing up and kill everybody for miles!"

"Angels shouldn't use language like that," Schwarz said. "That kind of talk will get back to heaven."

"Shut up!" Carver shouted. "Shut up and put down the guns, or I swear—"

"Do what he says, Gadgets," Lyons ordered.

Schwarz turned to Lyons and frowned. "Ironman, he'll just shoot us and then—"

"Do it!" Lyons ordered. Slowly he bent forward and set his submachine pistol on the carpet.

Schwarz stared into Lyons's eyes. The Able Team leader saw a sudden understanding cross the other man's face. Schwarz set his weapon down next to Lyons's.

Carver backed his way to the window. His gaze glued to Lyons and Schwarz, he set the Nerve Ending can on the floor but kept the .45 pressed against it. With his free hand he fumbled for the latch on the window behind him, found it, then lifted the glass.

A chilly wind blew into the bedroom from the backyard as Carver climbed through the opening backward. When all but his head and arms was outside the house, he reached back in and grabbed the canister. "Your friend was right, fool," he said to Lyons. "I *am* gonna kill you." The .45 rose away from the Nerve Ending gas and toward the Able Team commandos.

Lyons wore his own .45 and the Colt Python. Schwarz had his Beretta and S&W. But holstered as they were, they would be of no use. As the huge bore of Carver's Government Model pistol looked Lyons in the face, both men might just as well have been unarmed.

The explosion sounded, and Carver's gun hand jerked.

Lyons smiled; he had felt no pain. But more important than that, he had just seen the right side of

Carver's head blown to the side of the window. Carver slumped below the window, out of sight in the backyard.

Blancanales took the "archangel's" place in the open window and looked down at his feet. "Suppose he's a real angel now?" he asked.

Paris, France

BOLAN COULD SEE the C-17 Globemaster III taxiing along the other runway as the SR-71 set down in Paris. Pushing Toshiro Ohara in front of him, he deplaned quickly, followed by Bobcat Buchanan and Spencer Kiethley.

Jack Grimaldi would stay behind the controls of the supersonic aircraft and be ready to lift them off should they encounter political problems while in country. Brognola had already cleared them through customs, it appeared, and similarly to what Bolan knew the G-man had done for Able Team in Wichita, a phone call from the U.S. President should have the gendarmes here under control. But you never knew what kind of bedfellows politics would make when you crossed the borders of another country, and it wouldn't hurt to keep the SR-71's engines warmed up.

The Executioner pushed Toshiro Ohara ahead of him across the tarmac to where two sedans—one a Cutlass Brougham, the other a Ford Taurus—waited. Again Brognola had paved the way for transport, and the Paris CIA station had been instructed to leave the vehicles parked at the airport. They'd also been ordered to ask no questions.

Bolan watched his captive out of the corner of his eye as they neared the cars. Ohara had given them no trouble whatsoever since they'd left Okinawa. The man was a con artist, not a fighter; he'd proved that back at the castle even before Spencer Kiethley had a chance to mete out any of the bruises he owed the man. Kiethley had barely raised a fist when Ohara spouted out the locations of the central sarin and Nerve Ending storage bases in Paris and Wichita. Kiethley hadn't had to strike him once.

The American who had suffered so at the hands of the Followers of the Truth cult had looked a little disappointed as he lowered his fist. But he hadn't had the heart to beat the man for no reason once they had the information they needed.

Followed by his two fellow Americans, the Executioner hurried toward the sedans. He saw Phoenix Force sprinting toward the cars from the opposite direction.

They met at the vehicles; introductions were short.

"Guys," the Executioner said, "you've met Bobcat. This is Spencer Kiethley."

The men of Phoenix Force nodded. McCarter turned to Bolan. "You've got the directions?"

Bolan nodded. "According to our friend here—" he gripped Ohara's upper arm and saw the man wince "—they're in an old hotel in the Place Pigalle. I won't ask you if you're familiar with the area."

Buchanan, Kiethley and Phoenix Force all chuckled. Pigalle had long been infamous as Paris's primary area of prostitution.

"The Hotel Manet," Bolan said. "The public thinks it's closed for remodeling. We won't find a better place to get our act together than right here, so let's get the details out of the way right now. I'll take Buchanan, Kiethley and Ohara in the first car. The rest of you follow us in the other vehicle. The Manet is three stories and a basement, and sits on the corner. Three exits—front, side and one that leads out into the alley in back. When we get there I'll take Buchanan and Kiethley in the front. We'll go directly to the third floor and clear it. David, you, Gary and Rafael enter through the side and take the second floor. Calvin, you and T.J. take the alley, then cover the ground floor and basement. Ohara says it's just a lobby and storage downstairs."

All of the men nodded.

"Then, if there aren't any questions, let's get this over with before every person in town not wearing a gas mask is dead." Bolan dropped behind the wheel of the Cutlass.

Kiethley got in next to him, with Buchanan pushing Ohara across the back seat before sliding in himself.

"You do not need me anymore," Ohara whined. "Why not let me go?"

Kiethley snorted. "Just like that? After all we've meant to each other?"

"I think we'll hold on to you, O Great One," Buchanan said. "You might be lying about the hotel, in which case I won't show the mercy on you old Spence here did.''

Bolan twisted the key in the ignition and started the Cutlass's engine.

"It is the right address," Ohara insisted. "And it is over. I will never be able to get my organization back together after all this. But I still have money. I could make you all rich men...."

Kiethley swiveled in his seat and backhanded Ohara across the mouth. "Shut up."

The Cutlass led the way away from the airport into downtown Paris. With the Taurus trailing close behind, they zoomed down the Rue de Rivoli past the Louvre and Tuileries Gardens, passed through the opera district, then entered Montmartre and the Place Pigalle.

Hookers of every size, shape and description walked the sidewalks as Bolan guided the Cutlass onto a side street. A man wearing heavy women's makeup, a dress and a derby hat stepped out into the street, forcing the Executioner to stand on the brakes. The tires squealed, leaving rubber on the pavement. The man-woman didn't seem to notice.

Bolan pulled to the curb a half block from the Hotel Manet and killed the engine. Exiting the vehicle, he opened the trunk.

Brognola had come through again. Inside the trunk were six M-16s and several dozen extra magazines.

The Taurus pulled in behind the Cutlass. McCarter got out and opened his own trunk.

A few minutes later the men from Stony Man Farm were armed and walking down the quiet street.

"Spence," Bolan said, "watch over the Great One here. If this is a set up, I don't want him sneaking off."

Kiethley grabbed the braid at the back of the Japanese guru's head and jerked. "I'll do just that."

The few pedestrians they saw took one look at the armed men and headed the other way. When they reached the corner, Bolan, Buchanan, Kiethley and Ohara walked toward the front entrance. McCarter, Manning and Encizo angled off toward the side entrance while James and Hawkins broke into a jog toward the alley down the side street.

Bolan began running, too, as they reached the front steps. He held the M-16 in front of him as he looked up to see a sign announcing that the Manet was closed for repairs. Lowering a shoulder, he hit the front door and felt it burst open in front of him.

The lobby looked empty as the Executioner searched for the stairs. He spotted them to his left and hurried that way. The hotel was strangely silent as he sprinted up the steps, turned the corner at the landing and jogged on. Behind him he heard the running footsteps of the other three men. Below he heard McCarter and James kick the side and back doors.

Bolan had passed the second floor and was halfway up the steps to the third when he heard the first shots ring out behind him. He resisted the urge to backtrack and assist below—he had assigned the first and second floors to McCarter and James. They could handle the jobs, and it was his duty to continue to the top. No operation could be successful unless everyone followed orders, and that included the Executioner.

Bolan reached the top of the steps to the third floor. He came out in a small waiting area with chairs, couches and tables. Beyond it was a narrower hall. As the Executioner moved toward it, a door opened.

A glassy-eyed cult zombie bearing an Uzi was the first to step out of a room. He was also the first to fall to the Executioner's M-16. More doors opened along the third-floor hallway, revealing more cult gunners. More zombies appeared. Operating as if on remote control, they rushed Bolan, firing various weapons. A cult follower with a Heckler & Koch 93 fell to one 3-round burst. A cultist with a Japanese Howa fell to another. Still, they charged mindlessly forward, programmed to serve their master, the Great Hikari...or die trying.

By now Buchanan, Kiethley and Ohara had reached the waiting area. Buchanan and Kiethley fanned out to the Executioner's sides, and began firing. Together the three men downed cultists until their rifles ran dry, then dropped the magazines and inserted fresh loads.

Bolan fired the last 3-round burst into a bald man wearing khaki work pants, a matching shirt and a Greek fisherman's cap. The revolver in his hand dropped to the floor, and he fell clumsily to the floor on his back.

More shots rang out from the floors below, but the third floor suddenly went quiet. Bolan glanced to the side to see Ohara cringing in the corner of the waiting area. As he watched, Kiethley grabbed a fistful of the man's shirt and pulled him forward.

Bolan strode forward to the bald man, who stared up at the ceiling. A trickle of blood ran from the corner of his mouth. He had fallen awkwardly onto one arm, which was twisted and appeared to be broken underneath him. Other footsteps approached, and in his peripheral vision the Executioner saw Kiethley push Ohara up to his side.

The bald man's eyes saw the Followers of the Truth leader and focused on him. Even though he was dying, the Executioner could see his irises were clear. He wasn't one of the Great Hikari's followers but one of the hired criminals—the angels.

Ohara looked down at him. "Jean-Marc," he said. "I...am sorry."

"Yes..." Jean-Marc LeForce almost whispered. "You...should...be." The arm that had appeared to be broken suddenly shot out from under his back. The revolver he had dropped as Bolan shot him was in his hand once more.

Bolan and Jean-Marc fired at the same instant. The Executioner's 3-round burst from the M-16 obliterated the man's face.

The .357 Magnum round from Jean-Marc LeForce's revolver did the same to the Great Hikari. Toshiro Ohara was punched to his back on the floor, dead before he landed.

Bolan took the left side of the hall with Buchanan taking the right. They found no other cult members. But neither did they find any of the thirteen Nerve Ending canisters they were looking for.

The firing was still going strong on the second floor when Bolan led the way down the stairs. He heard footsteps running toward him as he neared the halfway landing and stopped, raising his rifle. A moment later a man in jeans and a black T-shirt turned directly into the barrel of the M-16.

For a moment the man froze, looking up at the Executioner. He was Caucasian, and his eyes were clear—an "angel." He confirmed it by saying in a resigned voice, "Oh, shit."

Bolan pulled the trigger.

The man danced on the end of the M-16, then fell to the ground.

The Executioner heard sporadic fire below on the ground floor as he moved on, turning the corner and looking down the hall at McCarter, Manning and Encizo coming out of rooms. Bodies littered both the waiting area and hallway. Some—the cultists—wore strange combinations of Oriental dress, and others— the angels—were dressed more normally.

The three Phoenix Force men walked forward. "No one left in the rooms," McCarter said. "At least not alive."

Bolan nodded. "Any sign of the Nerve Ending?"

"Not that we saw," Manning said.

The sporadic fire on the ground floor continued. "Let's go give Calvin and T.J. a hand," Bolan said, turning. He sprinted down the final set of steps and turned into the lobby. It was as empty as it had been when he first entered the Hotel Manet.

Bolan heard a final shot that sounded as if it came from the other side of the large room. Moving cautiously that way, he saw another set of steps leading downward. These stairs were narrow, and the M-16 would be hard to maneuver. He let it fall to the end of his sling and drew the Desert Eagle.

Voices came from the basement of the hotel. At first the Executioner didn't recognize them. But as he neared the end of the steps, James's deep baritone became distinct.

Several bodies lay at the foot of the steps, looking as if they'd been shot on the stairs and rolled to the bottom. Bolan stepped over them and into the basement.

He found himself looking down the barrels of two M-16s.

James and Hawkins recognized him and lowered their weapons. They stood next to a boiler and in front of an enclosed chicken-wire storage cage. Through the wire, the Executioner could see the tall canisters he knew were filled with Nerve Ending.

James produced an all-purpose multitool from his pocket and began to cut through the wire as Bolan pulled a walkie-talkie from his pocket and pressed the mike button with his thumb. The signal left the basement of the Hotel Manet in Paris, shot up to a satellite miles into space and was relayed back down to Stony Man Farm in the Blue Ridge Mountains.

"Striker to Stony Man Base," the Executioner said.

Barbara Price's voice came on loud and clear. "Stony Man Base. Go ahead, Striker."

"Mission complete."

James Axler

OUTLANDERS™

ICEBLOOD

Kane and his companions race to find a piece of the Chintamanti Stone, which they believe to have power over the collective mind of the evil Archons. Their journey sees them foiled by a Russian mystic named Zakat in Manhattan, and there is another dangerous encounter waiting for them in the Kun Lun mountains of China.

One man's quest for power unleashes a cataclysm in America's wastelands.

James Axler

OUTLANDERS™

DOOMSTAR RELIC

Kane and his companions find themselves pitted
against an ambitious rebel named Barch, who finds a
way to activate a long-silent computer security
network and use it to assassinate the local baron.
Barch plans to use the security system to take over
the ville, but he doesn't realize he is starting a
Doomsday program that could destroy the world.

Kane and friends must stop Barch, the virtual assassin
and the Doomsday program to preserve the future....

One man's quest for power unleashes a cataclysm
in America's wastelands.

A preview from hell...

JAMES AXLER

DEATH LANDS®

Dark Emblem

After a relatively easy mat-trans jump, Ryan and his companions find themselves in the company of Dr. Silas Jamaisvous, a seemingly pleasant host who appears to understand the mat-trans systems extremely well.

Seeing signs that local inhabitants have been used as guinea pigs for the scientist's ruthless experiments, the group realizes that they have to stop this line of research before it goes too far....